Also by Tina Folsom

THOMAS'S CHOICE

SCANGUARDS VAMPIRES – BOOK 8

TINA FOLSOM

Thomas's Choice is a work of fiction. Names, characters, places, and incidents are the products of the author's imagination and are used fictitiously. Any resemblance to actual events, locales, or persons, living or dead, is entirely coincidental.

2013 Tina Folsom

Published in the United States

Cover design: Elaina Lee
Cover photos: bigstockphoto.com
Author Photo: © Marti Corn Photography

Printed in the United States of America

1

Eddie tumbled into the studio apartment, the girl who'd introduced herself as Jessica in his arms. She'd come on to him in the nightclub he'd patrolled earlier. Behind him, the door slammed shut, helped by Jessica's hand. Her mouth was hot on his lips, kissing him passionately while her hands roamed his body, sliding under his T-shirt to caress his naked chest.

All the while, she pressed her curvy body against his, squeezing her generous breasts against him. The scent of her arousal filled the small room, which was furnished with a bed, a dresser, and a small table with two chairs. An open doorway led to a postage-stamp-sized kitchen and another door indicated that there was a bathroom, probably equally small as the kitchen. His sister, Nina, had lived in a similar place before she'd met her mate.

Jessica was pretty: long blond curls, plump lips, innocent-looking blue eyes. Anything a guy could wish for. On top of it, she was willing to put out. Major. No coercion was needed, no seduction necessary. In fact, she was more than eager and the one leading the charge, just as she now pulled her own T-shirt over her head and tossed it onto the nearby chair. For all he knew this was common practice for her: picking up a guy at a club and taking him home for no-holds-barred sex. Hey, he wasn't complaining!

Jessica took his hands, which had lain on her back, and made him cup her bra-covered breasts. Maybe *covered* was too strong a word—what she wore could barely be called a bra. It was a mere collection of specs of fabric, strings and an underwire to hold them together. Her nipples weren't even covered. Instead, her breasts were pushed up as if on a silver platter. Like a feast for him to indulge in.

He glanced down to where his hands squeezed the ample flesh in an almost mechanical fashion, as if he wasn't the one touching her. It felt as if he were watching a mediocre porn movie—explicit for sure, but barely tantalizing.

She threw her head back, closing her eyes. "Oh, yeah, baby!" she called out, placing her hands over his to make him squeeze harder.

He complied, if only because he thought it was what he should do, not because he felt like it. Maybe if he kissed her again, he'd get into it more. After all, he was out of practice. In fact, ever since he'd been turned into a vampire over a year ago, he'd not been with a woman. Funny that he noticed this only now. Well it didn't mean that he hadn't found sexual gratification; after all, what guy didn't masturbate in the shower after waking? Or before going to sleep? He was just like any guy, finding relief at his own hand whenever he needed it.

Eddie slipped his hand onto her nape and pulled her to him, pressing his lips onto her waiting mouth, and kissed her. His tongue swept in to explore her, yet the excitement that he expected to shoot through his veins didn't materialize. His heart beat as evenly as before—though at almost double the speed of a human heart. But that was normal for a vampire.

In an effort to get things going, he pulled on her bra and yanked it off her, allowing her boobs to spill from the inadequate cage. They looked almost rigid, which made him wonder whether they were real or not. Would a girl her age—and she couldn't be more than twenty-two—have silicone implants? Why would anybody put something so foreign into their body? He stared at them, still contemplating the question.

Jessica's hand on his crotch, running her fingers along the zipper of his cargo pants, jolted him from his thoughts and brought him back to the task at hand.

"Oh!" The disappointed sigh she let out when she squeezed him told him that something wasn't working the way it should.

Again she rubbed her hand over him, but Eddie snatched it, stopping her from touching him further.

"Is something wrong?" she asked, her lips pouting.

Everything was wrong. He wasn't hard. He should have a raging erection by now. Any twenty-five-year-old would under the same circumstances. When he'd been human, a passionate kiss had pumped enough blood into his cock so he could get down to business. And now, with a half-naked girl eager to please him, his dick hung there like an old ragdoll, limp and uninvolved. As if it were somebody else's appendage.

Why the fuck wasn't he getting hard? Why was his cock asleep? What the fuck was wrong with him?

He closed his eyes, trying to conjure up images that would make any man horny: naked women bent over furniture, women stripping, even women doing it with other women. Yet, his cock remained in its deathlike state, not a single blood cell rousing it.

Out of nowhere, memories from a few weeks earlier intruded again, memories he'd tried to push away each time they reared their ugly head. Only this time he couldn't push them away any longer. He had to face them head-on.

Several weeks earlier

Eddie marched along the corridor, heading for the conference room on the executive floor of Scanguards' Mission headquarters. Some major shit was going down, and he wasn't going to miss out on the juicy action. He loved this job, the camaraderie with his fellow vampires, the friendship with his mentor, and the admiration of his sister. Nina was finally proud of him, of everything he'd achieved after taking the gamble of becoming a vampire. Finally, everybody was happy: Nina was bonded to Amaury, a major player at Scanguards, and from what Eddie could see, he was going totally gaga over her. He'd never seen a man so in love with a woman. That fact had erased all of Eddie's doubts about whether a human-vampire relationship could work in the long run. Nina and Amaury made it look easy. They seemed made for each other.

As he walked along the hallway, his nostrils suddenly flared. Somewhere on this floor was a human. And that was a breach of security.

"Who else knows?"

Eddie recognized Blake's voice. Even though Blake was Quinn's grandson, and Quinn was a director at Scanguards, it still didn't explain why the human had been allowed onto this floor. It was his duty to check it out and get the situation under control.

"Thomas. But he isn't talking either. I already tried. Unfortunately he isn't gonna tell *you* either," Oliver responded, his voice coming from the alcove that housed a refrigerator and some shelves.

"But he might tell Eddie."

At the sound of his name, Eddie stopped in his tracks. What would Thomas tell him? What secrets were these two talking about? He couldn't help but remain where the two couldn't see him and listen in on their conversation. He knew it was bad form, but something was fishy, and he'd find out what it was.

"Eddie? My god, you're right. Why didn't I think of that? Thomas would tell Eddie anything. Everybody knows he's got the hots for him."

All air rushed out of Eddie's lungs. His vision blurred, and his heart stopped beating. He couldn't move, couldn't react, though he must have made a sound, because Oliver suddenly took a step out from the alcove and snapped his head toward him.

"Oh shit!" Oliver cursed.

Blake let out a heavy breath, shooting him a shocked stare.

"Thomas . . . he . . . " Eddie shook his head.

No, this couldn't be true! Thomas couldn't be attracted to him. This couldn't be happening! His mentor of over a year, the man he shared a house with, wanted to jump his bones? Fuck no!

Of course, Eddie had always known that Thomas was gay. Hell, everybody knew. Nobody had ever made a secret of it. And everybody accepted Thomas as he was: a generous man with a big heart, a brilliant mind. Nobody ever treated him any differently from any of the others. Neither had Eddie. He'd instantly felt comfortable with him when he'd first met him and been told that Thomas would be his mentor and help him get to grips with being a new vampire.

"Listen, Eddie, forget what you heard," Oliver tried to calm him.

The cords in Eddie's neck bulged. "How the fuck can I just forget that?" Nobody could take back words like that, words that shattered his cozy home life with Thomas. They'd lived alongside one another in Thomas's view mansion on Twin Peaks like the ideal roommates, sharing their love for motorcycles and tinkering with anything electronic.

"Believe me, Thomas is an honorable man. He'll never act on his feelings since he knows they're not reciprocated."

He tossed Oliver a furious glare. "God, I wish I'd never found out." Ignorance was bliss; Eddie realized that now.

"I'm sorry." Oliver put a hand on his shoulder.

The touch infuriated him even more, and he pushed him off. He didn't want to be touched, not by any man! "Don't touch me!"

Eddie turned on his heels and ran to the nearest exit.

He'd always looked up to Thomas, admired his intelligence, his street smarts, as well as his absolute loyalty to Scanguards. He'd never once questioned Thomas's motives for taking him in, for rearranging his own life to show a new vampire the ropes. But all this was different now. Had Thomas accepted the assignment Samson, Scanguards' owner, had handed him simply because even back then he'd wanted to get into his pants? Had his motives not been as altruistic as Eddie had assumed?

He couldn't help but wonder about all the incidents when he'd seen Thomas only half-dressed. Had his mentor done it on purpose to entice him to switch camps? Had Thomas tried to seduce him, and he'd just been too thickheaded to see it?

Eddie remembered one incident all too well. He'd spent the day at Holly's place—Ricky's ex-girlfriend—because he'd been out too late and missed sunrise. When he'd returned home, Thomas had stood in the living room, clad only in a towel, talking to Gabriel, who'd needed help with guarding the woman who would later become his mate.

Thomas's skin had glistened with water from his recent shower, and when he'd stretched his arms over his head in what seemed like a casual gesture, Eddie had admired the defined muscles of his stomach and torso. And it had stirred something in him, something he'd dismissed instantly. Had Thomas tried to tempt him even then? Had he purposely shown off his magnificent body because he got off on being looked at?

What about the many times that he'd seen Thomas walk to the refrigerator, dressed in his boxers, his bathrobe open in the front? Had Thomas behaved like that because it was his home, or because he wanted Eddie to look at him?

What would he do now? How could he go on living with Thomas, knowing what he knew? Every time he looked at his mentor from now on, it would be with the knowledge that Thomas had the hots for him, that Thomas wanted to strip him naked, touch him, kiss him, and make love to him.

"There, see, I knew it would be working," a female voice pulled him from his thoughts and brought him back to the present.

Eddie opened his eyes and stared down at Jessica. She'd opened his zipper and pulled out his cock—his fully erect cock— and was now wrapping her hand around him. He was as hard as an iron rod, but he knew it wasn't right, because he hadn't gotten hard for her. He'd gotten hard while thinking of Thomas. While thinking of a man.

Disgusted with himself, he gripped her hand and yanked it off him. "I can't do this."

"Of course you can," she purred and rubbed her naked breasts against him, an action that left him entirely unaffected when he should have dropped his head and sucked those hard nipples into his mouth.

Why wasn't he doing what she wanted him to do? Why wasn't he fucking her? At least then he could prove to himself that there was nothing wrong with him, that he was still the same person he'd always been: a straight man who desired women.

Jessica slid her hands onto his ass, drawing him closer. "Come on, Eddie, I know you want it."

Yes, he wanted it, but not with her. He was as horny as he'd ever been, but he knew instinctively that his dick would wilt like a dried-up flower if he tried to have sex with Jessica. And he wasn't going to add that kind of humiliation to his already-battered psyche.

No, he had to push all this away, pretend none of this had ever happened and go on as usual. He'd done so the last few weeks, he could continue the same way—by avoiding being alone with Thomas as much as he could, and by trying to forget what he'd overheard.

Maybe Oliver and Blake were wrong after all. Maybe they were only imagining things. What did they know about Thomas anyway? They weren't the ones living with him. They weren't spending any time outside of work with him. And even at work, they barely saw him, since Thomas rarely did any fieldwork and was working on IT projects most of the time, while Oliver and Blake were out patrolling or protecting clients.

Eddie stared into Jessica's eyes. "Listen carefully," he started, then sent his thoughts into her mind, erasing every memory she had of him.

If they met again, she would never know what had happened between them. Nobody would ever know that he hadn't been able to perform—nobody but himself. And he could always lie to himself and pretend everything was all right.

2

Thomas clicked the remote for the garage door from fifty yards away and saw the gate rise. Only slightly slowing his motorcycle, he drove inside, killing the engine as he came to a stop in his oversized garage that housed not only several motorcycles but also a large blackout SUV. He rarely used it, preferring to ride his bikes instead. Feeling the engine of his motorcycle hum between his legs and the wind blow through his short blond hair gave him a sense of freedom, a sense of a life without constraints. Even if it was all an illusion, because he was neither free, nor living without constraints.

He was content with what he had achieved—not happy, but then who was ever truly happy with their circumstances? He shook his head at his thoughts and dismounted from his Ducati. He'd spent most of the night in his office in Scanguards' headquarters in the Mission district and barely talked to anybody all night. Now he looked forward to a cold bottle of blood and to exchanging a few words with Eddie before he turned in and went to sleep.

His conversations with Eddie were something he looked forward to every time he came home. But at home wasn't the only place where he saw Eddie. Since he was still mentoring him, he often took him on training assignments. On other occasions they were paired up as a team and sent out on assignments together to apply what Eddie had learned. Thomas lived for those assignments.

Pride filled him every time Eddie showed that he was a quick study. It warmed Thomas's heart to see his mentee grow into his own and become an outstanding bodyguard with a quick mind and a steady hand. But it wasn't only Thomas's heart that was affected; his cock was just as involved. Just looking at the young vampire with the deep dimples in his cheeks when he smiled, made him hard in an instant. And Eddie smiled often. He was a happy-go-lucky kind of guy, laid back, and relaxed.

For over a year now, Thomas had tried to suppress his feelings, to no avail. He was irrevocably and hopelessly in love with Eddie. And there was nothing he could do about it.

Thomas climbed the stairs to the main floor of the house, leaving the garage and his priceless bikes, many of them restored antiques, behind. When he entered the great room which combined an open-plan kitchen with the large living room, he found it empty. He listened, but there was no sound in the home. Eddie had not returned from work yet.

Disappointed, he glanced at the clock over the mantle of the fireplace. In less than an hour, the sun would rise and the floor-to-ceiling windows that dominated one entire wall of the great room would display the waking city at his feet. Right now the San Francisco skyline twinkled in the dark. Only, the windows weren't real: they were monitors that played live videos from the cameras that were mounted around the perimeter of his house. A beautiful and realistic illusion, and the only way he could look outside during daytime without any UV light penetrating his home and burning him to a crisp.

Nevertheless, it was an illusion, one that helped him pretend he lived a normal life, when nothing in his life was normal. He was a vampire. He was gay. And he loved a man he had no right to desire. And underneath it all, his dark power slumbered, threatening to awake at any moment unless he kept the beast in check, a task that grew harder each year, almost as if he were a sleeping volcano, and the power in him the magma that was building up until the pressure became too strong and had to burst to the surface.

Thomas opened the refrigerator and pulled out a bottle of blood. Slowly, he popped the cap off and set the bottle to his lips, drinking the cold liquid and allowing it to coat his dry throat. He closed his eyes, letting his heart conjure up images that made his pulse race and his cock swell. His fangs lengthened involuntarily as the pictures intensified and blurred into just one image: Eddie lying underneath him, his head tilted to the side, offering his vein for a bite. And farther below, two cocks throbbed in concert, rubbing against each other in anticipation of what would happen next.

He shook the thought off—it would never happen, and he'd be better off if he stopped fantasizing about it. It only made the craving worse. Frustration howled through him.

Thomas gulped down the rest of the blood and tossed the bottle in the recycle bin where it clanged against the other empty bottles, reminding him that he had to dispose of them soon. Then he walked to the large leather sectional and plopped down on it, snatching the remote off the coffee table. He pointed it toward the flat screen TV and turned it on when he perceived something white in his peripheral vision. His head snapped toward the entrance door, the one he rarely used since he almost always entered his house through the garage.

His vampire vision zeroed in on the object that stuck out from underneath the door: a white envelope lay on the dark wooden floor.

He rose in one fluid motion and approached. At the door he sniffed, but whoever had pushed the envelope underneath the door was long gone. No residual scent remained. Thomas bent down and picked up the envelope, examining it from every angle. It was not addressed.

Curious, he tore it open and pulled out a single sheet of paper. Only a few words were written in a neat, but old fashioned handwriting: *You can't hide forever. One day you'll have to admit who you are.*

The letter wasn't signed.

The paper fell from his trembling hands. They'd finally found him. How, he didn't know. He'd changed his last name, his identity, even moved to another country, careful not to leave any trails. But even he couldn't hide forever. He'd always known it would happen one day. But it was too soon. He wasn't prepared to face the truth yet. The truth of what he was, what he would always be no matter how long and hard he fought it.

He sank to his knees and dropped his head into his palms. How long did he have until they came for him? And when they did, would he then succumb to them and the dark power inside him? Or did he have enough strength left to fight them?

London, England, Spring 1895

Thomas sat in the gallery of Old Bailey, the criminal courts of London, carefully watching the proceedings taking place below him. He'd been coming almost every day to attend the trial, not out of morbid curiosity like most of the other spectators, but because he had a stake in its outcome. Even though he didn't know the accused, Oscar Wilde, personally, his plight mattered to Thomas.

Oscar Wilde, the famous playwright, was a homosexual and accused of gross indecencies, and whatever happened to a man of his celebrity would have a lasting impact on the homosexual society of London. A society Thomas belonged to, whether he wanted to or not.

He'd always known he was different, but during his first year at Oxford, it had been confirmed: he loved men, not women. He'd tried to deny it at first, but no matter with which lies he'd tried to trick himself, he'd failed. He was what he was: a homosexual. A queer, a faggot, a fairy. Not a real man, but one who degraded himself and other men by performing acts of buggery.

Yet, it wasn't something he could turn off at will. His experiences with a young man at Oxford had opened his eyes to the joys of physical love and shown him the pleasures of the flesh. And once he'd tasted that forbidden fruit, there was no way back, no way to deny what he wanted: the love of a man, no matter how forbidden it was.

He hid it as best he could, never dressing as flamboyantly as other queers did, always participating in the most masculine of sports and entertainment to compensate for his *affliction*. He even courted women of the aristocratic circles of England and had turned into one of the most eligible bachelors not only because of his breeding and standing in society, but also because of his wit and charm, which he had no qualms about unleashing on any innocent debutante. They were swooning for him. If only they knew that their coquettish smiles, blushing cheeks, and rapidly waving fans left him as cold as a morning bath in an ice-crusted creek in the winter.

Underneath all the deception, he found time to meet other men of his penchant and give his carnal desires free rein. It was during those hours that he felt most at peace with himself. And most conflicted at the same time. Feelings of guilt and shame were never far away; yet whenever he made love to a man, he knew he couldn't deny who he was. He had no choice but to continue.

"May the defendant rise," a voice came from the courtroom below.

Thomas leaned forward, eager to hear the court's decision. Like him, others were doing the same, waiting with bated breath for the judge's ruling. It came down like a hammer on an anvil, just as loud and as crushing. Wilde hadn't been prosecuted for sodomy, but it might as well have been the case.

"Oscar Wilde, you've been found guilty of twenty-five counts of gross indecencies and conspiracy to commit gross indecencies."

An outcry ran through the crowd. Voices from below and from the gallery echoed against the walls of the courtroom, amplifying the sounds. Despite the judge's demands for order in the courtroom, the chatter didn't cease.

"Shame!" a young man next to Thomas called out, but behind him others voiced their approval of the verdict.

"Serves the bugger right!" a man proclaimed and shoved the young man to the side. "You're one of them too, aren't you?"

Thomas tried to rise and felt the young man bump into him. When he grabbed the man's shoulders to steady himself, frightened eyes looked up at him. For a moment, Thomas didn't move. This was what would happen to all of them: people would call them out for being homosexuals. Both he and the young man looking at him knew it.

"Yes, both of you!" the man behind them continued his tirade.

To Thomas's shock, others next to him joined in, pointing their fingers at him and the man, whose shoulders he was still clutching. Their eyes were filled with disgust, their mouths pulled up in sneers.

Thomas let go of the other man's shoulders and pushed him back. But it was too late. They'd all seen the flash of compassion that he'd felt for the young queer who'd expressed his opinion about the verdict. They'd all seen that Thomas felt the same. Because he was the same. He was no better than Oscar Wilde or the countless others who somewhere engaged in sodomy every night. The only difference was that he'd been more careful about his assignations, and hidden away his true nature from society better than others.

Thomas ran for the exit, desperate to escape the crowd's scrutiny. Had anybody recognized him? He glanced around, looking at the unfamiliar faces that he ran past. No, nobody from the aristocracy would have been in the courtroom. They found such events distasteful. It was his only consolation.

As he rushed outside, shouts followed him on his heels. He couldn't block them out.

"Faggot!"

"Poof!"

His lungs burned from exertion as he hurried down the broad staircase and crossed the foyer of the courthouse. He sprinted past the marble columns that flanked the entrance, and exited. Night had already fallen, and he was grateful for it. He would be able to disappear in the crowd that hung around the steps in front of the building, waiting for news of the verdict.

He kept his head down, not wanting to draw any further attention to himself. Unfamiliar faces passed him, and voices drifted past his ears. But he kept walking without engaging in any conversation, without breaking his stride. He pretended to be unconcerned about the goings-on around him. Even though he wasn't. The verdict had changed everything. From now on, homosexuals like him would be treated with less tolerance than before. People wouldn't look the other way anymore if they suspected a man of having an intimate relationship with another man. From now on he had to be even more careful or he would end up like Wilde—in prison.

"Wait up!" somebody called behind him, but Thomas kept walking without turning around.

Just a few more steps and he'd be able to cross Fleet Street and disappear into one of the many dark alleys in London. Then he could hire a hackney and get back to his rooms at St. James's Park. And nobody would be the wiser and know what had happened today.

"Young man!" a strangely insistent voice followed him.

He felt compelled to turn his head, but couldn't distinguish who had spoken. Nobody looked at him directly. Shaking his head in confusion, he turned back and bumped into somebody.

Strong hands gripped his shoulders. Thomas's gaze whipped to the person who'd stopped him. Panic surged and made itself known in form of a gasp. Penetrating brown eyes looked at him. The clean-shaven face of a man took on more definition as he pulled his head back by a fraction.

"There, there," the well-dressed stranger said in a surprisingly soothing voice, a voice that seeped into Thomas's body like rich wine or the comforting smell of a pipe.

The tension in his body eased as the stranger's hands smoothed over Thomas's shoulders, almost stroking him as if he were trying to massage the anxiety from his body. A pleasant tingling ran down his arms, spreading warmth in his body despite the cool spring evening.

"No need to be afraid of the mob back there," the man continued, tossing a look over Thomas's shoulder.

All the while, his hands caressed him, and Thomas allowed it even though he should push him away. They were in public, although the stranger now drew him into the entrance of a shop that had long closed. They stood in the shadows; still any passerby would be able to see them if he looked more closely. Yet Thomas didn't have the strength to resist the man's touch. Nor the press of his thighs as he now moved closer.

"So pretty," he cooed, his eyes perusing Thomas's face and body. "It would be a shame if they locked you up for what you are."

Thomas's breath hitched. Was this man taunting him? Was he a Charley? A policeman disguised as a gentleman so he could ferret out the queers in the society? Had the witch hunt already started?

Thomas straightened, making an attempt to push off the man's hands. "Sir, I must ask you to let go of me. You have me mistaken."

The man's face came closer, his eyes drawing him in. "No mistake." His lips parted and the scent of pure masculinity blew against Thomas's face, making his legs weak.

His gut clenched, and farther south, his cock twitched in anticipation. The stranger confirmed with a knowing smile that he was fully aware of Thomas's growing arousal.

"Yes, no mistake at all." One hand separated from his shoulder and, painstakingly slowly, slid down Thomas's torso.

He knew only too well where the stranger's hand was heading, but he couldn't stop him. No, not *couldn't*: didn't want to. For some perverse reason, Thomas craved his touch. He needed to affirm what he was, a man who loved men, and that it felt good, no matter what the mob in front of the courthouse thought.

When a hot palm slid over his now fully erect cock, Thomas groaned and pressed into it. "Christ!"

The man chuckled softly. "Not my name, but I'll take it any day." Then he squeezed harder.

Thomas's heart raced, his chest labored to bring much needed air to his body, and his hands clutched the lapels of the stranger's coat, pulling him closer. With every stroke, he panted more uncontrollably. And with every second his control slipped further.

"But I haven't even started yet."

As if to prove his words, the stranger unbuttoned the flap of Thomas's trousers, pushed aside his undergarments, and took his shaft into his hand. The firm grip, the contact of flesh on flesh, nearly undid him. His head fell against the wall behind him. He closed his eyes and surrendered to the alluring touch, knowing that fighting his own desire was impossible now.

Tender words drifted to his ears, giving him the illusion of floating. He'd never felt anything like it, not even during his most powerful orgasms. But the way this stranger stroked his cock and whispered sweet words into his ear while he kissed Thomas's neck, made him toss caution to the wind.

Forgotten was the fact that anybody passing by could see them engage in this indecent act, an act that could get them both thrown in jail. Forgotten was the fact that he didn't even know the man's name. Nothing mattered. Nothing but the immediate pleasure that this man was promising without asking anything in return.

"More," Thomas begged. "Harder!"

His companion complied without protest, stroking him more firmly, squeezing him harder and faster, bringing him ever closer to completion.

"Yes, yes, that's it."

Lips licked at the crook of his neck, teeth scraped gently against Thomas's heated skin. From somewhere a voice penetrated.

"Yes, come, my young friend. Spend for me. Surrender."

Surrender. Yes, it was all he wanted. Surrender to the touch of this man, give himself up to the pleasure, bathe in the lust of the moment. Without thinking, without regrets. Simply feel.

His balls tightened, and his cock jerked. Then he felt the rush of his semen as it traveled through his shaft as if shot from a pistol. Waves of pleasure washed over him and lifted him up as if he were floating. At the same time, a stinging pain shot through his neck. It was fleeting—too fleeting for it to be real. He had to be hallucinating, because the pleasure this stranger was giving him was making him drunk—drunk on lust, on desire, on sex. Drunk on the sensation of this man's lips locking on his neck, kissing him in a way that felt surreal.

As if the kiss were a bite.

3

Thomas opened his eyes and looked around. Startled, he sat up on a divan. He wasn't in the alley anymore. Instead he found himself in an opulently furnished salon. And he wasn't alone. Far from it.

He tried to take in what he saw, but his mind took a few seconds to process the scene in front of his eyes. There were close to a dozen people in the room—partially dressed people, mostly men, but there were several women among them too. If he were prudish, he would have found the entire scenario scandalous, but he couldn't quite conjure up such a feeling. Instead, he looked around with interest. A man had his trousers pushed down to his knees, his bare ass exposed as he was gripping the hips of another man, thrusting back and forth. Thomas didn't have to get any closer to realize that he was buggering the other man.

Nobody seemed to take any notice of the two, clearly too busy performing similar carnal acts. Thomas's gaze was drawn to a young man who lay on several pillows strewn on the floor in front of the fireplace. His shirt was open and an older man kissed his chest and tweaked his nipples while he rubbed his loins against the younger man. As Thomas continued watching, he felt his own cock rise at the erotic sight. He grew even harder when he saw the young man opening his trousers and pushing them down over his hips, letting his hard prick jut out. The man above him groaned and dropped his head to the man's cock, sucking it into his mouth.

Involuntarily, Thomas's hand went to the bulge that had formed under his trousers.

"Ah, you're awake."

At the sound of the voice, Thomas's head snapped to the side. It only took him a split second to find the man who'd obviously brought him here: the stranger who'd stroked his cock with such skill that Thomas must have fainted when he'd climaxed.

With wide eyes, Thomas stared at him. He sat in a large armchair, his shirt open, exposing his strong chest and dark hair, his trousers missing. Between his legs a half-naked woman kneeled, her head bobbing up and down in his lap, sucking him.

He laid his hand on the back of her head, pulling her up by her hair, then issued his command from between clenched teeth. "Do it like you mean it!" Then his gaze swept back to Thomas, and his hand waved him to approach.

Mesmerized, Thomas got up and crossed to join him.

"I'm Kasper," the man introduced himself.

"Thomas." He stared down at the woman. Why had he assumed that Kasper was queer like him? Clearly, the man liked women.

Maybe his facial expression had given him away, because Kasper chuckled. "Oh that?" He pointed to the woman who was working him hard. "I don't discriminate, nor do I judge. Whatever gives me pleasure." He paused and dropped his gaze to Thomas's crotch. "Earlier, you gave me pleasure, my young friend. I may call you friend, may I not?"

Thomas nodded automatically.

"And it also gives me pleasure to watch others." He waved his hand to indicate the other couples who were engaging in similar acts. Men cavorting with men, even two women touching each other, sliding their naked bodies against each other.

"Who are you?" Thomas asked. "And where are we?" He'd never been to a place like this, where people behaved without inhibitions, without fear of being detected. It seemed like an oasis. Like paradise.

"Safe," Kasper said. "Nobody will find us here. We can do as we please. Act out our wildest fantasies. Isn't that what you want? What you've always dreamed of?"

Kasper's penetrating gaze captured him. Thomas felt imprisoned by his eyes, as if they were shackles that chained him to a fence from which he was forced to watch what was going on around him.

Suspicion coursed through him. "How would you know?"

"I can see it in your eyes. Everybody can see it, if only they bothered to look. I've been watching you for a few days now. There's something about you that fascinates me. So much passion, so much pain buried inside you, wanting to burst to the surface. Just like it did earlier tonight."

Kasper groaned and shoved his cock deeper into the woman's mouth. "When I had you in my hand I could sense your need. So pure, so unspoiled." He tossed a glance around the room. "Not like the men here. They lost that innocence long ago. But you still have it. It's very endearing." He pushed his hips upwards, thrusting harder. "And more than just a little arousing. What man wouldn't want to taste that?"

His suggestive look sent a bolt of desire through Thomas's body. His initial suspicion faded. He had to admit that he was flattered. As well as turned on, not just by his surroundings, but also by Kasper's words. To be desired by a man with his obvious power and standing was exciting. He licked his lips, eager for a taste of what this man promised.

"There's a lot I can give you, if only you want it," Kasper offered and lowered his gaze to his own crotch. "I can give you some of it right now." There was no doubt as to what he meant by that.

And hell, if Thomas didn't want exactly that. Without hesitation he put his hand on the woman's shoulder and pulled her back. "Take a break. I'll take care of this."

Kasper smiled at him as the woman scrambled away and Thomas took her place.

"I'm not going to suck you like that woman. It will be much better than that," Thomas promised, running his hands from Kasper's knees up to the apex of his thighs, where a magnificent cock stood erect, glistening with moisture. It twitched as if acknowledging the words.

"Oh, I don't doubt that."

Thomas bent over Kasper's groin and licked over the head of his erection. A shudder went through his companion, and he smiled to himself. He would reduce this man to putty in his hands. A sensation akin to power jolted through him. It was new to him; yet he liked the feeling of knowing he could bring this man to his knees. It was a challenge he wouldn't shirk.

"But while I do this, you'll do something for me. You'll tell me about yourself. And with every bit of information you give me, I'll suck you harder." Thomas placed his lips around the head of Kasper's shaft and slid down on him, taking him in to the root.

Kasper trembled underneath him, before Thomas withdrew. "Start now," he demanded and cupped his balls, stroking a fingernail against the tight sac, feeling a thrill go through him as Kasper shuddered and a drop of moisture spilled from his cock.

Kasper panted heavily. "I'm a leader of a group of men who have certain . . . leanings."

Thomas sank his mouth back onto the engorged flesh and closed his lips around it, sucking him deep inside.

Kasper groaned and thrust his hips upwards. "We have our hideouts, safe places where we meet. Where we indulge in our fantasies."

Thomas wrapped his hand around the base and sucked again, letting Kasper's erection slide out of his mouth, only to capture it again a split second later, increasing his tempo. He squeezed his hand around him while his other hand gently played with his balls. He had yet to meet a man who could resist his intimate touch, a touch he knew was more tantalizing than that of a woman. Because he knew better than any woman what a man wanted.

"Nobody can touch us. We're strong. They'll never get us." Kasper panted heavily, his hips working frantically to increase the friction, pumping harder and faster in and out of Thomas's mouth. "Oh, fuck, you're good!"

Thomas's chest swelled with pride. This was what he lived for: to seek pleasure and to return it.

"And one day, we won't have to hide anymore. One day, they'll accept us."

Thomas heard the words and wanted to believe them, but he couldn't. Nobody would ever accept deviants like him. He would always have to hide. But at least if the hiding place was like this, a private den of iniquity, where sin was always on the menu and wickedness was expected, he could live with it.

Giving himself over to his task, he licked and sucked until Kasper finally surrendered and shuddered. It took long seconds before he stilled completely, his head falling back against the armchair, his body almost collapsing.

Thomas raised his head and looked at him. What he saw made him fall backwards onto his ass, trying to scurry away in horror. But he got no chance. As he fell flat onto his back, Kasper jumped onto him, legs spread-eagle, straddling him. Iron-hard hands encircled Thomas's wrists, pinning them to the floor next to his head.

Kasper flashed brilliant white fangs at him, snarling like a beast. "Now, my dear, you'll listen to me. Your little attempt at trying to control me was all good and fine, but make no mistake: I allowed you to control me for my own pleasure. Because sometimes, we all like to be dominated. Sometimes we enjoy being controlled and played with. But I decide when and where and how. Do you understand that?"

Numbly, Thomas nodded, unable to speak, because all air had rushed out of his lungs. What was Kasper? What kind of creature was this man? No, he wasn't a man. He couldn't be a man. He was a beast.

"I find you interesting." He rocked his still semi-erect cock against Thomas's groin. "And utterly sexy. But I don't let myself be controlled by my baser instincts. I'm the master. I decide what happens, when it happens, and how it happens. And it just happens I've decided to make you my companion." He let a smile quirk around his lips. "And not just because you suck cock so masterfully."

Thomas shivered involuntarily. Despite the fear he felt when he looked at the sharp teeth that were protruding from Kasper's mouth, the thought that this powerful man wanted him thrilled him. He was mature enough to admit it to himself: being controlled by another man excited him. It turned him on and made him hard.

Kasper ground against him again, and Thomas felt his cock swell as a result of it. He closed his eyes, swallowing the shame of it. Because he should be ashamed of what he wanted: to be dominated by this man.

"You know it, don't you? How much pleasure can be had from pain, from shame, even from fear. That's why you're so perfect. So perfect for what I need." Kasper released one wrist and stroked his knuckles along Thomas's neck, sending shivers racing down his skin.

The vein at his neck began to throb.

"Oh, yes, you know what I am, don't you?"

Thomas shook his head, trying to deny what his mind had already figured out. It wasn't possible. Creatures like him didn't exist. Not in real life, not in London, not anywhere in England.

"Say it, lover, say what I am." A long finger trailed along Thomas's pulsating vein.

"Vampire."

When the word was out, Thomas released a breath and felt the pressure on his chest ease. Kasper lifted himself off and pulled him up to a sitting position, cupping his nape with one hand.

"See? It wasn't that hard, was it?" He pressed a brief kiss on Thomas's lips. Then he placed his hand over Thomas's hard-on. "Even though other things are hard again."

Startled, Thomas pulled back, but didn't get far, Kasper's hand on his nape holding him close. "You're not going anywhere, don't you understand that? Everything you'll ever need is here. With me. I can protect you." He pointed toward one of the windows which was hung with heavy velvet curtains. "Out there, a man like you will always be in danger. But I can help you. And together we'll wait for the time when there will be no more persecution of our kind. We have time on our side."

Instinctively, Thomas knew what Kasper was proposing.

"I can give you eternal life. Don't you want to live in a time when queers like us will be accepted? When nobody will give a care about who we fuck? When kissing a man in public won't land you in prison?"

Thomas finally found his voice again. "You don't know that such a time will ever come! They'll always look at us with disgust!"

Kasper shook his head, smiling. "How wrong you are, my friend. My sweet Thomas. If only you could believe that the future will be bright."

"How can I when all I see is pain? When I have to hide from everybody who I am? When even my sisters would recoil from me if they found out?"

Kasper caressed Thomas's neck. The touch soothed him more than he liked to admit. Maybe his lover really could help him. If only to forget his troubles.

"All I ask for is a little trust. And patience. Our time will come. We will rise together. And in the meantime, we'll wring every last drop of pleasure from each other."

"Why me?" Thomas searched his lover's eyes for an answer.

"Because you have potential. You'll be strong. As strong as I am. And powerful. Together we can rule. But you'll have to become like me."

Thomas stared into Kasper's eyes, their darkness pulling him in as if he were being hypnotized. "You mean become a vampire?"

"Yes, I will drain you of your blood and give you mine. You'll be part of me. Strong, powerful, invincible. All you have to do is say 'yes.'"

Unable to tear his gaze away from Kasper's eyes, Thomas moved his head closer, his lips now hovering only an inch over his lover's. "Do you truly believe there'll come a time when we can be free to express our feelings without fear of punishment?"

"Yes. Soon that time will come."

"Yes." With a breath, he sank his lips onto Kasper's and kissed him, wrapping his arms around him and dropping back onto the floor with Kasper on top of him. "Do it while you make love to me so I won't see it coming."

"Whatever you wish, my sweet lover."

4

Today

Thomas pulled his motorcycle into the spot in front of Al's Motorcycle Parts and killed the engine. The one good thing about having to go shopping at night was that he almost always found a parking spot close by. The area south of Market Street was pretty much deserted by this time of night, and only clubbers were out now, most of whom didn't bother driving but instead took taxis or walked to the clubs in the area.

Al's was always open late. In fact, the shop only opened its door at sundown, even though Al could have easily opened during daylight hours. After all, the shop was windowless, and he would be safe in there even at daytime. But like many vampires, Al kept to the hours of his own species, shunning daylight.

He'd been coming to Al's shop for many years now, just about every time he needed to find a rare part for one of his motorcycles. Only recently, he'd completed the restoration of a WWII BMW, and Al had been a great help in sourcing some of the parts that Thomas had needed to replace. There was no place like Al's if he wanted to get authentic parts for his antique bikes. Where the guy found the genuine parts, Thomas didn't know, and Al had certainly never divulged his sources. It didn't matter. Thomas was prepared to pay a premium just so he could continue with his hobby.

Thomas pushed open the door to the large building and entered, accompanied by the sound of the chime above the door. The interior was well-lit, the endless shelves well-stocked, and the smells familiar: oil, solvents, and paints. He lifted his gaze to the counter, expecting the usual greeting from Al, but was instead hit with a wall of silence.

The man behind the checkout counter that was covered with faded linoleum wasn't Al, nor was he one of Al's employees. He was a vampire, all right, but Thomas had never met him. Had Al hired somebody new? It wasn't like him. Al didn't like change and hadn't taken on a new employee in years. Most of the time he worked by himself.

The vampire nodded at him. "Help you?" he asked brusquely.

Thomas crossed the distance between him and the counter, letting nothing in his gait betray the fact that he was curious. "Yeah. Al around?"

The vampire shook his head. "No."

"Will he be back soon?"

"No."

At the second monosyllabic answer, Thomas ground his teeth and had to relax his jaw so he wouldn't sound hostile. "When then?"

"Won't be back."

"Why?"

"Sold the place."

The news surprised him. Al had never mentioned that he had any intention of selling the shop. Selling meant changing, and there wasn't anything Al hated more than change, except for a stake in the heart or the rising sun on his heels.

Thomas perused the other vampire more closely now. There was nothing extraordinary about him. He neither looked very powerful, nor very bright. In fact, his speech pattern and posture made him look rather like a slow-witted cousin from the backwoods. Vampire trash if anybody asked him. The kind of man who'd never amount to anything.

"Sold when?"

He shrugged. "Last week."

"To whom?"

The vampire puffed his chest out. "To me."

Thomas kept his tongue in check so the next words didn't spill over his lips. There was no way in hell Al had sold out to the guy behind the counter. Something was fishy. But he was smart enough to know that any further questioning would only increase the guy's hostility. Maybe once he'd done some business with him, he could find out more.

"Well, in that case, I'd better deal with you." He pulled a piece of paper from his leather jacket and unfolded it, spreading the photocopy of an old magazine he'd found in front of the man. He pointed his finger at a spot on the drawing. "I need this part here for the front master cylinder. It's a 1956 model. Manufactured in Germany."

The vampire only glanced at the piece of paper then motioned to the aisles. "If we have it, it's on one of the shelves. Your guess is as good as mine." His bored look said it all.

Thomas shook his head. "It won't be on the shelves. It's a 1956 model. Nobody stocks those."

"Well, then we don't have it."

Thomas let out an annoyed huff. "I figured that much. What I'm asking is for you to find me one."

"How you want me to do that? Suck it out of my fingernails?"

"It's called special order. You must have contacts to some suppliers who do special requests."

The new owner of Al's Motorcycle Parts crossed his arms over his chest. "We don't do special orders. You can't find it here, go someplace else."

Thomas narrowed his eyes and leaned over the counter. "It's your fucking job!"

The other vampire moved closer. "I say what my job is. And it's not fetching shit for guys like you. I'm nobody's errand boy. You get that?" He flashed his fangs.

Clenching his teeth, Thomas took his piece of paper and folded it slowly and deliberately, keeping a lid on his anger. It would be so easy to simply crush the guy with one blast of mind control, so simple, yet so satisfying. Inside him, his two sides warred with each other, each fighting for supremacy, both sides almost equally strong. His chest heaved from the effort it cost him to reveal nothing of his internal struggle to the outside. He couldn't give himself away.

"My apologies," he pressed out instead. "I guess I'll have to take my business elsewhere."

Then he turned on his heels, hightailing it out of the shop as fast as if a horde of bigots were chasing him with stakes in their fists. He swung himself onto his motorcycle and engaged the engine. When it howled, he shot into the road and thundered down the one-way-street like a speeding bullet.

He had to get away from the temptation to teach the guy a lesson in manners—as well as in business. It happened more and more lately: the smallest things set him off and made the dark power surge within him, eager to break to the surface. Ever since he'd killed Kasper, his maker—or Keegan, as he'd called himself later—he'd started feeling the thirst for power well up more often. And every time, the struggle to suppress the evil became more violent.

5

The V-lounge at Scanguards' headquarters was buzzing with activity when Thomas arrived. Everybody was getting ready to welcome Haven, Yvette's mate, into Scanguards. After several months of sorting things out with his old life as a vampire hunter, he'd finally come to a decision and accepted the position Samson had offered him. Tonight would be his official first day, and the guys had decided to throw him a little party at the lounge.

Thomas glanced around. The large room looked like the lounge of a five-diamond hotel, complete with comfortable seating arrangements, a fireplace, and a bar and bartender. Only, no bottles lined the back wall of the bar, and no mirror decorated it. The drinks served from the stainless steel taps weren't alcoholic; the barrels underneath contained various types of blood that the sexy female bartender was serving in crystal glasses.

Just because Thomas was gay didn't mean he didn't recognize that the woman working behind the bar was what a straight guy would call *sex on legs*. Besides, he noticed the way the other vampires looked at her: as if they wanted to drink from her rather than from the glasses she handed them. Like randy dogs, they hovered around the bar, trying their various pick-up lines on her, almost drooling. Did Thomas look like that when he looked at Eddie? He hoped not. It was pathetic enough that he was in love with a straight man.

The ice princess, as some of the guys had started calling her behind her back, kept her cool and polite exterior despite the suggestive comments and the obvious propositions, not giving away what was going on inside her. With a sigh, Thomas approached, and smiled at her.

"Roxanne," he called her attention to him.

She turned toward him and gave him a genuine smile, her body visibly relaxing. "Thomas, what can I get you, love?"

Her British accent was still pronounced, and made him think of home and the two sisters he'd left behind. Regret for having left them flowed through him. But he couldn't turn back time. There was no use in thinking of it now.

"AB positive, please."

Roxanne pulled a glass from underneath the counter and operated one of the taps. "Dessert before dinner?"

He grinned. AB positive was considered the sweetest blood type. He winked. "If you don't tell, I won't."

As she expelled a warm laugh, Thomas heard the whispers of the other vampires beside him.

"What's he got that we don't?" one of them grumbled.

Roxanne's head shot toward the man who'd spoken. She nailed him with a glare. "Class. That's what he's got. So scram." She shooed them away, and to Thomas's surprise the men complied.

"You don't have to fight my battles for me, Roxanne."

She smiled at him softly. "You're constantly fighting mine. Just returning the favor, love."

Thomas jerked his thumb in the direction of the vampires who were now congregating near the fireplace. "If you smiled at them the way you smile at me, your tips would be better."

"I only smile when I mean it." She set the glass of blood in front of him. "On the house."

A heavy hand slid over his shoulder, making him turn.

"Is Roxanne plying you with blood again?" Samson asked, grinning.

Thomas laughed. "If only it worked!" he joked, knowing that if he were straight, Roxanne would make the moves on him. Yet, she respected what he was, and despite the fact that she was attracted to him, she treated him like a brother. He liked that about her.

He exchanged a long look with her.

"At least Thomas doesn't want to jump my bones. That's something I can't say for that bunch over there." She tossed her head in the direction of the fireplace.

Samson removed his arm from Thomas's shoulders and leaned over the bar. "If they're harassing you, you've gotta let me know. I'll take them to task."

She made a dismissive hand movement. "And make it even worse by tattling on them? I can handle them."

"As you wish."

"I would offer you a drink, but given that you're blood-bonded, I guess there's nothing I can do for you."

Samson shook his head, smiling. "Nothing at all." Then he winked at her. "Although I'm not blind, and can understand why the guys keep trying." Then he turned to Thomas. "We're almost ready. Haven and Yvette should be arriving any minute."

Together they walked away from the bar.

"Did Eddie come with you?" Samson asked.

"No, I had to stop by at Al's for a part, so I left earlier." He let his gaze sweep around the room, but couldn't see Eddie.

"I'm sure he'll get here in time. How is Al?"

Thomas rubbed the back of his neck, unease creeping down his back again. "Actually I don't know."

"But I thought you said—"

He interrupted his boss. "He's not there anymore. Somebody bought the place from him."

Samson's eyebrows pulled together. "I hadn't heard anything about that. When did that happen?"

"Apparently last week."

"That's what I heard too. But that's not all." Thomas turned to the voice coming from behind them and looked at Zane.

"What else did you hear?" Thomas asked.

Zane shoved one hand into his pants pocket. "That he sold awfully quick. Somebody saw a couple of guys in suits march into his office, and a half-hour later Al started packing. Doesn't look right, if you ask me."

Thomas could only agree. "The new guy who says he bought it doesn't look like the sharpest tool in the shed either. I get the feeling he's just a puppet. He has no idea about the business, and I can't help but think that he's a front for somebody. Maybe we should look into this." He looked at Samson.

Zane interrupted. "I'm way ahead of you. I made a few inquires and found out that he sold the place for next to nothing."

Samson grunted. "I don't like it. Do you think he was coerced?"

"Looks like it," Zane confirmed. "And he's definitely left town. I checked out his flat. Looks like he left in a hurry, only taking some personal items. His furniture is still there."

Thomas scratched his head, not liking at all what he heard. "Al isn't the kind of guy to make hasty decisions. Besides, he hates change. He wouldn't just move from one day to the next. That's not like him."

Zane rocked back on his heels. "Looks to me like he was shit-scared of something."

"But what?" Thomas asked.

"Zane, why don't you get a couple of guys on it to see what's going on?" Samson suggested. "Let us know what you find."

"Sure, will do." Then he pointed toward the door. "Looks like our guest of honor just arrived."

Thomas looked to the door of the lounge and saw Haven entering, Yvette by his side. The witch-turned-vampire was a big man, broad-shouldered, and strong. Even as a human he'd been able to hold his own, but now, as a vampire, he was among the strongest of them. Yvette was both his mate and his sire, a combination that made their bond even stronger if that was possible. While she'd always worn her hair short, after meeting Haven she'd stopped cutting it and it had grown back during her restorative sleep to the length it had had at her turning. She looked a lot more feminine now, and the hard edge she'd always had to her personality seemed to have softened too. Haven was good for her.

Haven had had his reservations about joining Scanguards after being a vampire hunter for most of his life. Luckily his love for Yvette had helped him see that his view of vampires, which had been influenced by a tragedy in his past, was too narrow-minded. Now that he had gotten to know their particular group of vampires, he'd finally accepted that even vampires could be good.

Thomas walked toward Haven and Yvette to greet them, Samson and Zane following him. Before he reached them, the door opened again and Eddie entered. Instantly, his heart started beating faster, and his fangs itched, wanting to descend.

Eddie looked as fresh and innocent as always. He wore a hooded sweatshirt over his jeans and immediately pulled it over his head to rid himself of it since the lounge was overly warm. As he did so, the T-shirt he wore underneath pulled up with it, exposing toned abs and a hairless chest.

Of course, he'd seen Eddie shirtless before, but no matter how often he got a look at his perfect body, it always caused the same visceral reaction in him: his mouth went dry, his palms became damp, his heart started beating into his throat, and he had to fight against his vampire side to stop it from bursting to the surface, wrestling Eddie to the ground, stripping him naked and driving his aching cock into him while sinking his fangs into his neck and drinking from him.

Eddie tossed the sweatshirt onto a nearby chair and pulled his T-shirt back over his jeans, depriving Thomas of the sight.

Maybe it was better that way. Maybe he should simply remove himself from temptation. Still, it wouldn't eradicate his daydreams, nor the fantasies he had about Eddie and himself: how they would shower together, stroking each other; how they would share a bed, making love; how they would feast on each other, sharing their blood.

So many fantasies, yet not a single one would ever turn into reality.

6

Eddie saw how Haven and Yvette were already beleaguered by their colleagues, who shook Haven's hand and congratulated him on his new position: bodyguard at Scanguards. Eddie remembered how proud he'd been when he had joined Scanguards over a year-and-a-half earlier. Back then he'd been human and had had no idea about the vampires that ran Scanguards. Much had happened since. Good and bad stuff.

He walked past the crowd, noticing that Thomas too was shaking Haven's hand. He'd known that he would find Thomas here. Nevertheless, his heart started beating faster, and nervousness crept up his spine, spreading over his entire body. He didn't know anymore how to behave around his mentor. Ever since he'd overheard Oliver and Blake, he felt awkward when talking to Thomas. And always on edge, as if he needed to weigh each word he uttered, careful not to say anything that might give Thomas the impression that Eddie was into him—because he wasn't.

Willing himself to calm down, he stalked to the bar and ordered a drink. "Hi Roxanne, O negative, please."

"Here for the party?" She started pouring his drink.

"Yeah, I never miss out on a party. Free blood, right?" He pointed to the taps.

"You bet. Just don't go overboard. The boss has instructed me to keep an eye on you guys. If anybody overindulges, I'm authorized to cut you off." She smirked.

He grinned back. "Spoil sport!"

She put the glass of blood in front of him and ruffled his hair. "Now go play with the others."

Eddie tossed her a mock-outraged look. "You make us sound like we're kids."

Roxanne chuckled and leaned over the bar, her ample bosom almost too close for comfort. He glanced at it briefly, but nothing stirred in his groin. "That's because *you* are."

He rolled his eyes. "I'm twenty-five!"

"Baby!" she cooed as if talking to an infant.

He grabbed the glass and downed its contents. The rich blood coated his throat, stilling his hunger. He instantly felt better, calmer. Maybe he'd just been overly hungry, and that was why he felt so apprehensive about being in Thomas's company. Hunger could do a lot of funny things to a vampire. He'd found that out the hard way when he'd first been turned. He'd never been so ravenous in his entire life. Nor as violent.

A hand tapped on his shoulder. Eddie spun around and released a shaky breath when he realized that it hadn't been Thomas's hand that had touched him.

Get a grip, he chastised himself.

"Hey, Cain."

"Wow, you're jumpy. What's up?" The dark-haired vampire with the permanent stubble on his chin and the penetrating dark eyes looked him up and down.

"Nothing. Why would something be up? Just getting my first drink."

Cain nodded toward the bartender. "I'm having what he's having."

Roxanne smiled. "Coming right up."

As she turned to the taps, Eddie caught the long lusting look that Cain raked over her body, lingering on her breasts, then dropping to her shapely ass. He could clearly see what his colleague was thinking. Oddly enough, when Eddie let his gaze sweep over Roxanne's curves, he felt nothing. The woman was exceedingly beautiful, but Eddie didn't feel any desire rising in him, nor any blood surging to his cock. Touching and kissing her held no appeal for him, when he should have the same lusty feelings as half the vampires in the lounge had for this extraordinary female specimen with the upper crust English accent.

Maybe something was wrong with him. Maybe a hormonal imbalance. Perhaps he should go see Maya and have her check him out to see if his testosterone levels were low. Maya, Gabriel's mate, was the only vampire physician—apart from the psychiatrist Dr. Drake—in San Francisco. Her specialty when she'd been a human doctor had been urology. If anybody knew a male body, then it was she. Maybe after the party, he'd pull her aside and make an appointment with her.

"Did you hear anything about that?" Cain's voice drifted to him.

Eddie fumbled for an answer. He hadn't heard what Cain had been talking about. "Sorry, can you repeat that?"

Cain narrowed his eyes and gave him an assessing look. "You wanna tell me what's wrong with you? First you're jumpy, and now you're distracted." His colleague leaned closer.

Eddie's breath hitched. Did Cain suspect the reason for his inattentiveness?

"You'd better pull yourself together, kid! I have the feeling there's some shit going down here soon. I just overheard Gabriel telling Samson he's calling a staff meeting later tonight. You'll need all your marbles. So whatever hot broad is distracting you, put her out of your mind."

Eddie sighed inwardly. If only it were a hot woman who was occupying his thoughts, then he would have nothing to worry about. He'd never been distracted by a woman. Sure, he'd fucked some of them, but now that he thought of it, he'd never been so into it that he'd forgotten about the rest of his life. Even as a teenager, he'd preferred hanging out with his buddies to sneaking off into some dark alley with a girl to get some action. His friends had actually teased him that he was too much of a good guy. And good guys didn't get laid. No wonder he'd been almost twenty when he'd lost his virginity.

It hadn't rocked his world. Maybe he was just not a very sexual guy. He shook his head. No, that couldn't be true either. After all, he masturbated daily. Didn't that prove that his sex drive was alive and well? Perhaps he'd simply not met the right woman. That had to be it. Roxanne was just not his type, that's why he didn't feel any spark in his groin when he looked at her.

"Why are you guys whispering?"

Heat shot into Eddie's cheeks as he heard Thomas's voice behind him. He took a steadying breath and turned slowly, trying to keep his face an unreadable mask.

"Cain was just saying there's supposed to be a staff meeting tonight," Eddie repeated Cain's words.

Thomas shrugged. "Hadn't heard anything. Must be a last minute thing."

Cain pointed toward the crowd around Haven and Yvette. "I should go say hello." But Cain didn't get a chance, because at the same moment, Samson asked for quiet in the room.

"Thank you! And thanks all for coming tonight," Samson started. "I'm very pleased to welcome our newest member into Scanguards."

Next to him, Haven stood smiling, his arm around Yvette who looked up at him with pride shining in her eyes. He bent to her ear and whispered something to her which made her eyes go wide. Eddie could only guess that it had been something very private, and something very erotic.

Thomas tapped his arm, sending a shiver through his body, then leaned closer to whisper to him. "Never thought I'd see Yvette like that."

Eddie forced himself to remain calm. "Like what?"

"All feminine and soft. You haven't known her as long as I, but she was one tough cookie."

"She seems happy. Haven's a great guy."

Samson continued, "Haven has been helping us in many difficult situations. And I'm therefore very happy to announce that he's finally accepted my offer to join Scanguards. Haven, would you like to say a few words?"

Haven nodded quickly. "Yeah, well, I'm not a man of many words. Just to say: I'm looking forward to this new challenge. Now let's party!" He waved to one corner of the lounge, where a band had set up.

Music filled the room. Eddie watched how Haven pulled Yvette to the area in front of the band, where some of the furniture had been removed to make space for a small dance floor. As Haven and Yvette started dancing and were soon joined by Zane and his hybrid wife Portia, Eddie turned away from the sight. His sister Nina wasn't here, nor was Delilah. Humans weren't allowed at the lounge. It was a strict rule that not even Samson broke.

However, the room wasn't completely devoid of women. Apart from Yvette and Portia, Maya and Rose, both vampires, were also present. They were mingling with the male vampires, but their mates were never far—both Gabriel and Quinn kept their eyes on the other Scanguards employees, ready to interfere if another male dared touch their wives inappropriately.

Next to Eddie, Cain and Thomas both chuckled. Eddie turned his head to see what they were finding so funny.

"Don't they look like dogs with a bone?" Thomas asked, motioning to Gabriel and Quinn.

Eddie rolled his eyes and cracked a smile. "Pathetic!"

"Let's drink to that!" Thomas agreed and turned back toward the bar. "Three of the . . . " He turned with a questioning look. "What are you guys having?"

"O neg," Eddie said.

"Same," was Cain's reply.

"And yourself?" Roxanne asked.

"Make that three O negs."

"You guys are easy."

Cain made a grimace. "Did she just insult us?"

One side of Thomas's mouth tilted upwards. "Sounded like it."

"What are we gonna do about it?" Eddie asked, grinning, glad that both Cain and Thomas were concentrating their attention on the bartender. It took the heat off him, and he could finally begin to relax.

"I think punishment is in order," Cain suggested.

Roxanne tossed them a *get real* look and continued filling the glasses with blood.

"I don't think she believes you," Eddie teased.

Thomas laughed. "That's probably because she knows we'd never punish her." He winked at her. "After all, she sits at the source." He motioned to the taps. "And you never bite the hand that feeds you. Literally and figuratively."

Roxanne finished pouring the three glasses. Then she took one and held it over the sink, tilting it a bit. "So, you want your drinks, or not?"

Eddie, Thomas, and Cain exchanged quick glances.

"That would be lovely, Roxanne," Thomas said, his voice softer than before.

Roxanne's look softened and Eddie could clearly see how Thomas's voice appeased her and made her melt. The reason he knew that was because he too could feel it: how Thomas's deep voice penetrated his body and sank deep into him. It made him want to lay back on one of the large sofas, stretch out, and settle in for a soothing massage. Strong male hands on naked skin. Smooth long strokes. Fire on his body. Electricity charging through his veins.

Eddie's fangs lengthened.

"Better give one to Eddie first," Thomas remarked. "Looks like he's hungry."

Eddie willed his fangs to retract.

Shit!

He should have more control over himself. After all, he wasn't a newborn vampire anymore. He was over a year old already, and he was past the worst cravings, past the most difficult time. But whenever he was near Thomas, his reactions were unpredictable.

7

A year earlier

Flanked by Ricky, Eddie walked into Samson's study. He couldn't help but fidget. After the mausoleum had gone up in flames, and Luther had been arrested and brought before the vampire council for sentencing, Eddie, as well another former Scanguards bodyguard, Kent, had been held under house arrest at Ricky's place—Scanguards' operations director.

Luther, the man who'd promised Eddie eternal life as a vampire, had lied to him and duped him into joining his evil plan to take revenge on Samson by killing his wife—a plan that thankfully had failed. He'd told Eddie that Samson and Amaury had killed Luther's wife, when in fact, she had refused Samson's and Amaury's offer to turn her into a vampire, and thus save her life, when she lay dying in childbirth.

Eddie had unwittingly chosen the wrong side and nearly paid for it with his life.

Finally tonight, Eddie had received word that his future had been decided. He looked at Samson, who sat behind his massive desk that housed two large computer monitors. He glanced up and motioned to the chair in front of the desk.

"Take a seat." He lifted his head to look at Ricky. "I'll take it from here."

Ricky nodded and silently left the room.

Eddie shifted nervously in his chair. His foot tapped on the rug beneath him, and he laid his hands on his knees to stop them from shaking. He already knew that they wouldn't kill him; his new brother-in-law, Amaury, had promised him as much. After all, Amaury had blood-bonded with his sister Nina and wouldn't do

44 Tina Folsom

anything to make her unhappy. And that meant he would not hurt her brother.

But they would punish him nevertheless. After all, he'd committed a crime under Luther's influence and had helped plot the attempted murder of Samson's mate.

"Relax," Samson said. "I didn't ask you here to rip your head off."

Eddie tried a smile and failed miserably. "Sorry. I mean . . . I didn't know what I was doing."

Samson held up his hand. "Stop right there."

Eddie pressed himself deeper into his chair. Shit, this wasn't going well. He sounded like some kid who'd been dragged in front of the high school principal, and not like the newly-minted vampire he was. Hell, he shouldn't have those concerns and fears right now. Weren't vampires supposed to be invincible? At least his sire, Luther, had seemed that way. Of course, now, he was sitting in a cell somewhere, not so powerful anymore. Probably crapping in his pants.

"I called you here because you'll need to be retrained. Luther is your maker, and I can never take that away from you, but the things he taught you are not the rules we live by. We don't kill indiscriminately; we protect the innocent. As Nina's brother, you're part of our family, and we can't ignore that fact. Luther used you and the others for his own nefarious plans, and the blame lies with him. But it is our duty to make sure this won't happen again."

Eddie nodded. "I won't do anything criminal ever again."

"You can't honestly promise something like that, because you're still not the master of yourself. There are many more temptations that will come your way. Many times you'll want to use your new powers for your own gain. Only when you've conquered those urges will you truly be able to make such promises. In the meantime, I'd like you to meet your new mentor."

Samson pointed to a spot behind him.

Eddie turned in his chair and jumped up in the same motion. Behind him stood a tall blond man dressed in leather gear: black leather pants, a white T-shirt, and a black leather jacket.

"This is Thomas. You'll follow all his orders. You'll eat when he tells you to eat, you'll sleep when he tells you to sleep. He'll teach you everything you need to know."

Eddie looked at the vampire. He'd seen him briefly during the fight at the mausoleum, but hadn't been formally introduced to him. Now the biker stretched his hand toward him, and Eddie clutched it immediately. His handshake was strong and firm, his hand surprisingly warm. His palm felt smooth, and the scent that emanated from Thomas now engulfed him.

When he spoke for the first time, the timbre of Thomas's voice drove deep into Eddie's chest. "Nice to meet you, Eddie. I'm sure we'll get along just fine."

Strangely enough, Eddie could only echo those words. There was something about Thomas that made him instantly relax. As if he'd known him all his life. Like a brother. A much wiser, older brother.

"You can let go of my hand now," Thomas said, smiling.

Heat shooting into his cheeks, Eddie dropped Thomas's hand. Jesus, what the fuck was wrong with him? Couldn't he just act normally? He had to make a good impression on his new mentor. After all, Scanguards was giving him a second chance, and there was no way he'd screw this one up. He'd make them proud of him and do whatever it took. Just like he'd always wanted to make Nina proud of him. In fact, he still did.

Turning to Samson, he said, "Thank you, Samson, you won't regret it."

Samson nodded. "Thomas will tell you when you're ready to resume your duties at Scanguards. In the meantime, we'll be paying your full salary."

Samson's generosity floored him. He hadn't expected this and had already wondered what he would do to survive once he was on his own again and not staying at Ricky's anymore. "I don't know how to thank you."

"No need. I practically had no choice. Amaury is a very persuasive man."

Thomas chuckled. "Who has no defenses when it comes to his mate."

Samson laughed. "Well, luckily, neither you nor I have to live with Nina."

Eddie felt the need to defend his sister, even though he knew well enough himself that she could be a pain in the butt. Stubborn as hell. And argumentative. "What are you saying?"

"Only that your sister has Amaury firmly wrapped around her little finger." Thomas pulled a set of gloves from his jacket pocket. "Let's go then. Do you ride motorcycles?"

"A bit."

"Well, you'll learn."

"Where are we going?" Eddie asked, curious and excited at the same time. He had the feeling that hanging out with Thomas would be a lot of fun. He seemed different from the other vampires he'd met. Not as intense. More casual.

"Home."

"Home?"

"Yes, you're moving in with me. Makes things easier. Any objections?"

Eddie shook his head. He was planning on complying with everything his mentor demanded. Not just to please Samson and Nina, but also, because he wanted Thomas to be proud of him.

"I hope I won't be cramping your style. I mean, if you have a girl coming around and need some privacy, I'm happy to stay out of your way."

Thomas stopped in his tracks. "A girl?" Then he looked back at Samson. "Didn't you tell him that I'm gay?"

Gay? Thomas was gay? Eddie looked him up and down. He didn't look gay at all. He looked ... masculine and not at all effeminate. A man's man.

"Is that a problem?" Thomas asked with a tightness in his voice that hadn't been there before.

For an instant, Eddie's heart stopped. He shook his head, not wanting to alienate Thomas. "No, no problem at all." He didn't care which way Thomas was swinging. All that mattered was that his mentor felt comfortable in his company. He wouldn't let Thomas's sexual orientation get in the way of their professional relationship. After all, they were both grown-ups.

"Can't wait to see your digs," he added, lending his voice a more cheerful note in order to dispel the awkwardness that had risen for a moment. "What kind of motorcycle do you ride? A Harley?"

Thomas smiled at him. "Not quite. I have a few others. I'll show 'em to you. If you like, we can go for a ride later."

8

Today

Thomas glanced at Eddie from the side as he watched the dancers, and occasionally sipped from his glass. Eddie appeared to be lost in his thoughts. Lately, he'd seen him like this quite often, almost as if something were bothering him. But Thomas wasn't one to pry into other people's personal affairs. If Eddie needed advice on something, he'd come to him when he was ready. From the beginning when he'd started mentoring the young vampire, he'd made a point of not coddling him. Nobody ever grew into his own and became a man if he was treated with kid gloves. And he wanted Eddie to become a strong and independent man with steadfast values. By all indications, Eddie was heading in the right direction.

"They make a great couple, don't they?" a familiar voice said close to him, a hand pointing at Yvette and Haven.

Thomas turned his head and smiled at Maya. "They sure do. As do you and Gabriel."

"Charmer!" she teased and walked to stand next to him. "Listen, Thomas, I wanted your advice on something."

He raised a questioning eyebrow, then allowed her to lead him a few steps away from Eddie and Cain.

"About?"

"I feel that some of us treated Oliver a little too harshly when this whole thing with Ursula and the blood brothel went down."

Thomas remembered all too well how everybody had tried to save Oliver from himself. They'd realized only later that he was stronger than they'd all assumed and was dealing with the temptation that Ursula's blood represented well enough on his own. "Don't remind me. But you know as well as I do that we had to be strict with him. His history—"

She raised her hand to interrupt him. "You don't have to tell me. We all had our reasons. But now that things have worked out for the best and he's conquered his bloodlust, I feel we should celebrate that fact."

Thomas smirked. "I have the feeling he's celebrating that fact every day in private with Ursula." His eyes searched the crowd, and he saw Oliver talking to his sire, Quinn. Oliver appeared relaxed and happy.

Maya nudged him in the ribs. "That's not what I'm talking about!"

"I know that. Just thought I'd throw it out there."

She rolled her eyes. "I'm talking about a party with more than two people."

"The usual suspects?"

Maya nodded. "It's just I need to find a pretense for this party. I don't want Oliver to know what we're planning, but I want to make sure he and Ursula will be there. And I'm not quite sure even what to tell him at the party. Sorry we weren't nice to you?"

Thomas contemplated her words. "Hmm. Not sure. Have you talked to Zane about it? From what I recall he was his usual asshole self. Maybe he's got some ideas."

Maya grimaced. "If I even mention it to him, he'll go ballistic. You know what he thinks of apologizing to anybody. I don't think he knows how it's done."

"Not his strong suit, you're right." He ran his hand through his hair. "Why does it have to be a party at all? Can't we just send him a gift?"

"A gift?"

"Yes, maybe an all-expenses-paid trip for him and Ursula to somewhere nice. I don't know, Venice, London. You tell me. I'm sure he'd rather go off somewhere with Ursula than hang out with us oldies."

Maya's forehead furrowed as she let his suggestions sink in. "Hmm. I'll think about it."

"You know he'll have to figure out something for his honeymoon anyway. Why not take it off his hands?"

"Honeymoon?" Maya repeated.

"Shhh!" Thomas cast a look around him to make sure nobody had heard Maya. "Yes, honeymoon. He's going to ask her sooner or later. Every idiot watching them can see that. I'm guessing we'll have another blood-bond before the year is out."

"You think so?"

"Absolutely. Actually, I'm a little surprised that it hasn't happened already. Just look at him now." Thomas pointed toward Oliver, who was still talking to Quinn and Rose. "See how he fidgets? He can't stand being away from Ursula. Ten bucks says he'll be the first to leave the party. And another twenty says he'll ask her to marry him before the week is out."

Maya grinned. "You're on."

"What are you guys betting on?" Cain asked, drawing closer.

Behind him, Eddie had turned to look at them too.

"Nothing," Maya answered.

"What if I want in?" Cain probed.

"Fine," Thomas caved, chuckling to himself. "We're betting on when Oliver is going to ask Ursula to marry him. I'm saying it'll happen within the next week."

"You're shitting me. He's only been with her for what, a month? And he's how old? Twelve?" Cain asked.

Thomas shrugged. "Twelve? I seem to remember that he turned twenty-five not too long ago. Besides, stranger things have happened." He noticed Eddie joining them, shoving his hands into his pockets, but saying nothing.

"Way too early. Those two are kids!" Cain said.

"Wanna put your money where your mouth is?" Thomas challenged, enjoying himself now.

"A hundred bucks says you're going to lose."

"Deal." He sealed the deal by shaking hands with Cain.

"And now to celebrate making money the easy way, how about a dance?" Cain addressed Maya. "Or is your mate going to kill me?"

Maya took his proffered arm. "Only if you put your hands where they don't belong."

As they walked off to the dance floor to join Zane, who was dancing with Portia, and Quinn, now twirling his wife Rose in his arms, Eddie looked at him.

"How come you're so sure that Oliver is going to ask Ursula so soon?"

Thomas winked at him and leaned closer so that nobody would be able to overhear them. As he moved his lips near Eddie's ear, he inhaled his male scent. His heart immediately began to race, and his pulse galloped. He had difficulty remembering what he wanted to tell Eddie.

"Because I saw Oliver buy a ring the other night."

He pulled back and took a step away from Eddie, putting distance between them so that he wouldn't be overwhelmed by his desire for the young vampire and do something stupid.

Eddie's mouth dropped open. "You dog! You just robbed Cain of a hundred bucks!" Despite his outraged words, his eyes twinkled, and his lips curved into a smile. Dimples appeared on his cheeks, and for a moment he looked exactly like the innocent kid Thomas had taken under his wings a year earlier. His heart clenched. Life had dealt him a card he didn't know how to play: he'd never loved anybody like he loved Eddie. And he'd never felt so powerless in the process.

You're not powerless, a voice deep inside him said. He knew all too well where this voice came from: from the dark power within him. A power so strong that he could force his will upon anybody, particularly a young vampire like Eddie. If he wanted to, he could use mind control to make Eddie think he was attracted to him. He could make Eddie desire him. But it wouldn't be right. It would be a shallow victory, because he'd never truly win Eddie's love. It would all be a sham. He would violate Eddie's mind. Just like he would violate Eddie's body. And that he couldn't do. He would hate himself for it.

He suddenly felt a hand squeeze his shoulder and blinked, looking into Eddie's brown eyes.

"Hey, I didn't really mean that. Cain's a big boy. He should know better when to bet with somebody."

Thomas forced a laugh over his lips. "No worries. Just keep it to yourself. I don't want the news about the ring reaching Ursula's ears before Oliver has a chance to kneel down."

Eddie laughed. "Kneel down? You don't really think he's going to get on his knees. That's old fashioned."

"Nothing wrong with being old fashioned. If I found the right person, I'd get on my knees too." He would fall to his knees for Eddie if it made a difference. But he knew it didn't. No amount of groveling would win him the love of the young vampire he couldn't banish from his heart.

Eddie lowered his lids and looked away. "Oh hey, look at that." He pointed to the dancers. "Didn't know that Quinn is such a good dancer."

Thomas sensed awkwardness in Eddie's gesture as well as his voice. Was he embarrassed that Thomas had talked about finding the right person? Maybe it was better not to bring it up anymore.

"I'm sure Quinn had plenty of practice in those ballrooms in London. Trust me, it can be torture for any guy!"

Eddie looked at him from the side. "Did you dance much when you were living in London back then?"

"I did, until I could fake a leg injury and had a valid excuse to sit at the gaming tables instead. Now that was fun!"

"Yeah, I'm not much of a dancer myself," Eddie admitted. "Nina tried to teach me when we were younger, but she gave up. She was quite disappointed in me that I was so clumsy. I hate disappointing her." He looked down at the floor, chuckling. "She claims I have two left feet. She's probably right."

"It's never too late to try."

"Well, we're short of girls here anyway." Eddie motioned to the few vampire females assembled.

"In hindsight it was probably a bad idea to have Haven's party at the lounge, given that none of the humans could join in." Samson had only intended for it to be a little welcoming celebration. How suddenly a band had been brought in, Thomas wasn't sure.

"And I'm afraid it'll be a short party," Gabriel added, approaching them. "I'm calling a staff meeting. Upstairs. In fifteen minutes." His boss looked casual in his black pants and black T-shirt, his hair as always pulled back in a ponytail, his scar that reached from his ear to his chin standing out against his olive skin. He'd been handsome once, very handsome. But the scar that marred one side of his face had put an end to that. Nevertheless, he'd found love. It just proved that the outside shell didn't matter.

Thomas nodded and pointed to Eddie's glass. "Drink up. Time for work."

Thomas was glad for it. How much longer could he have stood there talking about unimportant things with Eddie, when what he really wanted to do was ask whether there was a sliver of a chance that Eddie would one day return his feelings? Of course, it was a question he would never ask, because he knew the answer would only disappoint him more. Why was he torturing himself like this? Why couldn't he just go to one of the many bars in the Castro, the most famously gay district of San Francisco, and pick up some willing guy who maybe even looked a little bit like Eddie, and fuck him until he'd gotten it out of his system? Why couldn't he simply screw whatever guy wanted to be screwed, close his eyes, and pretend it was Eddie?

9

The staff meeting was held in a large conference room on the second floor that could hold over a hundred people if necessary. It was windowless. Tonight, only about fifty vampires were assembled, waiting patiently for Gabriel to start. Samson rarely chaired any of these meetings even though he was the owner of the company. Ever since bonding with Delilah and becoming a father less than a year later, he'd delegated most of the day-to-day running of the business to Gabriel.

Eddie sat down next to Zane and leaned into him. "You know what this is about?"

"Yep."

"So?"

"So what?"

"What's it about?" Eddie clarified.

"You'll hear in a minute."

"Thanks a lot for the info," he replied sarcastically.

"Anytime."

To Eddie's other side, Oliver sat down. Not exactly the person he wanted to see right now. After all, it was Oliver's fault that Eddie knew about Thomas's feelings for him. Feelings that made him uncomfortable and had made his friendship with Thomas feel awkward.

"Hey!" Oliver started.

"Hey!" Eddie kept looking straight ahead as if waiting with bated breath for Gabriel to start the meeting. Anything, just so he didn't have to talk to Oliver.

"How are things?"

"Fine." He sounded just like Zane. Maybe that was how he should react from now on: as if he didn't care about what anybody thought. It seemed to work for Zane, and nobody seemed to fault the bald vampire for it, knowing they couldn't change him anyway.

If he actually were Zane, Oliver would have probably shut up instantly, but Eddie wasn't that lucky.

"You sure? I feel awful about what happened. Maybe I was wrong and just reading too much into—"

Eddie whipped his head toward him and glared at him. "I said I'm fine. So get off my fucking case!" He felt his jaw clench and his teeth grind against each other. His neck muscles bulged and his hands balled into fists. If there weren't so many witnesses around, he would know exactly what to do with those fists.

"Sorry, man," Oliver quickly pressed out and turned to stare toward the front of the room, where Gabriel was getting ready to address the employees.

Gabriel cleared his throat and knocked on the wooden table to get everybody's attention. The whispers in the room subsided and it went quiet.

"Thanks for coming on such short notice. I've called you to alert you to a potential problem we've been made aware of. In the last week or so we've had an unusual influx of new vampires into San Francisco. Nobody knows these newcomers, and we're not quite sure what to think of them. It's just a gut feeling some of us have, but all these newcomers seem to be connected, like a clan."

Eddie listened attentively. A large clan was descending on San Francisco? The last time a group of strange vampires had come to the city, they'd brought blood whores with blood that made vampires high. It had led to carnage.

"While they could be entirely harmless, I want us to be prepared. A large group of vampires coming to our city and not integrating into our way of life can spell all kinds of trouble. We don't want a repeat of what happened with the blood whores. I'm therefore going to have to add to your workload."

Grumbles went through the assembled.

Gabriel raised his hand to stop them. "I know you're all exhausted because you've been on extra shifts in the last four weeks, patrolling to round up all the vampires addicted to the blood of the blood whores. But thanks to your thoroughness, we believe that the task has been accomplished. I wish I could give you all a break, but I'm afraid you'll need to continue with your patrols."

Eddie looked around, and while there were a few vampires who mumbled complaints to themselves, most seemed willing to accept their new assignments. Eddie didn't mind the new orders. Since he wasn't assigned to any particular client at the moment, he was glad to have something to do. Otherwise, Thomas would only have added extra training for him. And since Thomas always trained him personally, it would have meant spending more time with his mentor.

"Considering the concerns we're having about this," Gabriel continued, "I've assigned everybody who's not protecting a client to the patrols, including management. You'll all be patrolling in pairs. I don't want any of you out there on your own. That's a strict order. You don't stick to it, you might as well pack your things. Is that understood?"

Everybody nodded.

"Report anything suspicious immediately. And make sure the newcomers don't know they're being watched. We have no idea how they'll react. I've posted a patrol schedule out on the board in the hallway. You'll find the name of your assigned partner on it. Questions?" Gabriel swept a look over the employees, but nobody spoke up. "Dismissed."

Eddie got up from his chair as the crowd started leaving the room. He headed for the board, eager to find out who Gabriel had paired him up with. He sure hoped it wasn't Oliver. Even though he normally liked the guy, at the moment, he couldn't stand being with him, because Oliver's presence constantly reminded him of what he'd overheard.

Eddie squeezed through the vampires crowding around the board and searched for his name on the two sheets of paper.

Please let it not be Oliver, he prayed silently. Even Zane would be better than Oliver. At least Zane didn't talk much. In fact, the guy was as taciturn as they came. And that suited him just fine right now.

His eyes moved down the list of names until he finally found his own. Then he shifted his gaze slightly, reading the name of his partner next to it: Thomas.

"That's just great!" he grumbled to himself, not bothering to hide his displeasure, and whipped around only to bump into Thomas.

His mentor looked at him, startled, then let him pass, and approached the board, scanning the list of names himself. When he turned seconds later, there was an odd look on his face. He looked back at Eddie, who still stood there as if frozen to the ground. Their eyes met.

Eddie knew then that he'd hurt Thomas. And he felt like shit because of it. Thomas had never done anything wrong, never treated him badly. He didn't deserve how Eddie was treating him now. This was exactly what he'd been afraid of ever since overhearing Oliver and Blake: that he'd overreact and in the process hurt Thomas's feelings. He didn't want their relationship to change. He liked having Thomas as a friend, but how could he continue as before, knowing what he knew?

He ran his hand through his hair. How was he going to make it up to Thomas? He had to somehow apologize, but he didn't know how.

10

He and Eddie were scheduled for their first patrol the next night. Thomas pulled on his boots and tied them, sitting on his bed. His mind went back to the night before when the assignments had been handed out. Eddie had looked less than pleased about being paired up with him. Not just not pleased, he'd looked positively pissed off.

Thomas searched his memory to figure out whether he'd said or done something to insult Eddie, but couldn't find anything. Everything was as always. They hadn't had any confrontations or disagreements. In fact, they rarely ever disagreed on anything. They both enjoyed the same things: riding their motorcycles and working on their computers. Eddie was a great student when it came to anything related to computer software. He particularly liked hacking into systems, and Thomas enjoyed teaching him.

Thomas rose from his bed and snatched his leather jacket from the closet. He couldn't fathom why there suddenly was tension between him and Eddie, when over the last year they'd lived together like the most agreeable roommates. Shaking his head, he walked out of his room and knocked on Eddie's door.

"You ready?"

The door was opened immediately. Eddie appeared, dressed in leather pants, a black T-shirt and a leather jacket. Involuntarily, Thomas had to smile. His colleagues often remarked that they looked like twins with the way they dressed. Only today Thomas was wearing a white T-shirt instead of a black one.

"Rock n' roll," Eddie said and brushed past him, barely looking at him.

Thomas nodded and followed. "We're assigned to the Castro, so there's no point in taking the motorcycles. We'll walk."

The Castro was just down the hill from Twin Peaks. It wouldn't take them long to get there on foot. And once there, it would be easier to patrol, not having to worry about where to leave the motorcycles.

"Fine by me."

In silence, they left the house and hiked down the hill until they entered the Castro. It was still early and relatively quiet. The bars were half empty, and the shops were just closing up.

Thomas had often patrolled with Eddie in companionable silence; however, tonight this silence seemed full of tension. Eddie's breathing was uneven, and Thomas could hear his heart beating erratically. As if something were bothering him. Thomas tried to ignore the feeling of uneasiness and concentrated on his task: watching the people around him.

His senses were alert and sharp as always. For several hours, they wandered through the Castro, first through the commercial area, then the residential one, then back again to the area that was filled with bars, shops, and restaurants. The shops had closed now, but the bars were hopping.

"It's a bust," Eddie said next to him.

"Sometimes finding nothing is a good thing."

Eddie shrugged but didn't reply.

Thomas continued to survey the area, turning into a side street—it was a dead end. There was a boarded-up shop in the middle of the block, a restaurant to one side, and next to it, at the end of the block, there was a construction site: the frame for the three-story apartment building was already up. A Porta Potty stood in front of it, a tool shed next to it. A retaining wall about twelve feet high framed the other side of the street. Thomas glanced up and down the cul-de-sac and was about to turn back, when he saw a movement in the shadows.

He laid his hand on Eddie's forearm and turned to him, motioning him to be silent, then pulled him into an entrance way. From their hiding place, Thomas peered out to the spot where he'd seen the movement. Had he imagined it or was somebody there?

He held his breath and waited, Eddie by his side.

A few seconds later, another shadow moved, and this time Thomas could clearly see the person. His aura identified him as a vampire, and the light that shone onto him from a streetlamp confirmed that he wasn't anybody Thomas knew. He could be one of the newcomers Gabriel had mentioned.

Next to the strange vampire, another one appeared. They looked around, then moved toward the boarded-up building, when two more joined them. The first vampire pried one of the boards away from a window facing the construction site, then squeezed inside. The other three followed.

Thomas glanced at Eddie. "Ever seen those guys before?"

"No."

"Let's check them out."

Carefully, they advanced on the building. Thomas checked his boot, where a silver knife was hidden in a protective sheath. Then he stuck his hand into his inside pocket, verifying that the wooden stake was where it was supposed to be.

Waving Eddie to follow him, he walked to the other side of the boarded-up house the four vampires had entered. Without making a noise, he walked around it, Eddie on his heels. All windows were nailed shut with sheets of plywood, but as he reached the back of the home, which opened to a small garden that was filled with building materials, he noticed an open door.

He approached it with caution, then pressed himself to the wall next to it and peered inside. He heard voices.

" . . . without the boss's approval."

"But that one's ripe for takeover," another tight voice said.

"I'll advise him of it. If it fits into our plan, we'll take it."

Thomas strained to hear their low voices and felt a strange stirring in him. The dark power in him seemed to be awakening without any provocation, drawn out by the aura of the four strange vampires. He closed his eyes for a moment to try to push it back down.

"Never mind that. Whatever we can get, we'll take it. The more we take, the stronger we'll be when the time comes," the second voice replied.

A sound behind him echoed in the night. He swiveled his head. A board on the heap of building materials Thomas and Eddie had passed closely only moments earlier had shifted and caused the noise. His gaze collided with Eddie's, who motioned to the open door.

From inside, the voices suddenly stopped. The four strange vampires had heard the noise too.

Grabbing Eddie by the sleeve of his jacket, Thomas dragged him away, jumping over the low fence into the adjacent property. They were behind the construction site, facing another retaining wall.

"Shit," he hissed under his breath. There was no way out from the back. They'd have to make their way through the partially constructed building, where they would be seen by the other vampires.

At the sound of footsteps, Thomas whipped his head to the side. The four vampires were already approaching, though he couldn't see them yet. Which meant they couldn't see him and Eddie yet either.

One thing was clear: the vampires would suspect that they'd been overheard. And they wouldn't look at them kindly. "Gotta fight them," he whispered to Eddie.

His young friend shook his head almost instantly, pushing him farther into the corner they were backed into, farther away from the approaching vampires. Thomas glared at him.

"Too many!" Eddie whispered back.

"I'll use mind control," Thomas suggested. It would even out the playing field. Four against two weren't great odds, but if he could fight them with mind control, he and Eddie had a chance of winning the confrontation, should it come to a fight.

"No you won't! Too dangerous. Follow my lead."

Before Thomas could protest, Eddie pushed his back against the wall, then pressed his body against Thomas's and kissed him. Stunned, Thomas froze. This could not be happening! He had to be dreaming, hallucinating. But everything felt real: Eddie's hot lips on his mouth, his tongue pushing against the seam of his lips, demanding entry, one hand at his nape, holding him close, while Eddie's other hand circled around Thomas's waist to draw him into his body.

With a groan, Thomas parted his lips and invited Eddie in. When their tongues met, his entire body erupted in flames. Blood shot to his cock within seconds, bringing him to a full cockstand faster than he could have uttered a single word.

This was his dream come true.

11

Eddie realized that what he was doing was crazy, but he hadn't seen any other way out. He wouldn't allow Thomas to fight the four vampires with mind control. The last time Thomas had engaged in a mind-control fight with Keegan, his maker, he'd nearly died. And fighting four vampires with conventional means was suicide too. No, he owed him this.

And the deception might just work: after all, they were in the Castro, where gays behaved with a little less restraint than in the rest of the city. What they were doing here wouldn't seem out of the ordinary. With a bit of luck, they could fool the four strangers into thinking that they were just some horny homosexuals who couldn't wait to get into each other's pants.

As long as they made it look realistic.

Eddie angled his head to dive deeper into Thomas's mouth. To his surprise, he didn't feel disgusted about kissing a man. On the contrary, he loved Thomas's masculine taste, the firm stroke of his tongue against his, and the corresponding hard press of his hips. His lips were warm and welcoming, his breath hot and titillating. Lust shot through him, desire welled up. It was all for a good cause, he told himself. It had to look real, or the vampires would never believe it.

Allowing a moan to come over his lips, he released his hold on Thomas's waist and brought his hand to his own leather pants, popping the button open. If he had to show his naked ass to the four newcomers to make them believe he and Thomas were lovers, then he'd do just that.

Without wasting another minute, he pulled the zipper down and tugged on his pants. Thomas's hands stopped him. Eddie wanted to protest and make him understand why he needed to do this, when he felt Thomas's hand slide onto his ass, tugging on his pants.

In the front, his leather pants caught on something. Eddie's breath hitched when he realized instantly what had happened: his pants had caught on his erection which had created a massive bulge under his Calvin Klein briefs.

Fuck! He had an erection? How the fuck had that happened? But before he could follow that particular thought process, he felt Thomas's hands move to his groin, gripping the front of his pants and pushing them down. As one hand brushed over the bulge, Eddie hissed, "Fuck!" releasing Thomas's lips for a moment.

He inhaled sharply, but then Thomas's lips were back, his tongue thrusting back into his mouth, exploring him, sparring with him. God, he'd never been kissed like that, with such passion, such power, such determination. No woman had ever done that. Was that how men kissed? Was that what it felt like?

Before he knew what he was doing, words he had no idea he was going to say came over his lips. "Touch me!"

His moaned command was followed by Thomas's hand slipping into his briefs, pushing them down. Cool air blew against his cock a split second before a warm palm wrapped around him and squeezed. A bolt of electricity shot through him. His fangs descended without warning, and his hand gripped Thomas's nape tighter, pulling him closer for a deeper kiss.

Thomas's second hand pushed his briefs down fully, then palmed his ass. Fuck! He should make him stop, tell him that he wasn't wired that way, that he couldn't do this. He wasn't gay! This was all just to fool those vampires. But he couldn't stop his body from reacting to Thomas's touch and kiss. A kiss he, Eddie, had started.

Of its own volition, his cock pumped into Thomas's hand, thrusting as if he were thrusting into him, while he stroked firmly against Thomas's tongue, sucking it, as if he were sucking Thomas's cock instead. The thought shocked him. No, he couldn't think of something like that. He didn't suck cock! He ate pussy! Right! Only, at present he couldn't remember when he'd last even seen a pussy.

Thomas's hand worked him perfectly. As if he knew exactly what Eddie needed. The right pressure and firmness, the perfect rhythm and speed.

An enthusiastic "Yes!" came over his lips as he came up for air, only to lock lips with Thomas again a moment later. As he intensified the kiss, Eddie suddenly felt Thomas's tongue swipe against one fang. White-hot heat shot into his balls. Then Thomas repeated the action.

"Queers!" he suddenly heard a voice somewhere in the distance.

"Disgraceful for a vampire!" another voice added.

The footsteps moved farther away. The threat was over, but Eddie was unable to pull himself out of Thomas's arms.

"Come!" he heard Thomas growl as he squeezed Eddie's cock harder and faster, while he continued to lick his fangs.

Eddie had known that fangs were a vampire's most erogenous zone, but he'd never experienced it himself. Now that he felt it, he realized that he had no defenses against the sensual onslaught of Thomas's caresses. He was powerless to stop him, because all his body wanted was more: more of Thomas's kisses and his touch.

His hips worked frantically, thrusting his erection into Thomas's willing hand. He was aching now, aching for release, and had reached a point where he didn't care who was delivering it, be it a man or a woman. All he needed was an orgasm, or his entire body would go up in flames.

He was right at the edge—almost there, but not quite. Frustration howled through him and he threw his head back, groaning. "Fuck!"

Thomas seemed to understand what he needed and brought his second hand to Eddie's balls, cradling them. Then he started squeezing them in concert with the tugs on Eddie's cock. The touch was soft, yet firm at the same time.

"Kiss me!" Thomas demanded, and without thinking, Eddie followed his command, sinking his lips back onto his, thrusting his tongue into Thomas's mouth just as he was thrusting his cock into his hand.

His head swam with visions of them making love, of lying in bed together, naked, their limbs entangled, their cocks pumped full with blood. He felt their hands joining, rubbing their cocks together, moving them up and down in sync. He could firmly feel Thomas's cock rubbing against his own, just as he could feel the excitement build as they drove each other toward orgasm. But just short of that, Thomas suddenly rolled onto his stomach, coming up onto his hands and knees, offering himself.

Eddie moaned out loud as the vision in his mind blurred, ripping his mouth from Thomas's. He felt his seed shoot through his shaft and erupt at its tip. His body trembled under the intensity of his climax, and his knees threatened to buckle. Warmth and wetness engulfed him as Thomas continued to stroke his cock until his orgasm subsided.

Breathing heavily, he tried to gather his wits. Why was he here? Why had this happened?

He remembered the four strange vampires they'd followed and his plan to fool them. It had worked; they'd left, thinking that Thomas and Eddie were gay lovers and hadn't listened in on their conversation. Nevertheless, the plan had backfired. He'd gotten a hand job from Thomas! And he'd come so hard that he'd actually seen stars in front of his eyes.

Embarrassment swept through him. Panic wasn't far behind. Would Thomas now think that Eddie was gay? Oh God! Would he assume that Eddie wanted to be his lover? Had he just given Thomas carte blanche to make a pass at him? To seduce him again as soon as they were alone at home? Would this mean Thomas would come into his room, into his bed, wanting to repeat what they'd just done? And not just repeat, but do other things too, even more intimate things?

Eddie felt a shudder go through his body, and this time it wasn't an aftershock of his orgasm. As fast as he could, he pulled his briefs up and shoved his now flaccid cock into them, pulled his pants up, and zipped up. From the corner of his eye, he noticed Thomas wiping his hand on his T-shirt.

"About what just happened," Thomas said.

Eddie turned away. "It worked. They're gone. They bought it."

He felt Thomas's hand on his shoulder, drawing him back. "Eddie, please . . . "

"It's fine."

"I could have defeated them with mind control. So what we just did—"

Eddie narrowed his eyes. "You almost died when you fought with Keegan!"

Thomas noticed the defiant glare in Eddie's eyes and hesitated for a moment. Was Eddie concerned about him? Was that why he'd taken such a drastic measure and kissed him? To fool the other vampires into thinking they were lovers? Or did something else lie behind Eddie's actions? Could it be that Eddie felt a tiny flicker of attraction for him? Because what they'd done had gone further than necessary: a kiss and some groping would have been enough to fool the other vampires. It hadn't been necessary for Eddie to drop his pants and for Thomas to jerk him off. Certainly not that, particularly because the vampires had already left at that point. There'd been no need to make Eddie climax in his hand. But Thomas had been unable to stop, and Eddie had spurred him on, if not with words then with his moans and the relentless thrusting of his hips. Eddie had wanted this; he'd wanted Thomas to make him come. And Thomas had craved the feeling of Eddie surrendering in his arms.

For that one moment, they'd been lovers. Thomas had never had a more satisfying make-out session with anybody. Even though Eddie had barely touched him, and never once slipped his hand over Thomas's cock where he would have felt just how hard

Thomas had been, his kiss had been passionate and all-consuming. And for a while, Eddie had been completely under his spell and given himself over to the pleasure Thomas could deliver. It had been the sweetest of moments to feel Eddie come in his hand, to feel his balls contract and his warm seed shoot into his palm. At that moment, he'd wanted nothing more than to turn Eddie around, sink his cock into his virgin ass, and ride him to the point of collapse.

Thomas was still aroused, and he knew it would only take a few strokes for him to come just as violently as Eddie had come in his hand. But looking at Eddie right now, he knew this wouldn't happen, at least not by Eddie's hand.

He read regret in Eddie's face. Disappointed, Thomas dropped his lids. For a short moment, he'd hoped that Eddie was finally trying to tell him something, trying to show him that he felt the same way Thomas did. But he'd been wrong. All Eddie had wanted was to fool the four vampires.

Still, his lips formed words he shouldn't say. "But you let me touch you—"

"Forget what happened," Eddie replied brusquely. "It meant nothing."

It meant nothing? No, to Thomas it had meant everything. He sucked in a breath of air. "Forget? How the fuck do you expect me to forget this? You let me touch you like that. You should have stopped me." Because Thomas for certain hadn't had the strength to stop himself.

Eddie pressed his lips into a thin line. "I did it to stop you from doing something stupid! You couldn't have fought those four with mind control! It would have killed you!"

"Oh you think I'm weak?" Where those words suddenly came from, Thomas didn't know, but he uttered them nevertheless.

"I didn't say that!"

"You did." He grabbed Eddie by the shirt and pulled him close. "I'm older than you, and I'm stronger. So don't play with me, or you'll regret it. Next time you come up with a stupid idea such as kissing me, be prepared to go all the way. Provoke me one more time, and I'm going to take what you're offering. And next time I won't stop with a hand job. I promise you that."

Shocked, Eddie pulled back.

Thomas's chest heaved. Had he really just threatened to fuck Eddie if he ever laid hands on him again?

You should punish him now! a voice from deep within him suggested. *He deserves it for getting you all riled up.*

Thomas fought against the voice, pushing it back into the dark recesses of his heart, where it belonged. He wouldn't allow this temporary anger to get the better of him. Once he'd calmed down, he would only regret having given in to his evil side.

Eddie shoved both his hands against Thomas's chest, slamming him into the wall behind him. "You touch me like that again, you're a dead man!" He breathed heavily. "I don't swing that way, you get that? I was doing you a fucking favor! I guess from now on I should just let you get yourself out of your own jams and not lift a finger."

Thomas felt fury surge from his gut and travel to his chest. His jaw tightened. "Last time I checked, you were in the same jam as I. What were you gonna do without me? Run to your big sister and—?"

His next words were shoved back down his throat as Eddie's fist landed in his mouth.

Fuck! An angry flame shot through his heart.

Instead of returning the blow, Thomas straightened and glared at him, the dark power in him eager to push to the surface, demanding retaliation. His body hardened, preparing itself for a fight, a fight with himself. "Does that make you feel better?"

Eddie gave no answer; instead he simply stood there, glaring back at Thomas.

"Even if it does, it won't change the fact that you enjoyed being jerked off by a gay man."

Or that Thomas would play that image back next time he stood in the shower and stroked his own cock until he came.

Eddie turned on his heels and fled.

Thomas braced his hands on his thighs and fought against the feeling of nausea. The invisible battle inside him was already raging. His two sides, the good one and the evil one, faced off with each other. Thomas tried to calm his mind and bring peace back into his heart, but bright sparks started dancing on his hands. His vision now tinted red, and he realized that his eyes were glaring red. Sharp claws emerged from his fingertips and dug into his pants as he held on for dear life. The next attack knocked him on his knees, white sparks now flying around him.

The power within him was threatening to escape. It would attract other vampires if he couldn't contain it. With the last of his willpower, he slashed his right claw over his abdomen, cutting deep into his own flesh. The pain made him cry out, but it did what it was intended to do: it stopped the dark power and made it retreat into safety, deep inside him. The sparks of light extinguished and darkness soothed him. He'd conquered it once more. But each time the dark power made an appearance, it seemed to be stronger and harder to vanquish. It was time to beat it back into submission. Literally. And he knew exactly where to get what he needed now.

12

After running home as if the devil were chasing him with a stake, Eddie jumped onto his motorcycle and thundered down the hill into the city. Feeling the wind blow around his heated body made him feel a fraction better. However, it did nothing to wipe away the embarrassment he felt: he'd let Thomas touch him intimately. Hell, he'd encouraged him, spurred him on! What the fuck had gotten into him? Temporary insanity most likely! There was no other explanation for it. Because he wasn't gay! He'd never been attracted to a man before. So why the fuck had he enjoyed Thomas's hands on him? Why had he surrendered to his kiss and returned it with such passion? What was happening to him?

Without conscious thought of where he was heading, he made his way through downtown traffic and finally found himself in front of Nina's building. He lifted his head and looked up to the top floor. There was light. Somebody was home. He sighed. Maybe he needed to hang out with his sister for a while to take his mind off things. She would distract him somehow.

He parked and dismounted his motorcycle in front of the entrance. As he removed his helmet and locked it onto the back of his bike, he swept a long gaze over it. Thomas had given it to him. He'd said at the time that it was one of his older bikes anyway, and that he didn't ride it anymore. When Eddie had wanted to pay for it, Thomas had refused to take any money. Just like Thomas wouldn't take any rent for the room Eddie was calling his own. It suddenly hit him: he lived the life of a kept man. Thomas was showering him with gifts and paying for his living expenses the same way a man would treat his mistress.

Eddie tried to shake off the thought, not wanting to go down that road, but it was hard not to connect the dots now. From the moment he'd become a vampire, his life had changed. At first, when he'd been groomed by his sire, Luther, he'd not even thought of women because of the thirst for blood that had gripped him violently. Had something happened during his turning that had killed his desire for women? Had something gone wrong so that he now liked men?

Pushing these thoughts into the background, he walked to the entrance door, when it opened and one of the tenants stepped out. He'd seen the guy many times before and greeted him.

"Hey."

"Hey."

The tenant held the door for him and let him get inside.

"Thanks, see you!"

Slowly, Eddie strode up to the top floor. When he reached the landing, he walked to the only door on that floor and pressed the doorbell. He heard a curse from the inside and recognized Amaury's voice. It appeared he was interrupting his brother-in-law. Maybe it hadn't been such a good idea to stop by unannounced after all. Did he really want to be in the presence of these two lovebirds?

Eddie took a step back, half turning away, when the door opened. Amaury's massive body filled the entire door frame. His shirt was askew, his hair ruffled. Yep, he had definitely interrupted something.

"Hey Eddie."

"Amaury, sorry, didn't mean to disturb. Why don't I visit some other time?" He turned away, but Amaury's hand on his shoulder pulled him back.

"You're here now. Might as well come in."

"Eddie?" Nina's voice came from the living room. "Is everything okay?"

Eddie entered and saw his sister get up from the couch, her hands pulling her T-shirt straight. She shot him a concerned look. Behind him, Amaury closed the door.

"Yeah, sure, I'm all right. Why shouldn't I be? I was just in the neighborhood and wanted to say hi. Can't I say hi to my sister?"

"Of course you can." She came toward him and threw her arms around him, squeezing him.

He returned the hug, holding her for longer than usual, until he heard Amaury grunt behind him. Rolling his eyes, he released her. "How you can stomach that man of yours day in and day out, I have no idea."

Nina boxed him in the arm and admonished him, "Eddie!"

"So you've come to insult me?" Amaury asked and braced his hands on his hips.

Eddie grinned. "I hadn't planned on it, but you bring out the best in me every time."

Amaury laughed. "Cut from the same cloth as your sister." He ran a loving look over his mate.

When his and Nina's eyes locked, Eddie felt a never-known longing surging in him. He wanted what they had: a love so strong that nothing could tear it apart.

"I should go. You guys have better things to do than entertain me."

Amaury tore his gaze from Nina, then motioned to the couch. "No, stay. I would offer you some blood, but I don't have any here."

Eddie had figured as much. Since Amaury only drank Nina's blood, he didn't keep any supplies of bottled blood at hand. "Doesn't matter. I'm not thirsty." He dropped onto the couch, and Nina and Amaury joined him.

"Been out on patrol?" Amaury asked.

Eddie nodded. "Yeah. Aren't you on duty too? I thought I saw your name on the roster."

His brother-in-law shrugged. "I changed shifts with one of the guys."

Eddie tossed a sideways glance at Nina. "Nina's idea?"

Amaury chuckled.

"I'm right here, guys, so don't pretend I can't hear you," Nina interrupted. Then she put her hand on Amaury's arm. "Baby, why don't you get me a pint of chocolate ice cream from the store?"

"Now?"

"Yes, now. I'd be really grateful if you did." She batted her eyelashes at him.

"How grateful?" Amaury whispered, his voice softer than before.

"Very grateful."

Eddie groaned inwardly. Did those two really have to lay it on that thick? It was nauseating!

Amaury got up and walked to the door. "Back in a few."

The moment the door fell shut behind Amaury, Nina turned to him, her face serious. "Now tell me what's going on."

"What do you mean?"

She reached her hand out to him. "May I introduce myself? I'm Nina, your sister. And I've known you all your life. So don't bullshit me. You never show up here unannounced. In fact, I rarely see you unless there's a party."

"You've never complained before. Besides, I don't want to intrude on your little love nest."

Nina tilted her head to the side. "And I'm not complaining now either. I'm just stating a fact." She paused and sighed. "Eddie, I know this look. Something is bothering you."

He shouldn't have come here. His sister had a way of squeezing information out of him that he didn't want to share. Because how could he even start a conversation about what had happened between him and Thomas? No, nobody could ever find out about it.

"Nothing's bothering me. I just wanted to hang out with you."

"Mhm."

"What?"

Nina tucked her legs underneath her. "You were always such a bad liar, even as a child."

"What's that got to do with anything?"

"Spill."

He sighed. "Fine. I came to ask you for advice. I was thinking of getting my own place," he lied.

She raised her eyebrows. "You mean move out from Thomas's?"

"Yes. I mean, I've got myself under control now. I've learned to handle my vampire skills. I won't need any mentoring anymore."

"Well, it's been over a year. You haven't had any episodes of bloodlust, have you?"

He shook his head. "No, of course not. The bottled stuff is just fine. So, what do you think?"

"Think about what?"

"Me moving out. Getting my own place. I've got the money." It was true. He could certainly afford to rent a decent place by himself. What had started as a lie to pacify his sister could be just the solution to his problem. He wouldn't have to be alone with Thomas anymore. They would only see each other at work. And even there, he might not see him all the time. They wouldn't always be partnered up. Particularly if Thomas weren't mentoring him anymore. Maybe by putting a little distance between them, they could preserve their friendship.

"Do you want me to look around for you to see what's out there?" she offered with a smile.

"That would be great, Sis."

"Do you have a particular neighborhood in mind?"

He shrugged. "Just something central. I don't want to live out in the boonies. Somewhere in town, nothing too residential. And not in *Stroller Central* either."

Nina's brows snapped together. "Stroller Central?"

"Yes, Noe Valley. Don't tell me you've never heard that nickname?"

Nina laughed. "No, I hadn't. But now that you mention it, it's very fitting, with all the couples with small children running around. Okay then, I'll look around for you. I'm sure we can find you something nice and affordable."

"Find him what?" Amaury's voice came from the door.

"A flat. Eddie wants to move out and live on his own."

Eddie's gaze collided with Amaury's.

"Oh. Thomas hasn't mentioned anything about you moving out."

Eddie swallowed. "I haven't told him yet." And he had no idea how and when to tell him. This was not a conversation he looked forward to, even though he knew he had to have it—soon, before things got out of hand. In the end, it would be best. They could simply be colleagues and friends with a clear boundary between them that neither would cross again.

13

Thomas entered the windowless room and perused it. Nothing had changed. It was sparsely furnished with a couple of benches, a rack with various ropes and chains, and several whips, canes, and other tools used for flagellation. He possessed most of them himself and stored them in his basement in a room he'd used for sexual games with his various partners. Mild bondage and self-flagellation had all been part of his regular routine, but since Eddie had moved in with him, he'd barely used the room. Certainly not for any sexual games with other men. He'd only on occasion used it to flog himself whenever he'd felt his dark power rise. He'd beat it back into submission by using a cattail whip usually made of knotted cords, the same kind of tool the members of Opus Dei had used during private prayer. Only, he wasn't praying.

And tonight, he needed something more than just the mild flogging he could deal himself. He needed a firmer hand that could beat his dark power into submission.

Thomas walked to the sink in one corner and took off his jacket, letting it fall onto the chair next to it. When he pulled the T-shirt over his head, he could clearly see the deep cuts his claws had left on his stomach. They hadn't healed yet and would only do so once he'd had a few hours of restorative sleep and sufficient fresh human blood.

He opened the button of his leather pants and slid the zipper down. Tossing off his boots and socks, he finally stripped naked. His cock was semi-erect, a reaction to the smell of Eddie's semen that still clung to his hands. He'd not washed it off him, but simply wiped it on his T-shirt, although he'd run home to get his motorcycle and would have had an opportunity to clean up if he'd wanted to.

Thomas stared at the sink. He could wash his hands now and make this easier on himself by not being reminded constantly of what he couldn't have. But he'd never been one to take the easy route when there was a more challenging one he could choose instead. Did that make him a masochist?

The cracked mirror didn't give him any answers—there was no reflection in it.

Slowly he turned and walked toward the rack. It was of simple construction, with several bars anchored in the floor and reaching up to the ceiling. On a crossbar, several leather straps hung suspended. Thomas reached up and slid his hands into the loops, pulling down on them so they tightened around his wrists. While his vampire strength made it possible for him to rip free of the restraints, he liked the illusion of being tied up and feeling powerless.

It all helped him trick the dark power back into submission. The dark power felt everything his body felt. If Thomas was in pain and felt at the mercy of his tormentor, so was the dark power inside him. It would believe that it wasn't as powerful as it was and retreat, afraid of being destroyed. As long as he could pretend to be powerless, he had a chance of defeating the evil inside him. It was the reason he liked to play the submissive partner, even though he was anything but. Whenever his dominant side emerged, his dark power appeared with it and broke through the surface, just as it had earlier.

His true nature was to be dominant and strong. Kasper had seen that in him. That's why he'd chosen him and given him his blood. Blood that was evil to the core. Blood that made him want to do terrible things. He'd been fighting against it every day of his life, ever since he'd left Kasper. Back then, he'd thought that once he withdrew from Kasper's influence, the thirst for power would subside, but he'd been wrong. It was still there, running through his body like an undercurrent, like a dangerous riptide that nobody noticed until it was too late.

Thomas spread his legs and focused his gaze on the wall ahead of him. He took deep breaths, readying himself for what was to come. His heartbeat slowed. By the time the door opened a few minutes later, he was entirely calm and ready.

Footsteps approached. He didn't turn, not wanting to see who the man was who would deliver his punishment. When it was over, he would wipe the person's memory so nobody would ever find out what had happened here. He'd done it many times before, and tonight wouldn't be the last time.

"The leather cat," Thomas instructed simply. It was a flogger with nine long leather strips. The hardest leather had been used to fashion it. It was what he needed tonight.

The man didn't answer, but Thomas heard him take one of the tools from the wall and step closer.

Thomas's palms tightened around the straps. Simultaneously, he clenched his teeth, preparing himself.

Without warning, the first lash whipped across his naked back. Pain radiated through his body, making him cry out involuntarily. He sucked in a quick breath, but there was no relief in sight: the second lash followed instantly. Then a third and a fourth. His skin broke, and he smelled the blood that started oozing from the open wounds. It mingled with the scent of the human who was flogging him with unerring precision.

He felt the dark power inside him wanting to fight back against his punisher. Thomas gritted his teeth. "Harder!" he ordered the stranger.

The man complied without a word, slashing the flogger over Thomas's back with more ferocity now.

"Yes!" he cried out. He would beat the dark power. He would win this battle! He had to. Losing wasn't an option. Losing meant destruction.

As the pain became sharper and more intense, Thomas tried to separate his mind from his body. He focused on the wall in front of him as if wanting to drill holes into it. Every lash tried to pull him back and made him lose focus. Every bolt of searing pain that shot through his entire body made his gums itch. His fangs begged to be released, hungering for a vicious bite. They wanted to drive into the man who was flogging him, to punish him, to destroy him. But he fought against the urge to harm the man.

Instead, he focused back on the wall, on the emptiness of it. He inhaled, but the scent he picked up was Eddie's. It was still there, still tormenting him. He closed his eyes, and suddenly every lash of the whip felt like a caress by Eddie's hands. As if Eddie were stroking his back.

"Lower!" he ordered. And his mind gave the man another order. *Gentler!*

The whip moved lower, the leather strips lashing over his ass. He didn't feel the pain this time. He felt a firm touch, the touch of Eddie's hands on him. His fingers spreading over his backside, sliding down, caressing him.

"Yes!" Thomas cried out.

Every single leather strip felt like a finger sliding gently over his ass. When one caught in his crack, Thomas groaned out his pleasure. His cock hardened, curving against his stomach, yearning for release.

"More," he begged. "More!"

Again and again, the whip touched his ass and his mind conjured up the feeling of Eddie's hands stroking him with more passion, more determination. Again he felt the pressure between his ass cheeks. And again, he cried out. Bending forward as much as the restraints around his wrists allowed, he offered his backside for a more thorough flogging.

On the next stroke, his fangs extended and a bolt of lust shot through him. The whip lashed at him again, and this time it not only hit the full length of his crack, it also touched his balls, sending a shot of electricity right into his cock. His balls pulled up, tightening.

His eyes shot open. Fuck! He was going to come.

The flogger changed his angle, cracking the whip not from above, but from below now, hitting his balls again. His vision blurred. Without thinking, Thomas ripped his right hand free of the restraints and gripped his cock. With the same hand with which he'd pleasured Eddie, he now tugged on his own cock, jerking it up and down in vampire speed, while the flogging continued.

He closed his eyes, once again imagining the leather strips that slashed his ass and slipped into his crack to be Eddie's caressing fingers that drove into him to explore him.

With a groan, he exploded, shooting his seed against his stomach, letting it rain over his hand. He hadn't planned this. It was meant to be a simple flogging session. That he'd gotten so aroused that he hadn't been able to restrain himself, masturbating in front of the stranger who'd flogged him, hadn't been part of the plan. He could only blame his ever-growing need for Eddie. He had to do something to crush it.

14

Thomas closed the door behind him and stepped out into the street. He'd wiped the guy's memory and had gotten dressed in a hurry. Blood had started crusting over his wounds, but the pain was still fresh. His ass hurt like hell, but it had been worth it. He'd never come so hard and so fast before. He'd only needed a few strokes with his own hand before he'd climaxed. Eddie was the most powerful fantasy he'd ever had.

These days it didn't take much to get him aroused. One thought of Eddie was enough, and he was as hard as a crowbar. Each evening when he got up, the first thing he did was jump in the shower and masturbate to fantasies of Eddie and him making love. And every day when he went to sleep, he lay in his bed, his hand around his hard-on, imagining Eddie naked in front of him, watching him. And then he imagined Eddie lowering himself onto the bed and burying his head between Thomas's spread legs, sucking his cock into his mouth. Every day, he fell asleep to that image.

Now he had more details to add to his fantasies: he knew what Eddie's cock felt like, and how his body moved, how he'd thrust into his hand with such passion, as if he'd meant it. And he knew now how Eddie kissed. How soft his lips felt, how his tongue tasted. He'd felt Eddie shudder in his arms when he'd licked his fangs. It had been the sweetest of victories. But it hadn't lasted.

Thomas rubbed his chin. He could still feel Eddie's fist slamming into his face, raw anger shooting from his eyes when he'd come to his senses. He wasn't gay, Eddie had professed. And he'd only done it to fool the four vampires on their tail.

Bullshit!

There was something else to it. No straight man would kiss another man like this and respond to a hand job with as much enthusiasm as Eddie had if there wasn't something else going on. There had to be! He didn't *want* to believe that Eddie had simply put on a show. He wanted to hope that there was more between them.

Thomas reached his parked motorcycle and pulled the key from his pocket.

"Did it help?" a male voice asked from behind him.

Thomas swiveled on his heels and stared at the dark figure stepping out from the shadow of the adjacent building. The man was dressed in dark clothes that looked casual yet expensive. His hair was cropped short, his face even and somewhat pale. There was no doubt the man was a vampire—one he'd never seen. Dark power swirled around him, mingling with his aura. It was weak, but it was there nevertheless. He recognized its signature immediately.

But Thomas had no intention of engaging with the vampire who carried Kasper's blood. "I don't know what you mean."

A nonchalant smile played around the stranger's lips. "Oh, we've all tried it, and eventually given in. It doesn't work. Not for long anyway. The power is stronger. It'll break through when you least expect it."

"What do you want?" Thomas barked.

"Wasn't that evident from my letter? I'm sorry, I didn't sign it. I'm Xander."

That the letter had come from him was no surprise. Only one of Kasper's disciples could have written it. Because only they knew about the dark power that Kasper's blood had brought to all of them.

Thomas clenched his teeth. "Are you trying to threaten me?"

"On the contrary. I've been sent to ask you to join us. You're one of us, you can't deny that."

"I'll never be one of you!" he cried out, feeling his fangs lengthen.

"You say that now, but once you feel the power grow stronger, you won't be able to resist. His blood is strong in you, stronger than in the rest of us. You were one of his first."

"I destroyed that power. Just like I destroyed Kasper." Which wasn't technically the truth—Rose had shot Kasper, or Keegan as he'd called himself then, though Thomas would have killed him had Wesley not interfered in the fight and broken his concentration with a spell of witchcraft. But that was beside the point. He'd effectively brought about Kasper's death.

"Destroyed Kasper?" Xander asked, a look of confusion on his face. "Not likely."

"Yes, just like I'll destroy you if you don't get out of my life."

Xander's eyes didn't show any fear at Thomas's threat. "There are many of us. He created an army. More are coming each day. Collectively, we're strong. You'll soon feel it. You're nearly as strong as he. You can feel us already, can't you?"

Thomas shook his head, trying to deny Xander's claim, even though he knew it was true. He could feel the power coming from Xander. And now he also realized that he must have gotten a faint whiff of it from the four vampires he'd encountered earlier in the night. "I'm stronger than Kasper. Because I can resist the evil in me. He couldn't."

"Not all power is evil."

Thomas scoffed. Kasper hadn't done a single thing in his life that wasn't considered evil. He'd been rotten to the core. "Could have fooled me! If you believe that, then you obviously didn't see the atrocities Kasper committed with his power. You didn't see the pain he inflicted just because he could. Don't confuse me with Kasper. I'm nothing like him."

The stranger stepped closer. "It doesn't matter what you think you are, or what lies you're telling yourself. Over time, his blood will take over. It will make you into what you're supposed to be. You'll accept the dark power within you, and you'll come back to the throne he built." Xander's words were spoken with such determination that a shiver ran down Thomas's spine. He fought against the sensation of dread that tried to engulf his body.

"Throne?" Thomas expelled a bitter laugh. "I want no throne that's built on death and destruction and the tears of women and children. I want no part of it."

"You have no choice!"

Thomas grabbed Xander's throat and slammed him against the wall of the building behind him so fast, the stranger couldn't even blink. "I have a choice. I have free will. And I'm exercising it. You hear me? I've made my choice the day I left Kasper. He knew it, he just couldn't accept it." He released the man and took a step back. "Now leave. I never want to see you on my turf again. None of you. Leave this town, or I'll be coming after you."

Thomas turned in vampire speed and jumped onto his motorcycle, racing away without looking back. He would never do the things Kasper had done. Evil things . . .

London, England, 1897

Thomas let the entrance door to the mansion he shared with Kasper and a few others of their kind snap in behind him, shutting out the chilly night air. Jeeves, the butler, a spindly man with a crooked nose, took the cloak from his shoulders while Thomas stripped off his gloves and tossed them onto the table in the foyer.

He'd been out on his own, feeding, since Kasper had said that he needed to attend to some business. "When Master Kasper returns, have a bath prepared in our rooms."

The butler folded the cloak over his forearm and bowed. "But, sir, Master Kasper is already home."

"Impossible! He was on his way to Whitechapel when I left him. You must be mistaken."

Jeeves straightened his shoulders. "Master Kasper often surprises us by appearing unexpectedly. Maybe he simply changed his plans."

Thomas wrinkled his forehead. The butler was right. Kasper made a habit of showing up when and where he was least expected. He seemed to be ubiquitous. It was at times irritating and unsettling.

"Where is he now?" Thomas demanded.

"Downstairs. But he asked not to be disturbed."

Thomas's hackles went up. Was Kasper having an assignation with another man? While Thomas was fully aware that Kasper fucked whomever he wanted to, whether female or male, the thought that these trysts happened under the roof they shared was something Thomas couldn't stomach. They had agreed that whatever fornication happened outside of their relationship would take place outside of their home.

Thomas's fangs lengthened and a low snarl ripped from his lips. Jeeves took a step back. The human was aware that he worked for vampires, and had in fact been in Kasper's employ for many years, easily controlled by mind control and generous wages. He was loyal to Kasper.

"Who's with him?"

Jeeves lowered his lids halfway. "Nobody, sir."

"You're a worse liar than I am, Jeeves," he replied and strode toward the door that led into the basement of the building.

"Sir, please, the master . . . " he called after him, but Thomas ignored him, taking two steps at a time to descend into the cellar.

It smelled musty and damp. Electrical lights had been installed, lining the long corridor. It was an improvement over the old gaslights that he remembered from his father's country house. Kasper kept up with technology and whenever a new invention was publicized, Kasper was one of the first to give it a try.

A sound came from one of the rooms at the end of the corridor, and his feet carried him closer, his chest tightening, his hands balling into fists, jealousy charging through his veins.

Thomas ripped the door open without knocking. He smelled the human instantly, but Kasper wasn't feeding from a human, nor was he fucking one. Thomas's entire body revolted at what his eyes perceived within a split second.

A woman was tied to a rack on the wall, her pregnant belly sticking out prominently. He'd rarely seen pregnant women in society, since they confined themselves to their homes once they were increasing, but from a friend of the family he'd seen during her confinement, he realized, judging by the size of the woman's belly, that she was within weeks, if not days, of giving birth.

Yet, he instantly realized that the baby in her belly would never see the light of day, nor would she ever again see the sun shining on her face.

A vampire stood in front of her, a knife in his hands. And next to him Kasper's eyes were focused on the two.

"You can't have both! You can only save one of them. Choose! Either your mate or your child!"

Thomas rushed into the room. "What are you doing?"

Kasper's head whipped toward him. "Stay out of this, Thomas!" he snarled. Then his eyes narrowed and he focused on the vampire in his presence.

Thomas saw how flickers of light discharged from Kasper's body and shot toward the vampire.

"No!" Thomas cried out, realizing that Kasper was using his mind to control the vampire to execute his dirty deed.

"He needs to be punished!" Kasper cried out, his face distorting into an ugly grimace.

Less than an hour earlier, Kasper had been in an exceedingly good mood, but now, nothing of that good mood was evident. Almost, as if he had a split personality. Thomas had started noticing it more and more often. But this was the first time Thomas saw true ugliness within Kasper and recoiled from him. "What has he done?"

"He defied my orders! Now he's going to pay!"

Kasper whipped back to the vampire and shot a blinding ray of light toward him. The vampire cried out, but his hand holding the knife rose and his feet took a step toward his human mate whose eyes were wide with fear.

"No," she cried out. "Please don't do this, George, don't let him do this to you! You're stronger."

But her vampire mate advanced, his face distorted in pain as he tried to fight Kasper's control over his body. It was clear that he couldn't.

The knife sliced low into the woman's belly, her cries of pain echoing against the stone walls. Thomas's stomach lurched and he jumped toward the vampire, trying to kick the knife out of his hands. Kasper's kick to his midsection stopped him dead in his tracks.

"Stay out of it!" he ordered.

Thomas glared up at his lover. "Stop this now!"

But Kasper didn't listen. Instead he trained his eyes back on the vampire under his control and sent another burst of mental power to him. Again, the vampire cut into the belly of his mate, making a longer incision now. More blood spilled onto the floor and the woman merely hung from the rack now, her legs having collapsed underneath her.

Her cries deafened Thomas's ears as he tried to make another attempt to help her and her baby. A bolt of power hit him squarely in the chest, and instinctively he fought back, focusing his mind on Kasper.

"Finally!" Kasper grinned at him. "I thought you'd never find the power inside you. Isn't it wonderful? You feel it, don't you?"

Yes, Thomas had felt the force slumbering in him ever since Kasper had turned him and told him he'd help him harness it. Harness the dark power Kasper had given him with his blood. He'd suppressed it, because he didn't want it. But now, at the sight of injustice toward an innocent, it emerged.

Kasper laughed and pushed against him with his mental power, knocking him to the ground. "Maybe now you'll let me train you. Watch how it's done!"

Kasper looked back at the vampire he was still controlling. "So you've decided to save your child. Well . . . ." Kasper pointed to the bleeding belly of his mate. "Then take it from her body!"

The vampire followed Kasper's command and Thomas watched in horror as he stuck his hands into the woman's womb and pulled out the child. It was covered with blood, the umbilical cord still attached, but it was alive.

"Now kill it!" Kasper ordered as a bolt of white light shot from his fingers and hit the vampire's head.

Like a marionette, the vampire reached for his knife and aimed it at the child. His struggle was evident in his distorted face, the way he clenched his teeth, and the shaking of his arm as he tried to pull it back while an invisible hand drove it ever closer to the baby's throat.

The baby's cry was cut off a split second after it started. Then the tiny head fell onto the floor with a loud thud, the wails of its dying mother accompanying it.

Thomas felt a shiver as cold as ice crawling over his back and spreading over his entire body. He rose to his feet and stared at Kasper.

"You're evil, Kasper. Truly evil. I won't have anything more to do with you!"

Kasper expelled a bitter laugh. "You have no choice! I made you! You're just like me! You have the same power running in your veins."

"I don't want that power! I never asked for it!"

"It doesn't matter. You have it and you can't give it back."

Thomas shook his head. "I won't use it!" He turned on his heels and ran out of the room, Kasper's voice chasing him.

"You'll come back! The power is stronger than you! You won't be able to resist using it."

As Thomas rushed up the stairs and into his room to toss a few belongings into a suitcase, the horror of what he'd seen chilled his blood. No, he'd never be like Kasper. He'd rather die.

15

Thomas set the tin with the used oil he'd drained from the Ducati onto the edge of the workbench in his garage and bent down to pick up the screwdriver, when the earth underneath his feet started shaking. Instinctively, his hands searched for support to steady himself and ride out the earthquake. Tools and various containers rattled on the metal shelves along the garage, and the house moaned as the waves of the quake caused it to move.

Tools started falling from the open shelves and Thomas ducked, avoiding a falling wrench, and hitting his back on the leg of the workbench. The tin with oil he'd placed on it only moments earlier tipped over. Thomas dove away, but wasn't fast enough and the contents spilled over his T-shirt and the front of his jeans.

"Fuck!" he hissed as he felt the oil soak through his T-shirt.

Suddenly, the shaking stopped and all went quiet again. Thomas perused the garage. No major damage thanks to the fact that all the shelves were bolted to the wall and floor. He looked down at himself. No damage, except for his stained clothes. Shit, the stuff stank! He lifted himself up from the floor and instantly pulled the T-shirt over his head, careful that the oil didn't touch his head.

He tossed the shirt in the laundry sink and turned on the faucet while he popped the button of his pants open, lowered the zipper and rid himself of his jeans. It joined the T-shirt in the sink a moment later. At least the oil hadn't soaked through to his boxer briefs yet.

Thomas held his hands under the flowing water. The old faucet sputtered, and water splashed over his torso, washing away the drops of oil that had seeped through his T-shirt. A sound from the stairs made him whip his head to the side.

Long jeans-clad legs appeared from the stairs. "Everything all right? Fuck, that was a big one! Have you ever been through a big one like that?"

Eddie came into view just as Thomas felt the water run down his chest and soak his boxer briefs. It was too late to grab a towel: within seconds the soft white fabric was soaked and practically transparent.

Eddie froze at the bottom of the stairs, his eyes running over Thomas's virtually-naked body, and it was all it took for Thomas to get hard. Eddie's mouth dropped open, but his gaze was still focused on Thomas's groin. His Adam's apple moved. A hitched breath rolled over Eddie's lips.

Thomas felt more blood pump into his cock, which now stretched the fabric farther away from his body, tenting his boxer briefs. From the corner of his eye, he saw the towel that hung next to the sink, yet he couldn't bring himself to reach for it and wrap it around his lower body.

As long as Eddie stared at him without uttering a word, he felt frozen, like a statue unable to move. He didn't want to break the spell, because Eddie's eyes drinking him in made his heart beat in a frantic rhythm. He wanted to prolong this feeling, even though he wasn't sure what this was: was Eddie merely shocked at seeing him half-naked in the garage? Or did the sight excite him?

Only a day ago, he'd threatened Eddie that he would take what he wanted should Eddie ever touch him again. Maybe he should have warned him that if he ever looked at him like this, the same threat applied. Because at this moment, Thomas was ready to pounce on him, drag him to the floor and rip his clothes off him before he buried himself deep in Eddie's body and rode him until they both climaxed.

It was Eddie who finally broke the silence. "I see there's no damage." He turned back to the stairs. "I'll be going to sleep then."

Thomas reached for the towel. "There might be aftershocks. Keep a flashlight next to your bed, just in case there's a bigger one coming."

Eddie nodded. "Sure." He disappeared out of sight, and a few seconds later the door to the upper floor was closed, and Thomas was alone again.

His cock ached, wanting to feel Eddie's body, his hands, his mouth, his ass. Any which way he could get him.

Eddie rushed to his room and closed the door behind him, breathing heavily. Fuck, he should have never gone down to the garage! But when the earthquake had hit, a 5-pointer for sure, concern for Thomas had made him run down there, knowing he was working on one of his motorcycles. What if one of the heavy machines had fallen on him, or God forbid, what if the SUV had somehow shifted and pinned him against a wall?

He'd expected the worst when he'd run into the garage, but he hadn't expected to see Thomas in his underwear. In his nearly transparent underwear. Gazing at his wet torso had been bad enough: his mentor had a ripped, hairless chest with beautifully-defined muscles, sculpted so perfectly not even Michelangelo's David could compete with him.

But the package he was carrying between his legs had drawn Eddie to look for longer than he should have. He'd been able to see his erect cock clearly through the soaked fabric. In fact, he'd seen it grow hard in front of his eyes. It had taken only seconds for Thomas's shaft to fill with blood and curve upwards. He'd always guessed that Thomas was big—even when casually glancing at him when Thomas was dressed, Eddie had noticed it. But to see his thick long cock through the wet fabric had confirmed his guess. Eddie could easily guess what had caused Thomas's arousal: he'd enjoyed the fact that Eddie had surprised him and stared at him.

For an instant, a flicker of pride sparked inside him. *He* had made Thomas hard. Damn it, he shouldn't feel proud about that! He should feel repelled. No straight man should revel in the fact that a gay man was turned on by him!

Angry with himself, Eddie went into his en-suite bathroom and got ready for bed, trying to stamp out every thought about Thomas, and instead concentrate on other things. The earthquake. He should check whether everybody else was okay. Depending on where the epicenter was, there could have been damage in other parts of town. After all, Thomas's house stood on bedrock and therefore the shaking would have been less intense here than downtown.

Eddie sat down on his bed, wearing only his pajama bottoms, and reached for the phone, dialing quickly.

It took three rings before a female voice answered. "Eddie, something wrong?"

"Hey, Sis, sorry to disturb, but I wanted to make sure you guys are okay."

"Huh? Why wouldn't we be okay?"

"The earthquake. It was a big one. Was there any damage to your place?"

In the background he heard Amaury's voice. *"Earthquake?"*

"Oh, that was an earthquake?" Nina chuckled.

A deep rumble came from Amaury, then a giggle from Nina.

Eddie rolled his eyes. Those two hadn't even felt the earthquake because they'd been doing horizontal acrobatics. "Oh, you guys! Does he never give you a rest?"

"Who says she wants a rest?" Amaury's voice came through the line loud and clear as if he'd taken the phone from Nina's hands.

"Forget I called. Obviously, my concerns aren't welcome."

"Sleep well, Eddie," Nina's voice came from the distance. Then the line was disconnected.

Eddie put the receiver down. That would teach him not to call his sister during daytime hours when Amaury was home. Not that her possessive mate was always gone during the night either. It appeared that Amaury spent more and more time at home with Nina, and less and less time at Scanguards. Weren't those two getting sick of each other's company?

Slipping under the covers, Eddie shook his head. He reached for the bedside lamp and flicked the switch. Darkness surrounded him as he sank back onto the pillow and closed his eyes. He tossed, seemingly forever, visions of Thomas's half-naked body taunting him. He felt his cock harden and flicked an angry finger against the head to make it deflate. He would not masturbate to images of Thomas. He couldn't allow this madness to escalate. It was bad enough that the kiss, and now seeing him practically naked, were making him question his sexuality; he wouldn't top it off by actually giving into his urges. Instead he had to fight against those feelings in him. They weren't right. He was probably confused. They would pass if only he ignored them long enough.

Tired from the mental fight going on inside him, he let himself be lulled in by the creaking of the house as it responded to the aftershocks of the earthquake. He snuggled deeper into the pillows, the soft sheets caressing his skin. A scent drifted to him: tantalizing, arousing, tempting. So familiar, and so forbidden: Thomas's scent. A shadow moved toward the bed.

Then cool air blew against his body as hands lifted the bed sheet off his body and laid him bare. The mattress depressed and a warm mouth pressed soft kisses on his chest while gentle hands caressed him. With every caress they stroked lower, until they reached the top of his pajama bottoms. Fingers reached for the strings and undid the knot, then pulled on the fabric, pushing it down his hips.

Without thinking, Eddie lifted his butt to help him slide the garment off his body. It made a soft whoosh as it fell to the wooden floor. Thomas's hands were on his thighs and pushed them apart, so he could slide between them, settling his body there. His naked body.

Silently, Thomas's head dropped to Eddie's groin. He knew what his mentor would find there: a cock as hard as it had ever been. He was as eager to feel Thomas's lips around him as anybody could ever be. Anticipation made his pulse race, and tiny pearls of sweat built on his forehead and neck. His chest heaved as the lust that he'd been trying to hold back finally burst to the surface.

As if Thomas had waited for it, his lips finally wrapped around the tip of Eddie's cock, and painstakingly slowly, he slid down to the base. Eddie found himself engulfed in wet heat that threatened to consume him. A groan issued from his lips as he thrust upwards and deeper into Thomas's mouth. He'd never felt anything so good. So intense. So hot.

Hands urged him to bring his legs up over his lover's shoulders. It opened him up wider, exposing his sensitive balls fully. Warm palms cupped his sac, squeezing it gently, while his lover's head bobbed up and down, sucking his cock in a steady rhythm.

He couldn't help but mimic Thomas's movements and thrust in counteraction to him, fucking his mouth as if his life depended on it. Under cover of darkness, he could allow himself to surrender to his lover's touch, to his lips and his mouth. To simply give in to the pleasure Thomas was granting him. He shouldn't feel this pleasure. Yet he did.

Thomas's tantalizing tongue licked him, and his mouth sucked him with such perfect pressure, that he couldn't resist the urge to spur him on, to praise him by letting him hear the moans and sighs he could no longer keep contained.

"Yes, fuck, yes!" he cried out.

His cock pushed deeper into Thomas's warm mouth, harder and faster. Eddie put his hands on the back of his head, holding him there so he couldn't escape. His hips moved frantically, up and down. All the while a firm hand squeezed his balls in the same rhythm. Then he felt one finger slip along the crack of his ass, pushing against the tight ring of muscles that guarded his dark portal.

A bolt of lightning shot through him, sending an intense wave of pleasure through his body. When it hit his cock, his eyes flew open, his gaze zeroing in on the space between his legs. His own hand was wrapped around his cock, a cock that spurted hot semen in the air. Thomas was gone. No, not gone: he'd never been there!

It had all been a dream. A wet dream. The most erotic dream he'd ever had. And the most disturbing one at the same time.

He'd gotten off by imagining Thomas's mouth on him, his hand cradling his balls, and a finger rubbing over his anus. And everything had excited him, even the finger that had rubbed over the tight entrance that was buried between his butt cheeks. Particularly that had made him hot. So hot that he'd come without warning.

Distressed, he sat up and wiped his semen-covered hand and stomach on the bed sheet then threw it on the floor. Something was wrong with him. This couldn't be happening to him: he had gay erotic dreams. Did this mean he was turning gay?

He shoved a trembling hand through his hair. He had to figure out what was wrong with him so he could find a way to fix it.

16

Lights were ablaze in Samson's house in Nob Hill when Eddie entered the foyer. Delilah closed the door behind him, her baby daughter Isabelle in her arms. The little girl was awake and flashed a nearly toothless grin at him. None of her front teeth had grown yet; however, tiny fangs peaked from her gums. Isabelle was bigger, her gaze more alert than that of a human baby, as if she understood far more than regular children. As a hybrid—half vampire, half human—she had the traits of both species, yet none of their disadvantages. She could be out in the sun, but would one day be as strong as a vampire.

"Hi Delilah, hope I'm not disturbing," he greeted Samson's wife.

"Not at all. Come in. I haven't seen you in a while. How was the party for Haven?" She motioned him into the living room and he followed her.

"They should have really held it where you and Nina could have joined. And Ursula too."

Delilah made a dismissive hand movement. "Don't worry about me. I'm not one for parties. Besides, I would have had to find a sitter for Isabelle."

Eddie smiled at the baby. She was a cute little girl, and he was sure that one day she'd break a guy's heart when she rejected him. "I don't think you'd have any problems finding a sitter. She's one of the most well-behaved babies I've ever met."

Delilah chuckled. "And how many babies have you met?"

"Well, a few," he lied.

She rolled her eyes. "Anyway, my problem is that I need a vampire or a hybrid babysitting her. She'll drive any human crazy as soon as she realizes she's stronger than them. Won't you?" She gave her daughter a conspiratorial look.

Eddie laughed. "It's all a matter of discipline."

"If you're ever a father, I'll remind you of that, shall I?" Then she and her daughter locked eyes for a long moment, and Eddie realized that they were communicating telepathically. Isabelle had a special gift that allowed her to tell her mother what she wanted, even though she couldn't speak more than a few syllables yet.

"Excuse me, Eddie, but Isabelle wants her bottle now."

"No worries. I'm here to see Samson anyway. Is he here?"

She nodded. "In his office. Why don't you take Isabelle to him while I heat up the bottle?" Without waiting for his reply, she handed the girl to him.

Isabelle gave him an assessing look, then she smiled and threw her tiny arms around him.

"She likes you."

"I like her too." He stroked his hand over her soft hair. "Come, let's see what your daddy is doing."

"Dada," she said.

"That's right: Dada." He carried her along the dark wood-paneled corridor to the back of the house.

When he reached the door to Samson's study, he rapped on it briefly, and immediately heard Samson's voice.

"Come."

He opened the door and entered. On seeing them, Samson rose from his chair behind his massive desk and walked around it.

"Hey, Eddie." Then his voice changed, becoming softer and more playful. "And what pretty little lady did you bring me today?"

Something sounding like a chuckle came from Isabelle's lips as she stretched toward Samson, reaching her arms out as far as she could. "Dada!"

"Hey sweet cheeks!" he cooed and took her from Eddie's arms, pressing a soft kiss on her forehead while he rocked her in his arms.

"She's grown a lot," Eddie commented, feeling somewhat awkward at witnessing the tender exchange between the most powerful vampire in San Francisco and his daughter.

Samson looked up and smiled. "Faster than I would like. At this rate she'll be grown up and dating before I can blink."

"And she'll be a heartbreaker," Eddie speculated.

"Don't I know it? I'm going to have to fend them off with a stick."

Eddie winked. "Not all of them. There'll be at least one who you'll have to let get close."

"He'd better be a good man." He gave his daughter a mock-stern look. "You hear me, sweet cheeks? You'd better fall in love with a good guy or we're going to have a problem."

Isabelle turned her head into the crook of Samson's neck and Eddie heard her smacking her lips.

Samson laughed. "And if you think you can appease me with a kiss, you're wrong." Then he looked back at Eddie. "So, what's up? You wanted to see me?"

Eddie nodded. "It's about Luther."

Samson's expression instantly hardened. "Luther?"

"My sire."

"Oh, I know whom you're talking about. What is this about?" Samson asked tightly.

"I need to see him."

"Luther is incarcerated."

"I know that. But I still need to see him." Only Luther could answer the questions he had. Questions he needed answered as soon as possible. He couldn't wait.

"After all he's done to you, to your sister, to all of us?"

Eddie noticed how Samson held Isabelle even closer, and realized what was going through Samson's mind. Because of

Luther, he'd nearly lost Delilah, who'd been pregnant with Isabelle at the time.

"Despite everything, I have to talk to him," Eddie insisted.

"Why?"

"I'm afraid that's between me and my sire. It's private."

Samson raised an eyebrow and remained silent as if contemplating his answer carefully. "Are you having any problems?"

"There are things I need to clarify."

"You have a very capable mentor. I'm sure he can help you. Thomas has been around for a long time. He knows everything there is to know. You can—"

"No. This is between me and Luther." Thomas was the last person he could talk to about this.

"As you wish. I will talk to the council and request a visit for you. I can't promise that it will be granted. If I knew what it was about, you might have a better chance at swaying the council."

Eddie avoided his boss's gaze and studied his shoes instead. "Please, just ask them. It's important." When he looked up again, he met Samson's eyes.

"Fine. I'll take care of it."

"Thank you. I appreciate it. I really do." Then he turned on his heels and headed for the door.

"Eddie, if there's anything I can help you with, you'll come to me, won't you?"

Eddie put his hand on the doorknob and looked over his shoulder. "This is not something you can help me with, Samson." He turned the doorknob and left the study, hearing the echo of his boots as they pounded the wooden floor in the hallway.

17

Thomas looked up from his desk in his office at Scanguards' headquarters and stretched. He'd entered profiles of the four vampires he'd seen the night he'd been out patrolling with Eddie into the system for every Scanguards vampire to view, describing them as best he could. Should anybody else come across them, they would be warned and could take action.

Having done his duty, he'd searched for the deed of Al's shop online and found only the one that had been issued over twenty years ago, when Al had first purchased the place. If there was a new deed, then it hadn't been uploaded to the Assessor Recorder's online system yet. Most likely it was sitting in some clerk's inbox waiting to be scanned in.

Was it worth breaking into City Hall to rummage through the paper records? Or should he send a human employee during daytime hours to request a copy of the deed? The latter suggestion was probably more prudent. With security at City Hall being tighter than ever, after the Supreme Court had cleared the way for gay marriages in California, and the resulting clashes between proponents and opponents of same-sex marriage, a break-in was a last resort.

Thomas composed an email requesting an employee to procure a copy of the deed and sent the work order to the central dispatch unit at Scanguards. Then he pushed his chair back, rested his feet on his desk, and stared at the ceiling. His relaxing pose was interrupted by a knock at the door.

"Come in."

The door opened and Cain popped his head in. "Hey! Got a minute?"

Thomas motioned to the chair in front of his desk and lifted his boots off the desk. "What can I do for you?"

"I saw the profiles you uploaded."

Thomas pulled up straight. "Did you come across those guys?"

"Can't be a hundred percent sure. But I saw four vampires tonight. I only saw the system update when I got back a few minutes ago. Do you have any better description of those guys?"

Shit! Thomas felt annoyance surge in him. Because of what had happened with Eddie later that night, and then the encounter with one of Kasper's disciples, he'd not reported the incident earlier. He'd screwed up.

"Unfortunately not. I had to be careful not to be noticed and could only get a glimpse of them. But I overheard them talking. I'd probably recognize their voices. Where did you see them?"

"I saw them enter Sergio's Book Emporium."

"How long ago?"

"About a half hour."

Thomas jumped up from his seat and grabbed his jacket. "Did they see you?"

"No. We didn't go in; there were no other customers in the store at the time. We would have stuck out like a sore thumb. Besides, they didn't do anything suspicious. We saw them browsing through the stacks of books."

"Let's go. With some luck, they might still be there." Then he hesitated for a moment. "Who were you patrolling with?"

"Oliver."

"Where is he now?"

"Our shift was over; he said he was going home."

"Did you actually see him leave?"

Slowly, Cain shook his head, his eyebrows pulling together into a frown. "You don't think he would do anything stupid? Like play hero?"

He didn't think so, but it was best to verify. Thomas pulled his cell from his pocket as he ran out of his office, Cain on his heels.

At the elevator, the cell rang. He rushed into the elevator, Cain beside him, and pressed the button for the lobby level.

"Thomas?" Oliver answered the phone.

"Where are you?"

"Heading home."

Relief washed over Thomas. "Change of plans. Head back to Sergio's Book Emporium. But make sure you're not seen by the four vampires who went in. Wait for Cain and me. We'll be there in ten minutes."

At the ground floor, the elevator doors opened. Thomas and Cain crossed the lobby and exited the building.

"Shouldn't we get backup?" Cain asked.

"Call dispatch." He looked to his motorcycle, which was parked in front of the building, then addressed Cain, "Where's your car?"

"I'm on foot."

Thomas motioned him to follow him to his motorcycle. "Hop on. We'll be faster this way." He unhooked the helmet from the back of the bike and held it out to Cain, who shook his head.

"You take it," Cain said.

Thomas put his helmet on and mounted the motorcycle. The engine roared and Cain slid behind Thomas.

"Hold on tight."

Cain put one arm around Thomas's waist and Thomas pulled into traffic, racing down the busy street. At the next intersection, he turned right and headed toward North Beach where Sergio's was located. He heard Cain on his cell phone, calling the central dispatch office at Scanguards to ask for backup; Cain then put his phone away, wrapping his other arm around Thomas's waist too.

It was rare that he had anybody riding the motorcycle with him, but it didn't bother him. Nor did he sense any kind of desire or arousal when he felt Cain's thighs press against his, and his arms hugging his midsection. He liked Cain as a person, but that was all.

Thomas wound his way through traffic, dodging cars and bicycles, avoiding busses and taxis without blinking. Riding a motorcycle was like second nature to him. He could practically do it in his sleep. He leaned deep into the next curve, tilting the motorcycle almost forty-five degrees.

"Hope you know what you're doing," Cain said from behind him. "I'd hate to land on my ass."

"You won't. Promise." An involuntary smile stole onto Thomas's lips. If Eddie were riding with him, he would revel in the excitement of the drive, and the faster and more reckless the better.

When he turned onto the block on which Sergio's was located, a narrow side street off Columbus Avenue, he slowed the bike to a crawl and searched for a convenient place to park. In front of a dive, he pulled to a stop. Cain jumped off and Thomas parked the motorcycle, then perused his surroundings.

Raucous laughter came from the open door to the bar, and from the entryway of the house next to it, he saw Oliver emerge.

"What's going on?" Oliver asked and joined them.

"The four vampires you saw earlier, I saw them the other night. They were talking about a takeover. And some plans. Some big boss. I didn't like the sound of it."

"Let's check them out." Oliver seemed eager for some action.

"If they're still there," Cain interjected.

"One way to find out. Stay here and wait for reinforcements." Thomas crossed the street, and used the trees and parked cars to remain hidden from view.

The store looked closed—the sign in the door indicating as much—but a faint light was coming from the back of it, where the office and storage room were located. Ducking between two cars, Thomas trained his eyes on the light and focused on it. A door in the back seemed to be ajar, but he saw no movement.

Staying low, he took a few steps forward toward the entrance door of the bookstore and reached for the door handle. He pushed tentatively and was surprised to find it unlocked. Easing the door inside a few inches, he peered into the dark room. The shop was of a good size. There were six or seven rows of bookcases stacked over six feet high, a comfortable seating area in a corner for people to browse, and the checkout counter toward the middle of the room. The scent of books drifted to him. It reminded him of the library his father had kept in his old home in England. He closed his eyes for an instant, inhaling more deeply.

Shock made him roll back on his heels and almost lose his balance.

Fuck!

He turned and waved to Cain and Oliver to approach. They followed his command instantly, joining him at the entrance just as Thomas rose to his full height. There was no reason to hide now. He knew the vampires were gone.

When he opened the door wider and stepped inside, Cain and Oliver followed him. The scent intensified, but it wasn't the scent of books and paper.

"Oh shit!" Oliver exclaimed.

"Bastards," Cain pressed out.

Thomas pushed the door to the back room open, the scent of human blood assaulting him. Bound to an overturned chair, a woman lay in a puddle of her own blood. Her pregnant belly was riddled with stab wounds.

Thomas fell to his knees beside her, his hand stroking over her round stomach, his eyes searching his colleagues' in disbelief. He recognized her. He'd met her once or twice.

"She's Sergio's blood-bonded mate."

"Who would do such a thing?" Oliver cried out.

"There," Cain responded, and pointed to a spot on the floor a few feet away.

Thomas turned to look, and noticed the fine layer of ash that covered the floor. In its midst lay a few coins, a wedding ring, and keys—things that would remain when a vampire met his end.

"Somebody staked her mate," Cain guessed.

"And then they killed her and the baby," Oliver added.

A barely perceivable gurgle came from the woman on the floor. Thomas's gaze shot to her.

"Quiet!" he ordered his colleagues and listened intently. A heartbeat! It wasn't too late.

"Get Maya here! Now!"

While Oliver speed-dialed on his cell phone, Thomas bent over the woman and untied her from the chair, then helped her lie flat on the floor. He whispered to her, "We're here. We'll take care of you."

A breath blew against his cheek. "My baby." She attempted to lift her hand, but it fell back onto the floor.

Thomas laid his hand over the wounds on her belly, trying to stop the bleeding. "We'll do everything we can. You hear me? Just hold on." Then he turned toward Oliver who'd finished his phone call. "How long?"

"She's not far. Five minutes, ten tops."

"My baby," the woman groaned again. "Save my baby."

Thomas lowered his head to the woman's belly and listened, his hands still on her. All he could hear was the faint, irregular breathing of the injured woman. Nothing else. He closed his eyes, trying to push away the pain that assaulted him. An innocent had died tonight. If only he'd gotten the description of the four guys up earlier, maybe this could have been prevented.

Something bumped against his hand. Thomas's eyes flew open. There it was again, a tiny movement: a heartbeat. Faint, but it was there.

"The baby's alive!" He turned to Cain and Oliver. "Put some pressure on her other wounds; we have to try and stop the bleeding or we'll lose them both."

Cain and Oliver went into action, each of them pressing their hands onto the gaping wounds on her torso and neck.

"Give her some blood," Thomas instructed.

Oliver brought his wrist to his mouth and bit into it. Blood instantly dripped from the two puncture wounds his fangs had made. Quickly he held the open wound to the woman's mouth, but she turned her head away from him.

"Drink!" he urged her.

A tear ran down her cheek. "Sergio." Her voice broke. " . . . made him watch." A gurgle came from her throat. "Made him choose."

Thomas closed his eyes in horror. The memories of his past rushed back to him: he'd seen a similar scene before, where a vampire had been made to choose between his child and his mate. And then lost them both. He'd only ever known one person who was so cruel and heartless to do such a thing. A person who was now dead. But his signature was still alive. Alive in his followers. And they were trying to send him a message.

The moments ticked away until he realized that he could have done nothing to prevent this. They'd planned this all along: to show him the extent of their power and how far they would go to make him understand that their offer to join them wasn't an offer, but a command: *join us or everybody you know will die.*

"Make her drink," he ordered Oliver once more, but as much as his friend tried, the woman refused.

"Do it for your child if not for yourself. If you die before we can get your baby out, it'll die too," Thomas begged her. "Please!"

The woman's eyes stared at him. Had she heard him? Would she listen to him?

18

Maya arrived at the same time as Eddie and Gabriel rushed into the back office of the bookstore. With shock in her eyes, she stared at the scene in the small office for a second, then leapt into action, dropping to her knees next to the woman.

"Can you feel the baby's heartbeat?"

Thomas nodded. "It's getting weaker." He pointed to the stab wounds on her belly. "Chances are the knife injured the fetus too," he whispered, leaning closer to Maya so Sergio's mate wouldn't hear him. If she thought that her baby wouldn't make it, she would probably give up immediately.

Maya leaned over the woman and placed two fingers at her neck, feeling for her pulse. "Did somebody give her vampire blood?"

"Oliver did. But she didn't drink much."

Maya gave him a grave look. "We'll have to turn her to save her. Her injuries are too severe. We can't heal her."

"I was afraid you'd say that. I guessed the same." Thomas glanced back at the woman's face. He finally remembered her name: Helen. Her eyes were closed now.

"I have to get the baby out first. If we turn her while the baby is still inside her, it will die," Maya continued.

"What can I do?"

Maya reached for her bag and rummaged through it. "I've got no scalpel, and there's no time to get one from my office. I need a knife."

"You're going to do a Cesarean?" Thomas felt a shudder go through him. Without anesthesia Helen would suffer unbearable pain.

"We can't get the baby out through the birth canal. It'll take too long." She glanced at Helen's face. "She doesn't have that kind of time."

Thomas pulled the silver knife from his boot and handed it to Maya, careful that she didn't touch the blade. He noticed how she swallowed hard, her hand trembling. He wrapped his palm around her hand as it gripped the knife and squeezed it. "If anybody can do it, you can."

"She's in shock. She won't feel much of this. But just in case she does, I need you to distract her. Can you use mind control on her?"

Thomas nodded. From the corner of his eyes he saw his colleagues look at them with bated breath. "Give us some space, please. And somebody find us something clean to wrap the baby in."

Then he concentrated on Helen, laying his hand on her forehead. Going deep inside himself, he reached out to her.

Helen, can you hear me?

There was a soft murmur.

You feel gentle hands stroking you, massaging away all pain. Your body relaxes and you inhale a cleansing breath. You feel all tension flow from you, all anxiety gone.

Over and over, he repeated the words in his mind and noticed how Helen's breathing calmed. For an instant, he glanced back to where Maya bent over her belly, the silver blade slicing her open. He noticed how carefully Maya cut through the skin and muscle, not going too deep in order not to hurt the baby inside.

When Maya laid the knife to the side and reached her hands inside Helen's belly, Thomas turned his head. He didn't need to see this. Instead, he doubled his efforts to calm Helen with his mind, control her sensations, her feelings, and with them, her life.

Seconds ticked away, yet they felt like hours. Then a high-pitched cry cut through the silence in the room. Helen's eyes flew open.

"She's beautiful," Maya announced. "Beautiful and healthy."

Thomas looked at the bloody, moving bundle Maya held in her palms, the umbilical cord still attached to it.

"My baby," Helen whispered, her breath labored.

Maya brought the baby to lie on its mother's chest and Helen looked at it.

"The baby was lucky; the knife didn't get her anywhere," Maya said to Thomas in a low voice. She continued just as low. "Turn her now. Do it."

Thomas shook his head. He couldn't do it. His blood was evil, and he'd never subject Helen to the same kind of battles he was fighting each day. "Cain, please. You have to do it."

Cain instantly crouched down and opened his wrist, but Helen turned her head. "Sergio is waiting . . . "

"No!" Thomas said. "No! Helen! Your baby needs you."

Cain looked at him, hesitating. "What do you want me to do?"

"Sergio," she whispered as her last breath rushed from her lungs and her head rolled to the side.

Thomas felt a tear roll down his cheek. He pressed his hand to her neck, feeling for a pulse. Then he lifted his head. "She's gone."

"We have to cut the umbilical cord. Now," Maya said and reached for the knife again.

Thomas snatched her wrist and stopped her. "It's silver. The baby will feel it."

"What then?" She let her gaze wander around the room.

"Your claws, cut it with your claws," Thomas suggested.

The baby girl cried again, and Thomas stroked his hand over her head, soothing her while Maya cut the umbilical cord with her claws. Lifting the baby off its dead mother's chest, Thomas looked up.

"Do we have anything to wrap her in? A towel? Anything clean?"

Oliver came running from the store, two large sheets of paper in his hands. "Here, that's all I could find."

Thomas stared at him. "Gift wrap?"

Oliver shrugged. "It's clean, and it's almost as soft as tissue paper."

Having no choice, Thomas took the paper from Oliver's hands and wrapped the baby in it, then pressed her to his chest, rocking her.

When he heard hasty footsteps coming from the shop, his head whirled to the door. A moment later, Samson rushed in, his eyes darting to the body on the floor, then to the baby in Thomas's arms.

"Sergio?" he asked.

Gabriel pointed to the dust on the floor. "We have to assume that he was staked. His mate said that they made him watch."

Samson closed his eyes. "Oh God."

It was easy to see what he was thinking: being a blood-bonded vampire himself, the father of a small child, the horror of what Sergio must have felt was written on Samson's face. When he opened his eyes, he issued his orders.

"Gabriel, call the mayor. This can't be made public. Scanguards will deal with the cleanup and the investigation. We need our own forensics team here. Get the mayor to clear the way for us and use his powers to keep the police out of this. We need to find out who did this."

"We already know," Cain announced.

Samson's head whipped toward Cain. "Who?"

"Four of those newcomers. Oliver and I saw them enter earlier in the evening."

"And you didn't stop them?" Samson barked.

Thomas rose. "They weren't doing anything suspicious. Cain and Oliver aren't at fault. I am."

"Explain!"

"I saw those four last night, out on patrol. I didn't get a very good look at them. But I knew something wasn't right. I didn't enter them into the database until earlier tonight. Cain and Oliver didn't know they were already on our list of people to watch."

"I would have expected better from you!" Samson bit out.

Eddie took a step forward. "If this is Thomas's fault, then it's mine too. I was on patrol with him. And it's true, we didn't get a good enough look at them. Only their voices."

Surprised that Eddie stepped up to defend him, Thomas looked at him.

"Be that as it may, you know the procedure. Both of you."

Eddie nodded, dropping his head.

"What did you overhear?" Samson asked, looking back at Thomas.

"Talk about takeovers. And of a boss. Only fragments. Not much to go by." But it had sounded suspicious, particularly since he now suspected them of being Kasper's disciples, even though he couldn't tell the others that. Samson was right about chastising him. He should have reported it immediately. And as the more senior bodyguard at Scanguards, it was his duty, not Eddie's.

"We'll put a team together to search for them," Samson announced. Then he looked at the baby in Thomas's arms. "What are we going to do with the baby?"

"I have an idea," Maya said, her eyes locking with Gabriel's. A second passed, then her mate nodded. She smiled and announced, "She'll have a good home with parents who will love her like their own."

19

By the time the forensics team arrived at Sergio's bookstore and collected all the evidence there was, Thomas had replayed his decisions a hundred times in his mind. Could he have prevented this tragedy?

He stepped onto the sidewalk and inhaled the cool night air. The bar across the street had closed and his and Eddie's motorcycles were now the only ones parked there. When he heard steps next to him, he turned his head and saw Cain join him.

"They would have done it either way," Cain said.

"What?"

"Those four vampires. If not tonight, they would have gotten them on another occasion. It looked deliberate. Planned. And we can't be everywhere at the same time. Even if those descriptions had been up earlier, there's no guarantee that Oliver and I could have stopped them or been close enough to them to know what they were doing until it was too late."

Cain put his hand on Thomas's shoulder and squeezed.

Thomas gave a bitter laugh. "It's not making me feel any better." Because it still didn't wipe out the fact that the crime had Kasper's signature all over it. Were they trying to send him a message? Was this a direct threat?

"You and Maya saved the baby. Isn't that worth something?"

Slowly, he nodded. At least one innocent had been saved. "It is. Good night, Cain."

"Night, Thomas."

With a heavy heart, Thomas crossed the street and approached his motorcycle. He put the key into the lock and swung himself onto it, when he noticed that something was wrong. He looked down to the tires.

"Shit!"

Thomas jumped off the bike and inspected the damage. Both tires had been slashed, front and back, and were completely deflated. Angrily, he hit his boot against the back tire. Why would somebody slash his tires? Was this another message?

"Something wrong?" Eddie's voice addressed him from behind.

"Some asshole slashed my tires."

Eddie came into view and looked at the bike. "Oh, crap!"

Thomas shoved his hand through his hair, closing his eyes for a moment. Then he glanced back at Eddie. "Can you give me a ride home so I can get the van?"

Eddie's eyes blinked in the dark. The moment's hesitation confirmed to Thomas that he was apprehensive about being physically close to him again. Thomas was about to say that he could take a taxi, when Eddie suddenly nodded.

"Sure, no problem. Hop on."

Eddie mounted his bike and swept up the kickstand with his left foot before turning the bike toward the street, then turning the key. Thomas swung himself up behind him, putting his arms around Eddie's waist. When the bike accelerated and pulled into the street, Thomas felt himself jerked backwards and tightened his grip around Eddie's midsection. He noticed that as so often Eddie hadn't put his helmet on. They both liked to ride without it, and tonight the cool air blowing past his ears was exactly what Thomas needed.

He couldn't remember when he'd last ridden on the back of someone else's motorcycle, but he remembered that he'd never much liked it. But tonight, he was glad not to have to concentrate on traffic, and instead let his thoughts wander.

Holding onto Eddie gave him a strange sense of peace and comfort. Of feeling safe, when he knew that he was never truly safe, neither from the external threats that came from Kasper's disciples, nor from the threat the dark power within him

Thomas's Choice

represented. Still, feeling the warmth from Eddie's body seep into his chest gave him a feeling of home that he hadn't felt in a long time. Because Eddie represented home for him.

Thomas sighed and moved his head closer to Eddie, inhaling the scent of his hair and skin, his masculine odor. Of their own volition, his thighs pressed harder against the outside of Eddie's thighs, and it felt as if Eddie were pressing back into him. At every point where their bodies connected, Thomas felt as if on fire. If he didn't get off this bike soon and away from Eddie's tempting body, he would burn up. Or he would do something stupid, like pulling Eddie off the bike at the next stoplight and mauling him.

When the motorcycle leaned into the next curve, Thomas's hand slipped and landed on Eddie's thigh. He gripped it for support until Eddie pulled out of the curve, straightening the bike again. Underneath his palm, Eddie's muscles flexed, and he could sense his body stiffen as if trying to ward off an attack.

Disappointed at Eddie's reaction, Thomas removed his hand from Eddie's thigh and brought it back around his waist. Eddie's jacket was open in the front, and Thomas's hand accidentally slipped inside, feeling the hard abdominal muscles under Eddie's T-shirt. Heat radiated into his palm as he let his hand wander. He wanted to touch him so badly, wanted to explore his body, arouse him again.

Thomas shifted his hips and unintentionally rocked against Eddie. A grunt came over Eddie's lips. Quickly, Thomas brought as much distance between them as the seat of the motorcycle allowed, and was glad when they finally turned into his street.

Eddie pressed the garage door opener and the gate lifted. He drove in and brought the bike to a stop. Thomas hopped off as quickly as he could while Eddie killed the engine and engaged the kickstand, parking the vehicle as he got off.

Without looking at him, Eddie asked, "Do you need help with hauling your motorcycle back?"

Thomas headed for the van and opened the door. "No. I'm good." He could almost hear the silent sigh of relief that Eddie released as he walked toward the stairs leading up to the house. Clearly, Eddie couldn't get away from him fast enough.

Thomas jumped into the van and slammed the door shut. It was better if he was alone anyway. In his current state, there was no way of knowing what he'd do to Eddie.

20

The baby, now cleaned, dressed, and wrapped in a clean blanket, was sleeping. Cain looked down at it as he walked up to the garden gate and opened it. The barking of several dogs instantly sounded an alarm to the occupants of the small cottage. The baby began to wail and Cain rocked it softly.

"Maya had better be right," Cain mumbled to himself as he reached the door and rang the doorbell.

He only had to wait a few seconds before the door was opened. Haven, Yvette's mate, filled the doorframe. Behind him, two Labrador puppies barked, excitedly running through his legs. A larger dog popped his head out from the kitchen door, looking at the spectacle before disappearing again.

"Cain? That's a surprise," Haven greeted him.

From the living room, Yvette's voice called out, "Who is it?"

"It's Cain, baby."

Cain pulled back the blanket from the baby's head and turned it for Haven to see. "I come bearing gifts."

Haven's eyes widened as he stared at the baby and then back at Cain. His chin dropped and he took a step back. "You'd better come in."

When Cain walked into the living room—Haven following him closely, the puppies in tow—he almost bumped into Yvette. She wore leggings, accentuating her long, slim legs, and a casual T-shirt—without a bra, he noticed instantly. Yet her boobs were firm. Haven was one lucky son of a bitch to have landed such a beauty as his mate. Cain couldn't help but imagine what it would be like to have sex with a woman like her. Not that he'd ever dare touch another vampire's mate. It was practically a death sentence to any man who tried.

"Hey, Yvette. Sorry to disturb so late, but there was an incident."

Yvette inhaled sharply, her eyes instantly dropping to the bundle in his arms. Her mouth opened wider. "Oh my god!"

Cain looked down at the cute baby in his arms. "She's a hybrid. Her parents were murdered tonight. There's no other family. Maya had to cut her from her dying mother's womb. She's a perfectly healthy baby."

Yvette reached for the baby, and Cain passed her into Yvette's arms.

"That's horrible," Haven said. "What happened?"

"Four of the newcomers we've been tracking attacked Sergio in his bookstore, killed him and stabbed his blood-bonded mate. It's a wonder the baby survived. We have a description of them and are investigating."

Yvette caressed the soft hair on the baby's head. "She's perfect." Her eyes glistened with moisture as she looked up and sought Haven's eyes.

Cain smiled, glad about the reception Yvette was giving the baby. He set the bag he'd slung over his shoulder earlier onto the couch and pointed to it. "Delilah packed a few essentials. Diapers, formula, clothes. Just to get you started."

"To get us started?" Haven echoed.

"Yes. That is if you want her. She needs a home." His gaze moved from Haven to Yvette. "And a good mother."

A tear rolled down Yvette's face and her lips opened, but no words passed over them. Haven put his arm around her, kissing the top of her head. Then he looked back at Cain, moisture gathering in his eyes too.

"Of course we want her. She'll be like our own flesh and blood. I can promise you that." Haven's voice cracked.

A sob tore from Yvette's chest as she lifted her face to her mate. "Thank you." She stretched to press a kiss on Haven's lips.

"Baby, don't thank me. Thank fate for having blessed us with this gift." He stroked his hand over the baby's head. "She's precious. Thank you, Cain. I can't tell you what this means to us."

Cain pushed back the feelings that threatened to unman him. He wasn't one to give in to his emotions, but the sight before him tugged at even his heartstrings. Yvette glowed as if she were the woman who'd given birth tonight. He had no worries about the little girl in her arms. She would grow up in a loving home with parents who'd worship and protect her. She would be safe now.

Trying to break the tearful atmosphere in the room, Cain tried for a joke. "And you'd better be raising her with a firmer hand than those dogs of yours." He pointed to the two puppies running around in circles, swishing against his legs and tugging at his pant legs as if he were their favorite new toy.

Haven grinned. "Oh those, yeah, we made a few mistakes with them." He paused. "Want one?"

Cain lifted his hands. "You've gotta be kidding me! I'm not going to let those little buggers wreak havoc in my house."

Haven shrugged and chuckled. "It was worth a try."

"Maybe the baby will enjoy playing with them."

Yvette smiled. "Does she have a name yet?"

Cain shook his head. "There was no time. You're her parents now. You decide."

"Thank you, Cain."

He was about to turn toward the door, when Yvette's voice held him back. "One more question: who suggested that we should raise her?"

"Maya."

Another sob tore from Yvette's chest, as she repeated the name. "Maya."

21

The nearly three-hour ride on the motorcycle seemed to take forever, when it should have gone by in a flash. Eddie had looked up the address and left as soon as the sun had set over the Pacific. He could have taken the blackout SUV and left during daylight, but he needed to feel the wind blow past his body. It gave him a sense of freedom that being cooped up in a car couldn't provide. Not that it made his thoughts any clearer. They were still as muddled as ever. If not more.

When he'd seen Thomas fight for the life of the pregnant woman and her child, his heart had gone out to him. He'd felt Thomas's pain physically. Thomas had known her and Sergio, and even though they hadn't been close friends, Eddie had felt the compassion that had poured from Thomas's heart. Thomas had felt responsible for what had happened.

The drive home on his motorcycle, with Thomas hugging him from behind, had been pure torture. He'd wanted to lean into him, to let him know that whatever pain Thomas felt, Eddie would comfort him. But when he'd felt the hard outline of Thomas's erection press against his butt, he'd panicked and raced home as fast as the machine between his legs was capable of. He wanted to be Thomas's friend, but he couldn't give him more than that. Thomas had to understand that. There could never be more between them, because the things Eddie felt right now could only be short-lived. Some temporary confusion on his part.

Eddie pulled to a stop in front of a large windowless bunker-like, two-story building. It lay hidden away at the end of a dirt path somewhere east of Sacramento, bordering on the foothills of the Sierras. He switched off the engine and dismounted, ridding himself of the helmet and attaching it to the handlebar.

The building looked uninhabited and dark. Not a single light on the outside drew any attention to it. Looking around to see if anybody else was in the vicinity, yet noticing nobody, Eddie walked toward the entrance door. It was a simple, gray metal door without inscription. As if the only people coming here knew what lay behind these walls.

The door buzzed, and Eddie pulled it open. His visit had been announced, and he was sure there were cameras mounted along the building perimeter for the people inside to be alerted to any guests or intruders.

As he walked along the dark corridor and heard the door snap in behind him, Eddie inhaled. It smelled clean and sterile, and not musty like he had expected. He reached another door and again a buzzer sounded, allowing him to enter.

He stepped into a brightly lit room and squinted for a moment, allowing his eyes to adjust to the abundance of light. The room was a reception area with a counter and several uncomfortable-looking chairs. Clearly, this place wasn't built for comfort or luxury. No penitentiary was.

The vampire male behind the counter nodded to him. "Name?"

"Eddie Martens."

He looked down on the clipboard in front of him and ticked something off. "You're late."

"The traffic—"

"Sign in here." The clerk handed him the clipboard and pointed to a line.

Eddie signed his name then handed the board and the pen back to the curt vampire.

"You'll have fifteen minutes with the prisoner." The vampire pointed to a gray door.

Eddie walked to it and opened it. He entered, the door closing behind him with a loud thud. Surprise made him catapult back against the door. He'd expected to be led down another corridor, but instead he found himself in a bare room with two chairs. One was occupied.

"Eddie!" Luther jumped up, seemingly surprised and pleased at the same time. "They didn't tell me who my visitor was."

Eddie lifted his hand, stopping Luther from coming any closer. "Luther."

He ran his eyes over him. Wearing a gray prison jumpsuit, Luther's face looked washed out, lifeless. As if he'd lost his will to live. The light that he'd seen flicker in his eyes the moment Eddie had entered, seemed to have faded again.

"How have you been?" Luther asked. "Are they treating you well?"

Eddie nodded. "Scanguards has been good to me." He pushed himself away from the door. "And you?"

Luther shrugged. "I live." He sighed. "But somehow I get the feeling you didn't come to ask about my wellbeing."

"You're right. They've given me fifteen minutes with you. So let's not waste any time with chitchat neither of us is interested in."

"Let's not," Luther confirmed.

"I want to know what you did to me."

Luther raised an eyebrow as if he didn't understand the question. "What I did? Care to explain what you mean by that?"

"During my turning. You screwed something up."

Luther moved his head from side to side. "From what I can see, you turned out just fine. A perfect vampire. Strong. Invincible." He paused. "Although a little stubborn, but then you were stubborn even as a human."

Eddie clenched his teeth. "You changed something else about me. How I feel. What I feel." Fuck, there was no easy way to say this. No words he could use to make this any less embarrassing. Did he have to spell it out?

"I'm afraid you've lost me. Eddie, if there's anything you want to know you'd better ask directly. I'm afraid my mind reading capabilities aren't worth shit." Luther tossed him a look as if he wanted to challenge him to a fight.

"You changed something about me. You changed my . . . my desires," he pressed out.

"Are we talking bloodlust here?"

How could one man be so dimwitted! Eddie made an impatient hand movement. "I'm not talking about fucking bloodlust. I'm talking about who I'm attracted to."

Slowly, one of Luther's brows arched. Then his facial expression changed to one of understanding. "Ah, now I get it. You've switched camps."

Eddie made a step toward Luther and jammed his index finger into his chest. "It wasn't my choice! You—"

"It never is," Luther interrupted. "Being gay has never been a choice. Nobody chooses to be gay, nor to be straight. It's nature."

The word grated on him: gay. "I'm not gay!"

"Ah, so you have *gay tendencies*, just like that preacher. What was his name?"

Eddie ignored the question, his anger rising at Luther's flippant attitude toward his problem. "I thought as my sire you're supposed to support me. You screwed this up! You made me like this. Now change me back to how I was before."

Luther rocked back on his heels. "How you were before? Oh, Eddie, you're still the same way you always were. Turning you into a vampire didn't change who you are, or who you love. Whatever you feel now, it was already there when you were human. Latent, maybe. But you already had it in you."

Eddie pushed his hand against Luther's shoulder, making him stumble back a few paces. "What are you saying? That I was a fucking queer when I was human? I assure you, I wasn't! I never looked at another man! I loved women!"

"You did, huh? Well, you must have had girlfriends left, right, and center. With your looks and all, they must have been flocking to you. How was it? Lots of fucking?" A mocking expression spread over Luther's face.

Eddie sucked in a deep breath, his thoughts going back to his adolescence, his early manhood. He'd had the occasional girlfriend, and he'd certainly had sex with women before, but he hadn't been promiscuous. He just wasn't the type. He'd always respected women and wasn't one to take advantage of them. In fact, he'd had lots of female friends.

"I see," Luther continued. "Not so much, huh? Guess you didn't like fucking women so much after all, did you?"

Angrily, Eddie shoved Luther against the wall. "You're wrong! Just because I don't sleep around, doesn't mean I don't love women."

"Don't kid yourself, Eddie! If you've got the hots for men now, your true nature is finally coming out."

Before Eddie's eyes, the picture of Thomas standing half-naked in front of the sink in the garage flashed. It sent a bolt of desire through his groin, spreading heat in his cells. Suddenly he fought for air.

Unfortunately, his sire was perceptive as hell. "Oh, so it's not just any man. It's one in particular. Who is it who tickles your fancy? Do I know him?"

"There's nobody!" Eddie lied.

"Lying doesn't become you. Besides, you're not very good at it." Luther motioned his head to indicate the prison around him. "If I weren't tied up here, I would have taught you. Instead, I had to leave you to Scanguards. To continue your education there." He gave a crooked smile.

"You promised me to make me strong, invincible. This wasn't part of the bargain!"

"No, it wasn't part of the bargain, but that wasn't my doing. Can't you get that into your stubborn head? Guess not! Because as a vampire you're even more stubborn than as a human. Whatever traits you had before, they only intensified as a vampire. That's how it works! You were able to suppress whatever feelings for men you had when you were human, but now as a vampire, you can't do that anymore. Your desires are stronger, and they're growing stronger every day. Just give in and come out of the closet."

"No!" Eddie screamed. He couldn't accept this. There had to be another explanation.

Frustration howled through him. His fangs descended and his hands curled into fists. He watched himself as he slammed his right fist into Luther's face, whipping his head sideways. "You did this to me!"

Luther pushed him back into the middle of the room then came after him. "You wanna fight? Let's do it. But it won't change the facts!" His sire swung and landed a right hook under Eddie's chin.

Eddie tasted blood as his fangs pierced his own lip. It only made him angrier. Grabbing Luther by the shoulders, he catapulted him into the wall several feet behind him. Then he jumped at him and pounded his fists into him. But Luther was no willing punching bag. He fought back, attacking with his claws, slicing deep grooves into Eddie's chest and arms.

The scent of blood filled the room, and loud grunts mingled with the sound of breathing. It echoed in the nearly-empty room, bouncing off the walls.

"So who is your lover then?" Luther provoked him.

Narrowing his eyes and clenching his jaw, Eddie swung, aiming a blow at Luther's temple. His knuckles cracked at impact, but he ignored the pain and continued punching his sire, even though he knew beating him wouldn't change anything about the way he felt. It wouldn't eradicate the feelings he had for Thomas.

"Is he a vampire?"

"I'm gonna shut your fucking mouth for you if you can't do it yourself!" Eddie answered, and aimed for Luther's mouth to ram the words back down his throat. But Luther sidestepped him and instead landed a blow to Eddie's side, making him stumble.

Luther's taunting didn't stop. "Is he any good?"

Furious, Eddie fought to gain his balance back and threw himself onto Luther, tackling him to the ground.

"Are you taking it up the ass or is he?"

"Fuck you!" Eddie yelled and pinned him to the floor.

Luther grinned through the blood that ran from his cracked lip. "No, fuck him! Because that's what this is all about, isn't it? You wanna fuck him, but you need an excuse, because you can't admit what you are. You wanna blame somebody else for what you feel."

Eddie pulled back, breathing hard, his heart racing. But the fight was leaving him, deserting him like rats deserting a sinking ship. He was losing this battle.

"I heard they assigned you a mentor. Why didn't you ask him? He could have told you the same as I did. Would have saved you a trip."

Eddie avoided his gaze and rose. He wiped the blood off his face with the back of his hand, breathing hard.

Then a short laugh burst from Luther's lips. "Ah, now I see. You couldn't ask him, could you? You couldn't ask Thomas, because it's all about him. He's the one you want."

"Fuck you!" Eddie hissed and pressed the button next to the door to be let out.

A moment later, he left Luther and the prison behind. Was Luther right? Had he always had *gay tendencies* as a human? Eddie remembered his early childhood and his friends from back then. He and Nina had lived with foster parents, but his early years in foster care had been nothing out of the ordinary. He'd been just like other little boys: curious. Didn't all kids like to play doctor and examine each other's bodies? He and another boy had sometimes played like that, curiously touching one another. Of course, that had stopped when his foster mother had caught them and sent the other boy home. He wasn't allowed to visit again. And Eddie hadn't been allowed to watch TV for a week. That had taught him, and he had never done it again.

Later, when he'd joined the wrestling team of his high school, he'd always felt awkward in the locker room. Mostly because he'd gotten erections at the most inopportune times. It had been embarrassing, and some of the other boys had often locked him out of the showers because of it, not wanting him there when they showered. They'd bullied him because his body did things he had no control over.

He'd quit sports then, and Nina had been disappointed because of it. She'd accused him of not being able to stick with something. Of course, he hadn't been able to tell her what had really happened, because no 15-year-old boy talked to his sister about sexual stuff. He'd promised himself then that he wouldn't disappoint her again. She had fought to gain guardianship of him in order to move out of the last foster home they'd stayed in, after their foster father had abused her, and Eddie didn't want to seem ungrateful and load any more worries onto her shoulders.

Had those incidents been indications of what his true nature was? The true nature that Luther was claiming was now emerging because he was a vampire?

Had he hidden his urges so far in the depths of his psyche that he'd been completely blind to their existence?

What would happen if he stopped fighting his desires from emerging? Would they destroy his relationship with Nina, his friendship with Thomas, and the life he'd built for himself? Would people treat him differently if they knew? Most of all, would Nina look at him with disappointment in her eyes again?

22

Thomas stood in the shower and let the warm water run down his body as if it could wash away his worries. Another night had passed without any sign of the four vampires who'd killed Sergio and his mate. And while he knew intellectually that he couldn't have prevented this tragedy, in his heart he felt responsible.

He tried to put the thoughts out of his mind, but that only meant that other thoughts pushed to the forefront. Thoughts about Eddie. He hadn't seen him all night, and after checking the staff roster, he'd realized that Eddie had taken a vacation day. Samson himself had authorized it. Strange, neither Eddie nor Samson had mentioned anything to him. And Eddie had left on his motorcycle as soon as the sun had set.

Thomas reached for the soap and lathered up, cleaning the grease from his body after he'd tinkered with one of his motorcycles for a few hours. It had helped him focus. He had to do something. Sitting around and waiting for the next atrocity to happen was not an option. Tomorrow night, he would go out and search for Xander, the man who'd asked him to join Kasper's disciples. He would use him to ferret out the others and then figure out how to destroy them.

Feeling better about having formulated a plan, he rinsed the soap off his body and turned off the water. There was silence now, but it was interrupted by the even breathing of a man other than himself. He inhaled and recognized the scent.

"Leave!" he ordered and continued to stare at the tiles that lined his oversized shower stall.

But no sound of footsteps followed his command.

"Eddie, get out now! You can't be in here. I don't have the strength to suppress my desire for you, not today. You're better off locking yourself in your room. Leave! Please leave!"

He braced one hand against the tile wall, steadying himself while his body betrayed him, his cock pumping full with blood, making it rise like a Phoenix. There was no way he could turn around now. It was bad enough that Eddie could see his naked backside. Showing him his erection and admitting that he was powerless in his presence would only make things worse.

When he heard bare feet on the floor, he almost let out a sigh of relief—until he realized that they were coming closer instead of moving away. He closed his eyes and clenched his jaw, fighting against the urge to turn around and pull Eddie into the shower with him.

"You have to leave," he begged once more, but it was too late.

Eddie's hand touched his shoulder, turning him around to face him. Eddie's brown eyes looked straight at him, connecting with his gaze, before they wandered down his body, stopping at the place, where Thomas's cock stood erect.

Thomas's heart stopped beating as he let his gaze travel over Eddie's body. His chest was bare. Tight abs flexed just above his low-riding pajama pants. The thin material tented at Eddie's groin. Thomas's throat went dry. He was unable to swallow.

Nor was he able to move when Eddie's hand stroked over his chest, grazing his nipple and turning it rock hard in an instant. But Eddie's hand didn't remain on his chest. It dove lower, went past his navel, and reached the thatch of hair that guarded Thomas's sex. When his fingers combed through the coarse hair, Thomas held his breath, afraid of breaking the spell. At the first contact of Eddie's hand with his cock, Thomas let out an involuntary groan. Then his breathing went into overdrive.

Eddie's hand wrapped around him, the warm skin of his palm covering him like a blanket.

"Fuck!" Thomas hissed under his breath.

Eddie's eyes shot up to meet his gaze. His lips moved. "You like that?" His pink tongue licked his lips, making Thomas let out another sound of pleasure. Was he dreaming? Because this couldn't be happening. Why was Eddie suddenly in his shower, touching him when only two nights ago, he'd made it clear that the kiss at the construction site had been merely a diversionary tactic? What had changed Eddie's mind?

Eddie tightened his grip around Thomas's hard-on, then slid up and down on it. "If we do this, you have to promise me something," he demanded.

"Anything," Thomas replied without thinking, since his brain had already shut down and his dick was doing his thinking for him now.

"Nobody can ever find out."

"Nobody," he whispered back, his breath deserting him as Eddie moved closer.

"Undress me."

Thomas reached for the strings that held up Eddie's pajama pants and untied them with trembling fingers. When the knot was open, he loosened the waistband and pushed the pants past Eddie's slim hips. From there, they fell onto the wet shower floor, pooling around Eddie's feet.

Thomas dropped his gaze and stared at Eddie's cock. It was fully erect and more beautiful than anything he'd ever seen. Pumped full with blood, plump veins snaked around the shaft, its purple head glistening with pre-cum. He took a deep breath, inhaling the tantalizing scent, sending a shockwave through his body.

"Eddie," he murmured, unable to form a coherent sentence.

Instead, he slipped his hand between Eddie's legs and palmed his balls, then gripped his erection. Eddie's breath hitched, and for a moment, his hand on Thomas's cock stilled in its movements.

Eddie let go of Thomas's cock, then laid his hand over Thomas's and pried it off him. Disappointed, Thomas stared at him.

"Together," Eddie whispered and pushed his cock against Thomas's, then put his hand around both cocks at the same time, though his palm couldn't span the combined girth fully.

Thomas added his hand, and together they moved their hands up and down their joined erections. Feeling the soft skin of Eddie's cock against his own hard-on, Thomas felt overwhelmed by the sensations racing through his body: fire shot through his cells, electricity fueled the flames in his body, desire surged.

Eddie let out a ragged breath, his lids lowering. Thomas slanted his head and brought his lips to Eddie's, brushing against them. A moan left Eddie's throat and Thomas captured it, closing his lips over Eddie's mouth.

The moment their tongues met, pleasure so intense he thought it would kill him rushed through him. He'd dreamed of this so many times, spent so many days in his bed imagining how it would feel. But now that it was happening, now that he and Eddie were making love, he realized that his fantasies had been pale copies in comparison to what he was experiencing now.

Eddie's hand stroking him, his tongue dueling with him, his thighs pressing against him, made his pulse race. And if vampires could suffer heart attacks, Thomas would surely die from one. Sliding his free hand onto Eddie's ass, he ground against him, making him aware of his unquenchable desire for him.

Eddie's hand started moving at a faster tempo as he slid up and down their cocks. Thomas matched his strokes to Eddie's, feeling his excitement rise along with his own.

Thomas intensified the kiss, sucking, stroking, exploring his lover with more fervor, diving deeper into the sweet caverns of his mouth, nibbling on his lips, then licking his tongue over them.

When Eddie's head fell back, severing the kiss, Thomas kissed the tempting column of his neck, his lips latching onto the plump vein that pulsed there. He could sense the blood rushing through the vein, the pulsing sensation that indicated the heartbeat, just as he could smell the blood. It called to him like a beacon that guided a lost soul to shore. Taking a lover's blood was part of what many vampires did during the sex act. It heightened their arousal and intensified their coupling. Temptation roared through Thomas as his fangs extended and brushed against Eddie's hot skin.

Eddie felt Thomas's mouth on his neck and his sharp teeth sliding along his skin. The sensation sent a spear of heat through his core and right into his cock. He'd never felt anything better in his life, and all they were doing was rubbing their cocks together, their hands joined, their rhythms in perfect harmony.

Maybe this was the way to get this out of his system. At least that's what he'd thought at first when he'd walked into Thomas's bathroom. Just one quick fuck and he would realize that this wasn't what he wanted, and then he'd finally kill his desire for Thomas and get back to being his friend. Unfortunately, the moment he'd touched Thomas and wrapped his hand around his magnificent cock, he'd realized that it wouldn't be so easy. Maybe they would have to fuck more than once for Eddie to satisfy his *gay tendencies*.

Eddie's free hand wandered over Thomas's body, exploring the hard ridges on his abdomen and the smooth, hairless skin that covered his chest. Then he roamed his back, sliding down to the curve where his firm ass waited. His cheeks clenched as Eddie palmed him, and a corresponding moan rolled over Thomas's lips. He felt Thomas's hand tighten over his ass and tried to suppress his reaction to it, but a sigh left his lips nevertheless. The possessive touch did something to him, urging him to react to the call of his lover like animals answered the mating calls of their mates.

Thomas's hips pumped, thrusting his cock harder and faster as his hand tightened over Eddie's hand, pushing their cocks harder together. Already now, he could feel the moisture that was lubricating them. Whose cock it had seeped from, Eddie couldn't tell for certain. Probably from both.

"I'm coming," Thomas ground out, his breath labored. He lifted his head from Eddie's neck. "Can't hold it back."

Eddie let go of the control with which he'd held himself back, and thrust harder. "Yes!" he cried out, proud of the fact that he could bring a strong vampire like Thomas to lose control just by pumping his cock in his hand. "Come," he urged him and captured his lips with a passionate kiss.

Then he felt wetness spread between his fingers, and a loud groan come from Thomas's chest. The pleasure of feeling Thomas surrender in his arms did him in: hot semen shot through his cock and exploded from the tip, raining over his and Thomas's hands as they continued to stroke each other more slowly now. His body shook with pleasure, his knees going weak at the same time. He ripped his lips from Thomas's mouth, trying to catch his breath, when he felt Thomas's free arm wrap around his waist, catching him before his knees could buckle.

"I've got you," Thomas murmured, pressing his forehead against Eddie's.

Eddie closed his eyes, unable to return Thomas's gaze. He'd just made love to a man, and fuck, he'd liked it. What did that make him? He didn't want to answer that question. He wasn't ready for the answer. Besides, all they'd done was masturbate together. Didn't guys do that in college all the time?

Right, a sarcastic voice in his head answered. *And they probably touch each other's cocks all the time.*

Eddie pushed away the thought when he felt warm water run down his body and Thomas's hands gently cleaning him. Without thinking he leaned into him.

"I loved it," Thomas said.

Eddie couldn't bring himself to reciprocate the words, even though deep inside, he knew he felt the same. Instead he buried his head in the crook of Thomas's neck.

He felt Thomas reach for the towel that hung just outside the shower and put it around Eddie's back, patting him dry. Eddie let it happen as if he were a helpless child. He was unable to sever the contact with Thomas's body and realized that it was because he was hungry, hungry for more. This . . . *episode* had only whet his appetite.

23

"Don't go," Thomas said.

Eddie stood at the door, a towel wrapped around his lower body, about to leave Thomas's bedroom. It had taken him all his remaining willpower to make the few steps to the bedroom door after Thomas had dried them both. But he couldn't bring himself to turn the doorknob and exit. What Thomas was offering was too tempting to turn down. His body wanted this, but his mind was fighting him.

Thomas stood behind him, his hands on Eddie's shoulders, sliding them gently down his arms, his fingers caressing him. Goosebumps appeared on Eddie's skin and a sigh escaped his lips. He hadn't realized that a man could have such a tender touch. There was nothing rough about it.

"I should go."

"Why?"

He had no answer, no matter how long he searched his mind for one.

"What are you afraid of?" Thomas's hands stroked down his back, his fingers sliding underneath the towel, loosening it, sending hot tendrils of lava running down his butt.

Eddie's breath hitched. If he stayed, he knew what would happen. Thomas would take him the way only a man could. He wasn't ready for that. Hell, he didn't think he'd ever be ready for that. How could he allow another man to do that, to take him like that?

"I won't do anything you don't want."

The towel fell to the floor and cool air blew against his heated body. Thomas's hot hands slid over his ass, palming him, making him press into them even though his mind was telling him to escape while he still could.

"I'll only do what you want me to do." Thomas's hands moved around Eddie's hips, sliding to his groin, his fingers combing the thatch of hair around his cock, promising more pleasure.

Eddie closed his eyes, his body almost trembling now. He couldn't think straight anymore. He almost had to laugh at that thought: not thinking *straight*. How twisted his mind was!

"I love touching you," Thomas confessed and covered Eddie's cock with his hand, stroking him.

Under his touch it grew harder. Eddie tried to fight against it but to no avail. As Thomas's hands caressed him, Eddie's cock rose to its full size and curved upwards, demanding more. Lust spread in his body, boiling up from his gut. He was unable to contain it much longer. Soon it would take over his body and make decisions for him.

"Let me suck you. I promise you you'll like it."

Eddie had no doubt about it. But if he let it happen, wouldn't that only reinforce his feelings? Wouldn't it make things even worse? Having another man suck him—wasn't that considered gay sex? Even more so than just having Thomas jerk him off? Was he getting deeper and deeper into this? Wouldn't it be better if he left now and chalked this up to a one-time stupid act? A lapse in judgment. Everybody made mistakes. Wasn't he allowed one too? Okay, maybe two mistakes, if he counted the kiss at the construction site and the subsequent hand job Thomas had given him.

Thomas turned him so he had to face him. His eyes bored into Eddie's. "Stay."

Unable to make a decision, Eddie simply stared at him and didn't protest when Thomas led him to the bed. Eddie lowered himself onto his back, looking up at Thomas. Naked and aroused Thomas stood above him, the most beautiful specimen of maleness

Eddie had ever encountered. Could he really resist Thomas and deny himself the pleasure of being desired by a man like him?

Without another word, Thomas lowered himself and pushed Eddie's thighs apart. Eddie felt exposed. Yet when he saw the hungry look Thomas raked over him, he shivered with pleasure. He'd never felt so wanted in his life. And it felt good—too good to put up a fight even though he knew he should.

When his lips parted, Eddie had no idea why. Only when he heard his own words, did he know he'd come to a decision. "Suck me."

At least for today he'd give into his body's desires. Tomorrow he'd figure out what it all meant.

Eddie lay on the bed like a sumptuous feast. Thomas let his eyes roam, drinking in the sight of the naked body before him. Just like he drank in the scent of Eddie's arousal. Hard and heavy, Eddie's cock curved toward his navel. Thomas had felt him come hard in the shower and was pleased to see that Eddie was ready again so soon. Particularly since he'd sensed Eddie's hesitation. Eddie was still afraid of his feelings; there was no doubt about it. Even the way his eyes looked up at him now told him that Eddie hadn't fully surrendered to his new self. And Thomas wouldn't push him today. As much as he wanted to sink his aching cock into Eddie and fuck him until the sun set over the Pacific Ocean, he knew that his lover wasn't ready for it. Eddie would need more coaxing to accept the inevitable.

A small sliver of guilt crept up Thomas's back as he sank his head between Eddie's legs. Was he seducing an innocent? Was he inadvertently using his power to lure Eddie into his bed? For a moment, he pulled back and searched within himself for any signs of his dark power having risen to the surface. He let his senses flow and felt the peace that surrounded him. No, he hadn't used his power to make Eddie come to him. All he'd done was show Eddie the pleasure a man could give him. At any time during their tryst, Eddie could have walked away. Yet, he'd stayed, just like he'd lain down on the bed out of his own free will.

Thomas lowered his head again, his tongue darting out and licking over the tip of Eddie's cock. Under him, Eddie jerked, a groan coming from him at the same time.

"Easy, easy. There's more where that came from," Thomas murmured.

He noticed how Eddie's hands were gripping the covers as if holding on for dear life. Sliding his hands down Eddie's thighs, he spread them wider and urged him to angle his legs. The position opened him up wider, freeing his balls for Thomas to touch.

With a sigh, he sank his lips onto Eddie's hard-on and pulled the head into his mouth. His tongue licked over and around the tip, gently lubricating the skin before he slid down his entire length, taking him inside his mouth as deep as he could.

"Fuck!"

Eddie's single word was encouragement enough to repeat the action, releasing his cock for a split second before sucking him back into his mouth, while he flattened his tongue against the underside of his shaft, gliding down.

Another groan came from Eddie. Then he shoved his hand into Thomas's hair and urged him up. Eddie's cock popped from his mouth as he hit him with a questioning look. "You don't like that?"

"You continue like that and I won't last more than ten seconds."

Thomas felt a smile tug at his lips. "Don't worry. I have ways to make you last."

Then he sank his mouth back onto Eddie's erection and sucked him even harder. He would make sure that Eddie would thoroughly enjoy this and come back for more. And with each slow seduction, they would grow closer and their lovemaking would become more intimate.

Thomas was nothing if not patient. He'd waited for this for over a year, and now that Eddie was in his bed, he could be patient until Eddie surrendered fully.

Feeling Eddie's cock pulse in his mouth, hearing his moans and sighs, and feeling his hips thrust upwards, gave him almost as much pleasure as when Eddie had brought him to a roaring climax with his hand. Already Thomas's cock was rock-hard again, but for now, he had to ignore it and concentrate on Eddie. He had to show Eddie the kind of pleasures men could give each other, and that there was nothing wrong with it.

Thomas gripped Eddie's erection at the base without removing his mouth, and pulled upwards, then stroked down again, adding more pressure with his hand. With the knuckles of his other hand, he stroked over Eddie's balls, which had tightened and pulled up, an indication that he was getting close to coming. Not wanting this to end too soon, Thomas palmed his scrotum and gently pulled the sac downward again. He felt it relax under his grip, and continued licking up and down Eddie's cock.

"Fuck, that's good!" Eddie cried out.

Thomas heard a ripping sound and noticed that Eddie's hands were shredding the sheets as he tried to hold on to his control. Pride filled his chest: he was bringing out Eddie's vampire side— his primal instincts, the side of him that controlled his drive for blood and sex.

A thin sheen of perspiration had built on Eddie's neck and chest, and tiny rivulets now formed and made their way down the channels of his muscled chest. He was lean and less bulky than Thomas—only an inch or two shorter—but perfect in every way. A hairless chest, a flat stomach, strong legs. And then his shaft. He hadn't expected Eddie to be so big. And so beautiful.

Thomas couldn't get enough of him. The more he sucked and licked, the more he pumped Eddie's cock up and down, the longer he wanted it to continue. Eddie's taste was intoxicating, and the tiny drops of moisture that had leaked from the tip were addictive. Whenever he'd sucked other men, he'd eventually wanted it to end so they could get on with other things, but this was different. This wasn't simply a prelude to something else. This was no mechanical blowjob that he gave a lover so he'd bend over for him later. No, this time Thomas wasn't expecting anything in return, other than seeing pure pleasure spread over his young lover's face. All he wanted was for Eddie to acknowledge that it was Thomas who gave him this pleasure.

When he felt Eddie's hand on his head again, he wondered whether he wanted to pull him back once more, but then it slid to his nape, his warm fingers caressing him. A shiver ran down his spine all the way to his tailbone where the tingling spread and reached his cock.

Fuck! He was no novice. An innocent touch like that shouldn't have such an erotic effect on him, yet it felt as if Eddie were caressing his cock instead. Involuntarily, he moaned and the breath he released blew against Eddie's erection, which jerked in his mouth.

"I'm coming, Thomas! I'm coming!" Eddie let out in a breathless moan while he tried to pull his cock from Thomas's mouth.

But Thomas didn't allow it. He sucked him harder, holding onto the base of it, so he couldn't escape.

"You don't have to . . . " Eddie started, but his words died as he arched his back and his cock spasmed.

Hot spurts of semen shot into Thomas's mouth. Like electrical pulses, they came, and Thomas swallowed the liquid just as quickly. With it, his fangs lengthened and pushed past his lips, grazing Eddie's skin. Without thinking, he let Eddie's cock pop from his mouth and sank his fangs into his thigh, driving them deep into his flesh.

A startled cry-and-jolt came from Eddie, but then he settled back onto the bed, and his limbs relaxed. Thomas drew on the plump vein and tasted the rich red liquid that filled his mouth. Sex always made him hungry, but this time it was more than that. This time he wanted to intensify Eddie's pleasure, and his own, with a sensual bite.

Eddie's blood was tangy with a scent of musk to it. Rich and young. He let the liquid run down his throat and coat it, closing his eyes to savor the feeling. If he could live off Eddie's blood, he would. Unfortunately, vampire blood provided little nourishment to another vampire, though he knew that Maya only drank Gabriel's blood. However, since Gabriel was part satyr, his blood had other nourishing qualities that could sustain Maya. Thomas and Eddie would always be forced to drink human blood. It didn't stop him from enjoying Eddie's blood now—from savoring every drop.

His entire body was ablaze, every cell of it recharging with strength and hope. His mind calmed and for the first time in almost a century, he could barely sense the dark power within him. As if it was shrinking. While sex had always been a distraction and taken his mind off the evil that lived within him, it had never managed to push it down to such a depth that it was barely noticeable. Was Eddie giving him the strength he needed to defeat the evil within?

Thomas took one last, long drag from the open vein before he retracted his fangs and licked over the tiny puncture wounds to close them.

Then he lifted himself up and laid down on the bed next to Eddie, pulling him into his arms. Eddie's eyes opened, looking at him in wonder, and his lips parted, but nothing came from them.

"Thank you," Thomas whispered. "You have no idea what this means to me."

Eddie's hand moved up to Thomas's nape, pulling him down. Without a word, he pressed his lips on Thomas's and kissed him— a kiss more passionate than Thomas had ever felt from Eddie before. Had something finally changed between them? Was Eddie accepting him and the feelings that grew between them?

24

Eddie swung himself onto his motorcycle and rolled it out of the garage, closing the garage door behind him before he switched on the engine. Even though the sun had just set, Thomas was still asleep, and he didn't want to wake him. He didn't know how to act around him after what had happened less than eight hours earlier.

He hadn't planned on sleeping in Thomas's bed, but after Thomas had sucked him with such passion, he'd been unable to lift a single limb to leave. He'd wanted to continue feeling Thomas's body close to his. And Thomas had accommodated: he'd spooned him the entire time, pressing his front to Eddie's back, tucking his legs underneath Eddie's knees, his groin lining up with Eddie's butt. And he'd liked feeling Thomas's protective arms around him like a cage. Did that make him the girl?

Eddie pushed the thought aside. No, he was a man. Just because he'd let Thomas hold him like that didn't make him a girl.

Eddie stopped at the next stoplight and waited for it to turn green, plotting out his route in his head. Nina had sent him an urgent text message to meet him at an address in the Mission, and he was wondering whether something was wrong. Had she and Amaury argued, and was that the reason she didn't want to meet him at home?

Somewhat concerned about his sister, he continued his drive down the hill. He'd always felt responsible for Nina, even though she was three years older than he. But after the horrible events at their last foster home, he'd felt the need to watch out for her just like she'd watched out for him after they'd lost their parents. They'd stuck it out through thick and thin and finally managed to get away and start a new life.

Eddie found the address easily, even though he couldn't see the house number on the two-story house. But since Nina was standing in front of it, waving at him as he approached, he knew he was at the right place. He pulled to a stop in front of the garage and turned off the engine, removing his helmet a moment later, and hanging it on the rearview mirror.

"Hey Nina! What's going on? Are you in trouble?" he asked, dropping the kickstand as he dismounted.

She shook her blond curls. "Why would I be in trouble?"

"Your message made it sound urgent."

"I've got to show you something," she answered and motioned him to come closer.

He approached, giving her a quick hug before she turned to the entrance door and produced a key from her jeans pocket. She stuck it into the lock and turned it, pushing the door open.

He followed her inside and noticed that the place was empty. Not a single piece of furniture stood in the large, open living area they entered. Realization washed over him. He knew why Nina had brought him here: this place was available for rent.

A pang of guilt slammed into him out of nowhere. Looking at an apartment after what had happened between him and Thomas earlier suddenly felt like a betrayal. It shouldn't, because he hadn't made his mentor any promises. Nothing had been said between them, nothing had been discussed about how or whether they would continue their sexual relationship. Still, sneaking around behind Thomas's back, clandestinely looking for a place to live made him feel like a jerk.

"I don't know, Nina," he started, quickly glancing around the room.

"I know it doesn't look like much right now. They didn't stage it, but just imagine it with some cool furniture. And it would need some new paint too, but I'm sure you can get a few of the guys to help you with that," she interrupted.

She sounded like a real estate agent, touting a rat-infested fixer-upper.

"Come, I'll show you the kitchen." She grabbed his arms and pulled him to the back of the house.

"The kitchen isn't really my big concern," he answered as he followed her. "As you know, I don't eat; hence I don't cook."

She turned her head and rolled her eyes. "It's important for resale value. Kitchens sell homes," she claimed.

"Resale?"

"Yes, the place is for sale. I figured you might as well buy a place here, rather than rent. Rents have really gone up in the city, and if you don't buy now, you won't be able to afford anything decent in a few years. Trust me on that!"

Nina stomped into the kitchen. He entered behind her and had to admit that it was large and roomy, despite the fact that it looked dated.

"Original 1960's tiles, but all that can be changed. Imagine some stainless steel appliances, a granite counter top and some new cabinets. You can even put an island in the middle and there'll still be enough space to move around comfortably."

Eddie sighed. "Nina, I'm not really interested in buying. I just wanted . . ." Well, he wasn't sure anymore what he wanted. Things had somehow changed. But he couldn't tell his sister any of it. And if he suddenly told her that he didn't really want to move right now, she would smell a rat and continue digging until she'd unearthed the truth. It was best if he lied.

"If you're worried about the money, Amaury said he'd give you a loan, so you won't have to apply to a bank," Nina said.

"That's nice of him, but I really don't want this. I'm not ready for a house. I just wanted a small flat." And if he were honest, he'd admit right now that he wasn't even sure he wanted his own place. Having spent the day in Thomas's bed had made things complicated and confusing.

"If you don't like this house, I can look around and find you others. And it doesn't have to be as big as this either. Maybe just a little cottage like the one Yvette and Haven have?" Her eyes suddenly sparked. "Oh, I bet now that they have the baby, they'll probably want a larger place. They only have two bedrooms, and I know the second bedroom isn't large. Maybe they'll want to sell their house. I can ask them."

"No!" That was all he needed: everybody at Scanguards finding out that he was looking for a place to live. It would take all of two seconds to reach Thomas's ears.

"Why not? Telegraph Hill is an excellent neighborhood."

Eddie let out an exasperated breath. "Nina, I just told you that I don't want a house."

She shrugged, sighing. "Fine. But you know that with a flat you'll always have neighbors and have to be more careful so that nobody finds out what you are."

He nodded automatically. "I'm aware of that."

"Well, I guess your mind is made up. I'll have Amaury tell the agent it's not what you're looking for." She walked toward the exit.

Relieved, Eddie followed her. "How did you even get the key? Aren't real estate agents supposed to accompany prospective clients?"

Nina opened the entrance door and stepped through. "You forget that Amaury has a real estate license too. He gets keys from other agents whenever he wants one. Trust me, they're happy not to do an evening showing when they'd rather be at home with their families."

Eddie waited on the stairs while Nina locked up and stuffed the key back into her pocket.

"Can you give me a lift?" she asked. "Amaury dropped me off earlier, but he needed to get to the office to take care of a few things."

"Sure, I'll drive you home." He walked to the parked motorcycle and swung himself onto it, raising the kickstand in the process.

"Oh, I'm not going home. Can you drive me over to Portia's? She and I wanted to go shopping to get a few things for Yvette's baby." Nina mounted behind him. "We're throwing her a shower."

"A shower?"

"Yes, a baby shower, you know, where all the girls get together and bring gifts for the baby."

Eddie shook his head. "As long as I don't have to attend," he mumbled under his breath. Then he took the helmet off the handlebar and handed it to her. "You've gotta wear this."

She took it without protest and put it on.

"Ready?" he asked and felt her arms wrap around his waist.

"Let's go."

He pulled into the street, watching his speed as he did so. It was one thing riding with another vampire, it was another having a human on the bike. He never took any risks when Nina was with him. While he could easily walk away unscathed from any accident, a fragile human woman like Nina would not necessarily be as lucky. And Amaury would have his hide if anything ever happened to Nina under Eddie's watch, just as Eddie would never be able to live with himself if one of his actions resulted in Nina being hurt.

"Does this machine not go any faster?" he heard her complain from behind him.

"It does, but there are speed limits in town," he deflected, knowing that she would only get pissy if he told her he was driving this slowly because of her.

"You've never followed speed limits before."

"I do now," he grumbled. "So stop complaining or I'm going to make you walk." He wouldn't, of course, but there were few other ways of making Nina shut up.

It took less than five minutes to reach Portia and Zane's house in the Mission. Eddie pulled into the driveway and stopped, dropping his feet to the ground to support the bike while Nina jumped off. She removed the helmet and handed it to him.

"Do you want to come in for a moment?"

He shook his head when he saw the garage door lift. Moments later he saw Portia walk out of the garage, Zane not far behind her.

"Hey!" she greeted them. Her next words were drowned out by the crazy Labrador puppy chasing her and barking at the motorcycle as if it were an intruder he had to defend her against.

"Z!" Zane chastised the dog. "Get a grip!"

The dog turned his head toward his owner and stopped barking for a second, then turned back to the motorcycle and continued just as loudly as before.

"Z!" Portia now reprimanded him and bent down to lift him into her arms. The dog instantly stopped barking.

Zane approached, putting his arm around Portia, then giving the dog a stern look. "One of these days you'll find yourself locked out of the house, and I won't let you in anymore!"

Portia chuckled and grinned up at her mate. "You know that those threats don't work with him, because he knows that you'll never make them true."

Zane grunted, then looked at Eddie and Nina. "Hey guys, what's up?"

"Oh, I just showed Eddie a house. And now Portia and I are going to do some shopping for the baby shower," Nina answered before Eddie could stop her.

Zane tossed him a surprised look. "You're moving out of Thomas's? He never mentioned anything."

"Yeah, well, it's not decided yet," Eddie replied quickly. "Anyway, I've gotta run. See you at the shooting range in half an hour?"

Zane nodded. "I'm just getting ready to leave."

"Shooting range?" Nina asked, staring at Eddie in surprise. "Since when do you like shooting?"

"Eddie's been taking almost daily lessons in sharpshooting from me. He's getting pretty decent," Zane answered.

"Decent?" Eddie repeated. "I'm more than just a decent shot!" Hell, he'd been working his ass off to perfect his target practice.

Portia laughed. "I guess, Eddie, you haven't quite figured out Zane's rating scale. 'Decent' is a huge compliment coming from Zane."

Zane rolled his eyes. "Don't listen to Portia. She's just trying to make you feel good. You've still got stuff to learn."

Before Eddie could protest again, Nina put her hand on his arm. "How come I'm always the last to find out what you're up to?"

Eddie shrugged. "Hey, no big deal. It's just part of my job." Though his job didn't require him to be a crack shot. But after Thomas had fought with his maker a few months earlier, and Eddie hadn't been able to shoot his attacker for fear of hitting Thomas instead, Eddie had promised himself to perfect his shooting skills.

"Anyway, better run. See you!" he said quickly, before his sister asked any more questions, and put on his helmet.

"Thanks for the ride!" Nina called after him as he turned the motorcycle and raced into the street.

Maybe he should have told Nina right there and then that he'd changed his mind about the apartment search. Or at least that he wanted to put it on hold until he could figure out what he wanted. But he wasn't prepared for the questions his change of heart would have raised. Besides, he really didn't know what he wanted: stay with Thomas or leave?

25

Thomas set the piece of paper he'd studied for the last minute down on his desk and started typing on his keyboard. The new owner of Al's shop was a corporation, and only a PO box had been given as an address on the deed. Like hiding behind a PO box could really prevent him from finding the people who had bought out Al. He'd already checked the California Secretary of State's website, but again only found a PO box. Now he brought up a trusted website he often used to investigate companies and individuals who had something to hide and went to work.

K Industries was a Delaware corporation, which indicated that whoever had set it up liked the tax-advantaged status of that East Coast state. Again, only a PO box was given as the address of the company, but upon further digging, Thomas found more. The name of an attorney in California appeared on one of the company documents filed with the state of Delaware, though he was unable to find the names of any individuals who owned the company. It appeared that the company was owned by other companies— definitely a ploy to keep the real owners of K Industries hidden. He followed the trail of the companies which led him to various off-shore tax havens and finally to a dead end.

This only left the attorney who'd filed the papers. Thomas typed the attorney's name into the Bar Association's website and hit return.

"Bingo!" he said as the web search returned the attorney's name with an address in San Francisco. He jotted it down on a piece of paper and slid it into his pocket. At least he had a place to start. The attorney would have files on his clients in his office. Somebody had to have paid him.

Thomas rose from his chair and walked toward the door. He'd check in with Zane to see if his colleague had found anything else, and then head out to see what he could find in the attorney's office.

As he opened the door and took a step into the hallway, he noticed Eddie standing at the board where the assignments were posted. Two other vampires walked past him. Desire awakened instantly.

"Eddie," Thomas called out to him.

Eddie's head immediately whirled in his direction, his eyes wide as if he'd gotten caught.

"Do you have a minute?"

Looking around himself, Eddie approached hesitantly. "I should be getting ready for my patrol."

"It'll only be a minute," Thomas added and motioned to his office.

Eddie dropped his lids as if to avoid looking at him directly, then brushed past him and entered. Thomas squeezed in behind him and closed the door.

Inhaling, he took in Eddie's scent. It was just as enticing as earlier in the day.

"You left early."

Eddie's Adam's apple bobbed. "I've got lots of work to do."

"You should have woken me before you left the bed." Thomas leaned in closer, noticing how Eddie pressed himself against the wall at his back.

"I just couldn't sleep anymore."

"Was I keeping you awake by snoring?"

Eddie shook his head. "You didn't snore."

"I'm glad." Thomas brought his face closer to Eddie's, dropping his gaze to his parted lips. Were they trembling slightly, or was he imagining it? "It would be awful if you didn't want to sleep in my bed because I snore."

Eddie's chest heaved. "I, uh, I . . . "

"Of course, there are other things that may keep you awake in my bed. I won't always be able to guarantee that you get a lot of sleep when you're with me." Thomas let his lips hover less than an inch over Eddie's and inhaled his heady scent. He felt him suck in a breath. Without pressing against his mouth, he continued, "I enjoyed what we did. Every single second of it."

Eddie's eyes closed. "Thomas, I'm not sure . . . I don't think I can . . . "

"Shhhh. I'm not making any demands." Not yet, he thought. But soon he wouldn't be able to hold back and would ask for what he wanted. "I hope you're not mad at me for biting you. But the temptation was too great to resist. You tasted too good." Even now he could still taste Eddie's blood on his tongue, and the mere thought made him hard.

Without thinking, he pressed his hips into Eddie's.

A hitched breath escaped from Eddie's mouth, and his eyes shot open, his gaze colliding with Thomas's.

"Oh God, Eddie, I've wanted you for so long. I want you even more now."

In slow motion, he pressed his lips onto Eddie's. Tilting his head to the side, he drove his tongue between Eddie's parted lips, stroking gently against his counterpart. The contact sent a heat wave through his body and straight into his cock, making him grind his hips against Eddie.

With long and sure strokes, he explored Eddie's mouth and dueled with his tongue, feeling how the young vampire in his arms gave up resistance and rubbed his body against Thomas's. When Thomas felt Eddie's hands grip his ass and yank him even harder against him, a groan slipped over his lips.

He plundered Eddie's mouth, reveling in his taste, the firm strokes of his tongue, and the hard press of his lips. He'd always loved the way a man kissed: with determination and strength. And Eddie was no different: he kissed like he meant it, even if Thomas had been the one to initiate the kiss.

Eddie palmed his ass, squeezing his flesh in the same rhythm with which he ground his groin against Thomas. There was no mistaking the heavy bulge in Eddie's pants. His lover had a hard-on of massive proportions. That fact shot another flame of white-hot heat through his body: he could arouse Eddie within seconds. It gave him hope that things between them would progress quickly and become even more intimate soon.

All of a sudden, the ring of a telephone tore through the sounds of heavy breathing in the room.

Eddie ripped his lips from him, releasing his hold on Thomas, and pushed him back a foot. Panic shone from his eyes. "People will find out."

Another ring sounded.

Eddie turned to the door and ripped it open.

"Eddie, please . . . "

But Eddie rushed outside and down the corridor. Thomas slammed the door shut, frustrated. Maybe kissing him in the office, where anybody could walk in on them at any time hadn't been the smartest idea. Clearly, once Eddie had heard the phone and regained his senses, he'd panicked.

Thomas shoved a hand through his hair. He'd talk to him at sunrise when they were both home, and tell him that he would from now on confine his displays of affection to their home, where they had all the privacy they needed.

The phone rang a third time. Thomas turned to the desk and lifted the receiver. "This is Thomas." His voice sounded huskier than usual. No wonder—after all, he'd been ready to fuck Eddie against the wall in his office.

"Please stop your people from looking for me," a familiar voice came through the line.

Thomas was instantly alert. "Al!"

"Listen, I can't talk long, but just forget about me."

"What's going on, Al? Why did you sell the shop?"

There was a brief pause during which Thomas could hear a heavy breath being expelled. "It was safer that way."

"Safer? Did anybody threaten you?"

"Don't get involved, Thomas. You'll only regret it. I did what I had to do," Al shot back.

"We can protect you. Scanguards can—"

"Nobody can protect me from them," Al cut him off. "It's better to get out of their way. They're too strong."

"What did they threaten you with?" Thomas asked, hoping to get through to him.

"It doesn't matter. Just let it rest, or people will get hurt."

Thomas sighed. "People have already gotten hurt. Sergio and his mate are dead."

A gasp echoed through the line. "Fuck! He must have resisted them. But I'm not stupid enough to play hero. Let them have what they want and get out. You can't stop them."

"I can and I will! But I need your help. Where can I find them now?"

"I don't know. And I'd rather keep it that way. It's safer not knowing."

"Al—" But the click in the line indicated that Al had disconnected the call.

"Shit!" Thomas cursed. He didn't have to be a brain surgeon to put two and two together: Kasper's disciples were behind this. They were the newcomers and they had scared Al into selling and leaving town. They'd tried to do the same to Sergio. Only Sergio hadn't complied.

Thomas ripped the door open and stalked down to Zane's office. He had to find the nest of vampires who were forcing the good vampires of the city to leave so they could replace them with their puppets.

At Zane's office, Thomas rapped his knuckles on the door. "Zane?" Without waiting for a reply, he opened the door and saw Zane sliding a silver blade into the sheath strapped to his ankle.

"Going out?" Thomas asked.

Zane nodded. "Patrol."

"Change of plans. Tell your patrol partner to find a replacement."

"What for?"

"I need you for a little breaking and entering."

Zane's lips curled up in an almost-smile. "Sweet."

26

Thomas looked over Zane's shoulder, watching how he worked on the lock of the entrance door. The building was a run-down, two-story house on a busy street along one of the streetcar lines in the Outer Parkside neighborhood. The attorney's name, Wilbur Wu, was stenciled in gold letters on the large window facing the street. Parts of the letters had stripped and faded, adding to the unappealing look of the law offices behind the uninviting facade. Somehow Thomas couldn't imagine that this attorney attracted much walk-in business.

"Got it," Zane murmured and pushed the door open, sliding inside the dark interior.

Thomas followed without a word and eased the door shut silently behind him. To the left was a staircase leading up to the second floor; ahead of him lay a dark corridor, and to the right was a door. He pointed to it.

"Let's start here."

They walked inside what turned out to be an office. Several filing cabinets lined one wall, a massive desk dominated the center of the room, and two rickety old chairs stood in front of it, presumably meant for clients, though Thomas couldn't imagine what person in their right mind would want to sit down in a chair that looked like it would be crushed under the weight of a cat.

"The blinds," Zane advised and walked to the window, lowering the shades, then adjusting them so they were fully closed.

Thomas pulled out a flashlight from his pocket and switched it on, pointing it at the filing cabinets. "Let's get started."

They rifled through drawer after drawer, starting with the one labeled 'K'. Thomas shone his light at the labels of each file contained in the drawer, looking for K Industries.

"Nothing here," he commented.

Zane grunted. "If he wanted to hide something, he wouldn't be filing the documents under K."

"Good point." Thomas continued his search, painstakingly thumbing through file after file.

"Did Al have no information at all?" Zane asked out of the blue.

"If he did, he didn't want to share. All he said was that he didn't want to fight them. And Al is no coward."

But knowing what he knew, Thomas couldn't fault him for his caution. The dark power that those vampires possessed could frighten anybody. There was no defense against the mind control they could unleash on an unsuspecting vampire. Only somebody like Thomas, who possessed the same kind of dark power, would have a chance of fighting them. But first he had to find them.

Zane closed another drawer. "Nothing here either."

Thomas let out a resigned breath. "Upstairs then. There must be more."

Leaving the office behind, they walked up the creaking staircase. Thomas's nostrils picked up a scent as they reached the landing.

"You smell that?"

"Not a good sign."

Thomas followed the smell that led him to a door at the end of the hallway. The stench was strongest here. He braced himself for what he was about to see and pushed the door open.

A Chinese man in his fifties, presumably Wilbur Wu, lay on the floor, his body lifeless. There was surprisingly little blood, despite the wounds on his face. His mouth had been cut from his face, exposing his white teeth. His tongue was missing.

Zane pointed to the injuries. "Looks like a warning sign."

Thomas couldn't agree more. "He knew something he wasn't supposed to know."

"And was about to talk about it," Zane added. He pointed to the manila folder the dead man clutched in his hand.

Thomas bent down and took it from him. The label had been ripped off. He opened the file. It was empty. He had expected as much. Why kill Wu and leave evidence behind? "Too late. Whatever was in there is gone."

Thomas rose, bracing himself at a filing cabinet that was labeled 'Banking'.

"He probably got greedy and blackmailed somebody. Looks like what they paid him in the first place wasn't enough."

"Greed is a terrible thing," Thomas confirmed.

"Yep. Couldn't take his bank account with him, could he?"

Suddenly something clicked in Thomas's mind. "His bank account! That's it!"

"What are you talking about?"

Thomas turned to the cabinet behind him and pointed at the label. "If Wu's gotten paid, there should be records of transfers or checks." He ripped the top drawer open and looked at the neatly organized files. "Perfect, they're in date order."

He remembered the date of the Delaware filing and pulled out the files around that period, tossing one to Zane while examining one himself. "They would have had to pay him for doing the company filing for them, and most attorneys work on a retainer— which is always issued prior to any work being done. And since the company couldn't have a bank account prior to the filing, somebody would have had to issue a check from their personal account."

"That's why you're the genius at Scanguards," Zane remarked.

"Hardly."

"Now, now, why so humble? You do know that everybody looks up to you, don't you?"

Thomas shook his head. "I don't think so."

"Okay, blind and a genius! You should look around you occasionally. Especially the young kids at Scanguards look at you like you're their god."

"Zane, you're so full of shit. Is there anything you want, or why are you sucking up to me?"

Zane rolled his eyes. "Sucking up? Me? Not likely. However, now that you mention it, can you get Maya off my back about that whole apology thing to Oliver?"

Thomas sank his head back into the file and continued scanning the documents. "It wouldn't do you any harm to apologize. Besides, I thought I had convinced Maya to forget about the party and buy him and Ursula an all-expenses-paid trip abroad instead."

"She's still on about throwing him a party. And you know how I hate anything sappy."

"I'll talk to her."

"Thanks."

Thomas closed the file, having found nothing. "Anything?"

Zane pulled out a sheet and looked at it more closely. "Maybe. It's a photocopy of a check and there are some notations in the margin."

Thomas reached for it and shone his light on the words Wu had scribbled next to the check. *Del filing, K I,* then a date of about two weeks before the filing date.

"Looks like it," Thomas murmured and shifted the light so it illuminated the check.

An address was printed on the left hand corner of it. The address was local; however the name could not be read. Whoever had photocopied the check had placed it incorrectly on the photocopier and cut off the top section of it that contained the name of the issuer.

Thomas's eyes drifted to the signature on it. In a rather old-fashioned script, a name was written in blue ink. He couldn't decipher it. Nevertheless, his heart skipped a beat. The handwriting looked familiar. He shook off the shiver that crept up his spine. He had to be mistaken. Lots of people had similar handwriting.

27

The address they'd found on the check was located on the edge of Chinatown where it bled over into Little Italy, or North Beach, as it was officially called. The streets were narrow here, the buildings mostly three stories, or occasionally four stories high. Storefronts were interspersed with restaurants, and above them, apartments were located from which laundry hung to dry. The area was colorful to say the least.

Even at this late hour, many of the shops were still open, and pungent smells drifted from their entrances. Thomas turned up his nose and glanced sideways at Zane.

Zane's lip curled up in disgust. "What now?"

"Let's check it out." Thomas motioned his colleague to follow him up the steep side street until they reached the building. It was nothing special, a simple, rectangular, gray, three-story building, most likely built in the sixties or seventies, with small windows and no distinguishing architectural features. There was a garage on the entry level, a rarity for this part of town, where parking was at a premium.

Thomas looked at the house and noticed that the street lamp in front of it wasn't working, making this part of the street darker, and effectively hiding the entrance from human eyes. His vampire vision, however, still enabled him to see the door clearly. He lifted his head to look up at the windows. There was light behind them, and no curtains or blinds were drawn on the first and second floors. On the third floor, blinds obstructed any view into the interior.

He lowered his gaze to the floor above the garage and focused on one window. The room behind it was well lit. Silently, Thomas stood in the dark delivery entrance of a store and waited, Zane, next to him, not making a sound either. They were used to this. Waiting and watching was part of their work. They'd done it a thousand times, and while they hated waiting, both knew it was necessary.

It took a few minutes before he saw a movement in the house. A man walked past the window, a phone pressed to his ear.

"Somebody seems to be home," Zane said, rocking back on his heels. "Wanna visit?"

Thomas was about to nod when a second person appeared. He recognized him immediately: Xander, the man who'd cornered him a few days earlier. He wasn't at all surprised to see him at the house. It only confirmed what he already knew: Xander was behind K Industries. He was the driving force trying to restore Kasper's empire after his demise. If he could take out Xander, then the rest of them would retreat into the holes they'd crawled out of. If none of them possessed more power than he'd sensed emanating from Xander, he could easily defeat them.

Yet, he wasn't going to bring Zane into his. While Zane was a mean fighting machine, even he couldn't win a fight against a vampire carrying Kasper's blood.

"No. Let's wait. I'm going to talk to Samson first," he lied. He motioned to the house. "They're not going anywhere. We'll come back after we've formulated a plan."

"Fine," Zane agreed. "Let's go talk to Samson."

"I'll take care of it. Why don't you go back to the office and organize the clean up at the attorney's office? We can't leave him like that."

Zane narrowed his eyes, looking at him with suspicion. Could Zane tell that this was merely an excuse so he'd get out of his way?

"Your call. See you later."

When Zane turned on his heels, Thomas breathed a sigh of relief and walked in the opposite direction toward Nob Hill, where

Samson's house was located, just in case Zane turned around to make sure he was doing what he said he'd do.

After two blocks, Thomas turned around and returned to the house in which he'd seen Xander. Looking left and right, he crossed the street and approached the entrance door. In front of it, he paused, inhaling deeply. Then he closed his eyes and let his mind travel, reaching past the door and into the building's interior.

He clearly could sense several vampires on the premises. Xander and whoever had been on the phone were not alone. That fact didn't deter him. As long as he could take down Xander, the others would be easy pickings. All he needed to do was keep Xander in the belief that he intended him no harm. Then once he dropped his guard, Thomas would attack.

Clearing his mind, Thomas rang the door bell and waited, his entire body alert and ready to engage the enemy at any time. Footsteps from the inside alerted him to the approach of a vampire. There was a slight hesitation of the person who stopped just behind the door, but then the deadbolt was turned, and the door opened inwards.

Xander stood in front of him. Thomas had expected one of his minions to open the door. But he didn't let the surprise show on his face. Nor did Xander show any surprise at seeing Thomas at his doorstep.

"So you've found me," he simply said and motioned him to enter.

Thomas walked past him, never letting his guard down, and forcing his senses to remain engaged, constantly scanning for any sudden movements his opponent might make. Turning back to Xander, who closed the door and locked it again, he waited.

"This way," Xander instructed and led him to the living room, where only minutes earlier, he'd seen him and another vampire. The room was empty.

"Where are the rest of your followers?" Thomas asked, letting his senses explore. He could clearly feel the presence of other vampires in the house.

"My followers?" He chuckled. "You give me too much credit."

"We both know you're not alone."

Xander nodded, lowering himself into an old-fashioned armchair in front of the fireplace. He gestured to the armchair opposite his. "Please. I hate craning my neck."

Cautiously, Thomas sat down.

His host gave him an approving look. "You're right, of course. I'm not alone. But I've asked my . . . associates to withdraw upstairs so we can have an opportunity to talk in private."

Thomas moved his head in agreement. This situation was even better than he'd planned it: being alone with Xander would make it easier to take care of him. And by the time the others in the house figured out what was happening, Thomas would have collected his strength again and be ready for another attack.

"Yes, let's talk," Thomas started. "I know what you're doing."

"Well, I should hope so. After all, we made sure of it. What would be the point of doing things to bring you to our side if we hid them from you?"

Was Xander implying that he'd deliberately left a clue at Wu's office for Thomas to track him down? "You have a funny way of trying to attract new followers."

"Followers? You wouldn't be a follower. I thought I made that clear during our earlier conversation."

"Just as I made it clear that I want you to leave my turf."

Xander smiled. "I'm afraid we can't do that. You see, we have plans at dominating the vampire world."

"By threatening law-abiding vampires and running them out of town? Killing them when they don't comply?"

Xander shrugged. "Casualties are to be expected. People are killed in every war."

"This is not a war. And you'll fail," Thomas promised.

"What makes you so sure?"

Thomas rose and turned his mind in towards himself. "Because I'll destroy you!" Concentrating on Xander, he bundled his mind's energy and unleashed it on his opponent. Xander shot up from his chair and the air vibrated between them. Then a blast sent Thomas into the wall behind him, breaking his concentration.

The sudden power that had come from Xander stunned him. How was this possible? He'd only sensed a low level of dark power within Xander, but what his enemy had fought back with was magnified.

Xander laughed, the sound bouncing against the walls, creating an eerie echo. "You haven't learned, have you? The more of our kind are together, the stronger the power grows. It's like gravity. It attracts more and more of the same kind, and as we join forces, we get stronger. You have no choice in the matter. You'll soon be one of us! You'll join the family."

"Never! I already have a family!"

"Oh, you mean Scanguards? Or are you talking about the boy you're fucking?"

White hot anger shot through Thomas's body as he peeled himself away from the wall. Xander knew about him and Eddie?

"You think he's your salvation?" Xander mocked. "Dream on. Not even he can save you from yourself. Just admit what you are!"

Blind with rage, Thomas charged him and grabbed him by the throat, lifting him in the air, and slamming him against the fireplace. "You touch one of them, you're dust."

Footsteps sounded on the stairs from above. Knowing he couldn't defeat their collective powers, at least not in the state he was in, Thomas ran out of the room and to the entrance door, unlocked it, and barreled outside before they could reach him.

***

Kasper charged into the living room and saw Xander getting up from the fireplace. Luckily no fire had been lit in it, otherwise his trusted follower's clothes would have caught fire.

"I see Thomas is still as hotheaded as ever," he remarked.

Xander rubbed his backside. "I don't know why you couldn't talk to him yourself."

Kasper narrowed his eyes. He didn't tolerate insubordination from anybody. "Because I think it was better this way. So unless you would like to meet the same fate as some of your predecessors, you'll do well not to question my decisions. Do we understand each other?"

Xander bowed his head in submission. "Yes, Master Kasper."

Kasper turned to the six men who'd followed him. "Get back upstairs! I'll call you when I need you!"

They turned without protesting and marched back upstairs. He'd trained his minions well. They were scared of him. And fear produced obedience. He'd sired them, all of them, but his blood wasn't as strong in them as it was in Thomas, because their minds were weak, and the power couldn't thrive in a weak mind.

He turned back to Xander. "Very well then. What else do you have to report?"

"Your suspicion was correct: he has a lover, a young vampire who lives with him. When I confronted him, he went ballistic."

Kasper felt a wave of jealousy boil up in him and pressed it back down. This wasn't the time for weakness. He would have Thomas back, and together they would rule the world of vampires. Just as it was always meant to be.

"He's strong, just like you said. If you hadn't channeled your power through me when he attacked me, he would have killed me."

"I know." He pulled his lip up in a snarl. "Let that be a lesson to you. Now, join the others. I need time."

Xander bowed and quickly left the room, shutting the door behind him.

Kasper walked to one of the chairs and inhaled. Thomas's scent drifted into his nose. "I'm coming for you. You had your fun. But it's time to come home now."

28

Thomas rang the doorbell at Samson's Nob Hill home and was surprised that it was opened almost instantly.

Samson, holding his nine-month-old baby daughter Isabelle in his arms, greeted him and motioned him to enter. "Hey Thomas, you're just the man I need."

"What's happening?" Thomas asked and stepped inside, closing the door behind him.

"Maya and Delilah are upstairs weeding out Isabelle's toys and clothes to give to Yvette."

Thomas grinned. "Looks like they've got it in hand then. Leaves us to sit back and sip a glass or two."

"I wish! They've roped me into it." He waved toward the hallway. "I've gotta get something from the storage downstairs."

"I'll come with you."

As they walked down the stairs into the basement where the garage, a storage area, a weapons arsenal, and a safe room were located, Thomas noticed Samson exchanging a brief look with Isabelle. Could they both sense his unease?

"Something wrong?" Samson asked him as he opened the storage room and switched on the light.

"Zane and I were following a lead on who's purchased Al's place. We found the lawyer who filed the papers for the company that bought Al out. He's dead."

Samson froze. "Foul play?"

"Somebody cut his tongue out. Looked like a message."

Samson shuddered visibly. "Is the body still there?"

"Zane is sending a cleanup crew as we speak. But we found something else. An address for the people who are behind the company."

"Let's check them out."

"I already did. They're the same vampires who killed Sergio and his wife."

"Let's put a team together and go in to take them out. Good work finding them, Thomas."

"I'm afraid it won't be that easy. There's something else."

Samson raised an eyebrow in inquiry. "What is it?"

"We need to talk, in private." Thomas motioned to Isabelle.

A frown spread over Isabelle's face. Samson's baby daughter seemed to understand way too much. Her telepathic skills also meant that if she heard something she wasn't meant to hear, she would be able to communicate it to her mother. And what Thomas wanted to tell Samson was not meant for anybody else's ears.

"Why don't you grab the buggy here and bring it up? I'll bring Isabelle back to Delilah." Samson didn't wait for Thomas to acknowledge his request, and walked to the stairs.

Thomas took in a deep breath, inhaling the dusty air in the basement. He hoped he wasn't making a big mistake, but he really didn't think there was any other way. The power Xander had displayed had made him reconsider going it alone without Scanguards' backing. He'd thought it would be easy to destroy Xander and his followers by himself, but his opponent had proven him wrong. He needed Scanguards' help.

Thomas grabbed the buggy Samson had pointed out and carried it upstairs to the foyer where he set it down and waited. It took only moments until Samson descended from the upper floor again.

"My office," he instructed and marched down the long corridor.

After Thomas entered his study and closed the door behind him, Samson turned to him, remaining standing.

"What's bothering you?"

Thomas let his gaze wander over his old friend and boss. "As you and some of the others know, I have special mind control skills."

Samson nodded. "You proved that when fighting your maker not too long ago. I wasn't there, but Quinn told me everything."

"I'm not the only one with those skills."

Samson leaned back against his desk. "It's clear your sire had the same skills."

He acknowledged Samson's words with a quick nod. "What I'll tell you now can't leave this room. Nobody can ever find out, not even Delilah. Can you promise me that?"

"This sounds serious."

"It is. I need your word."

"You have it."

Thomas trailed a hand through his hair and felt the perspiration that had built on his nape. He'd never told anybody about his dark power, and revealing this now was a risk. But he had to in order to keep everybody at Scanguards safe.

"My skill comes at a price. Every day and every night I fight against the evil that's inside me. It's a dark power that fuels my skill, an evil power that makes me strong and able to destroy others with my thoughts alone. If I don't continuously beat it back down, it will rise and demand its due." He searched his friend's wide eyes. "If I allow it, it will take over and turn me into a cruel, violent, heartless man. A man who will destroy those he loves."

"Thomas," Samson murmured, clearly shocked.

Thomas lifted his hand. "I'm not finished. There's more." He filled his lungs with air. "The one who gave me this dark power is Kasper, or Keegan, as you know him. I'd hoped that his death would bring me peace, but it didn't. He sired many protégés, and they all have the same dark power within them. And they're using it for evil. They're here, Samson, they've come to wreak havoc."

"The newcomers?" Samson asked, understanding dawning in his eyes.

"Yes. It's them. The vampires who bought up Al's, the same ones who killed Sergio. They've come to take over, and they want me to join them."

Samson pushed away from the desk, his chest heaving. "You're part of us, Thomas!"

Thomas squeezed his eyes shut. "Scanguards is my family. There's no doubt about it. But there are things beyond my control. The more of them who are coming, the more their collective powers will lure my dark power to the surface. I felt it tonight when I confronted their leader."

"You went in on your own? Are you crazy?" Samson raised his voice.

"I thought I could defeat him. His power had seemed so weak that I was convinced I could overpower him and take out his followers right after, but I'd miscalculated. His power was too strong. Stronger than mine. He must have learned to harness it better than I can." He sighed. "I never honed my skills." He'd always been too afraid of the outcome, afraid of growing too powerful and letting that power drug him and turn him into something he didn't want to be. "I failed, Samson. That's why I'm here. You can't send a team in without knowing what you're up against. They'll annihilate us."

Samson's face had turned serious, concern etched in it, a frown on his forehead. "What do they want?"

"What Kasper tried before: to rule the vampire world. He tried, but perished in the process. Now his followers are back. They're taking over business after business, driving all good vampires out of town, building a stronghold. Once they control this city, they'll expand."

"We have to stop them before they even get that far."

"I tried, Samson, but I'm too weak."

Samson gripped Thomas's shoulders and shook him. "You're not weak, Thomas. You're Keegan's protégé. That means you have the power within you, just like those others do. You're a strong man, and there's no reason why you can't hone the power inside you to get stronger than theirs. You have to try."

What Samson was suggesting was too dangerous to contemplate. "I can't, Samson. It's not safe. It means releasing the power from its cage. I won't be able to control it. It will automatically pull me toward them. It will make resisting them even more difficult."

"We need you, Thomas," Samson pleaded. "If they are as dangerous as you say, then our conventional weapons will have little-to-no impact. We'll be hopelessly disadvantaged if they can fight us with mind control. There's nobody apart from you who could offer any resistance."

Thomas pulled free of Samson's hold. "Don't ask this of me! You don't know what you're conjuring up." He balled his hands into fists and clenched his teeth. "Even now, I can feel the dark power rattling at the doors of its cage. I can feel it getting stronger. It'll overpower me and force me to do things I don't want to do. I've seen the evil it unleashes. What happened at Sergio's could happen again. Only next time *I* could be the culprit. Don't you see? I have to keep the power chained up. There's no safe way to hone it."

He pointed to the window, indicating the world outside, his mood turning grimmer by the second. "Those vampires were able to hone their skill because they weren't concerned about who they hurt in the process. They don't have families they care about. They don't know what love is."

Thomas's thoughts instantly turned to Eddie. If he unleashed his dark power, he'd hurt Eddie, because his desire would drive him to force Eddie to fully surrender to him, whether he was ready for it or not. He'd break his trust and lose any chance he'd ever had at love.

"You have to prepare the others for what they'll face. But I can't be part of this. I have to stay away from Xander's people. Just being in their presence awakens my dark power, and I don't know how much longer I can control it."

Samson's Adam's apple bobbed up and down, his eyes wide. "God help us."

29

Eddie pulled into the garage and heard the garage door lower behind him. He turned the key in the ignition, switching off the engine and closing his eyes for a moment. He'd been paired up with Cain for patrol, and while he liked Cain, he'd missed working with Thomas. Cain had been called off early to attend to the cleanup of a murder scene, and therefore Eddie had had to terminate his patrol early. The edict that nobody was to patrol on his own was still in place.

Nina had called him on his cell just before he'd headed out for his patrol, wanting to clarify more what kind of apartment he was looking for so she could narrow down the search. He hadn't had the courage to tell her that he wasn't at all sure anymore whether he still wanted to move out of Thomas's place. He wasn't sure about anything right now.

Eddie dismounted from the bike and took off his helmet, placing it on the bench next to the stairs, then hung up his jacket next to it. He set his foot on the first step when a sound coming from the other direction reached his ears. He froze, his ears perking up. Holding his breath, he listened intently. Was there an intruder in the house?

A sound akin to a groan came from the room that was built into the hillside. The cave, as Thomas called it. When Eddie had first moved into the house, Thomas had told him that this was the only place that was off-limits to him. Eddie had respected Thomas's wishes, but had always been curious about what lay hidden in that room.

Quietly, he approached the door and pressed his ear to it. Odd noises he couldn't identify drifted to him. He inhaled deeply and took in two very distinct scents: the smell of a human, and the scent of vampire blood. Thomas's blood! Somebody was hurting Thomas.

Eddie ripped the door open and charged into the room, his eyes quickly assessing the situation, his body readying itself to fight the intruder who had somehow overpowered Thomas.

His eyes found Thomas bent over a rack near the wall, his wrists bound to a pole above him, his body naked, his legs spread wide. His lower back and ass were covered with streaks of blood, which undoubtedly had been delivered by the human, who cracked a leather whip with several lashes.

Eddie rushed toward the man, snatching his hand and preventing him from delivering another painful lash to Thomas's back. The man whirled his head to him, shocked at being caught.

"What the fuck!" Eddie hissed and hit the man across the face, slamming him to the ground.

"Eddie!"

He jerked his head in Thomas's direction, noticing how he'd turned his head.

"Don't hurt him!" Thomas ordered.

Eddie narrowed his eyes. "He's beating you!" He pointed at the man who was now trying to get up. "He deserves everything he's getting!"

"No, Eddie! Leave!"

"Leave? Are you crazy? He's tied you up, and you want me to leave?" What was happening to Thomas? Was he under some sort of spell? Had somebody overpowered him with mind control? "What the fuck are you saying?"

"He asked for it," the human ground out, collecting the whip that had fallen from his hand.

"What?" He looked from Thomas to the human, then back, now realizing that the straps around Thomas's wrists were made of leather, not silver. Thomas could free himself at any moment if he wanted to. However, it appeared he didn't want to.

Then his eyes took in more of his surroundings. All kinds of flogging instruments hung on the walls around the cave, which was furnished with racks and benches, a chaise longue and several cabinets. What else was hidden behind the doors of those cabinets? More torture toys?

Realization dawned on Eddie. Was Thomas doing this to get turned on? Furious, he glared at the human. "Get out! Get out now!"

He flashed his fangs at the man, causing him to fall backwards in horror. "Out!" he screamed once more, and pointed to the door. Before the man turned, Eddie concentrated his mind on him, wiping his memory of the event.

Only when he heard the door to the garage close again and knew the man had left the house, did he turn back to Thomas.

He ran his eyes over his mentor's back. The wounds seemed superficial. Several cuts on his lower back bled, as well as one on his ass.

Thomas glared at him. "I told you never to come in here."

Eddie ignored Thomas's reprimand and approached, slowly putting one foot in front of the other, his entire body tense. As he came closer, the scent of Thomas's blood intensified.

"Why would you do such a thing? Why let yourself be beaten by a human? What's gotten into you?" As he spoke, he couldn't tear his eyes away from Thomas's naked body. He'd never seen such a muscled ass, such shapely thighs, on anybody. His skin glistened invitingly.

"You wouldn't understand."

"Try me!" Eddie challenged.

Thomas pulled one wrist from the restraints above his head, then the other. As he turned fully, Eddie's gaze immediately fell to Thomas's groin. Anger shot threw him as he saw Thomas's erection.

"You were going to let him fuck you, weren't you!?"

"No!"

"Don't lie to me!"

Thomas glared back at him. "It's the truth! I had no intention of having sex with him!"

"The evidence says otherwise." He motioned to Thomas's erect cock.

Thomas stepped closer, bringing his body almost flush with Eddie's, his breathing harsh and uneven. "I got hard the second you walked in here. As soon as I smelled you. The only man I wanna fuck is you."

Eddie's heart stood still, Thomas's words filling it with warmth. Had he just flown into a jealous rage? Did that mean what he thought it meant? He stopped himself, not wanting to let his thoughts wander any further. He didn't want to know what it meant.

"I don't want anybody else but you," Thomas said, his voice softer now, his face coming closer.

"Then why?"

Thomas sighed. "There are moments in my life when I need to be dominated. When I need to submit to another's will. To forget that I'm powerful."

Eddie listened to the words, but didn't fully understand. "What does it do?"

Thomas brushed his fingers over Eddie's cheek. "It helps me control my urges."

"Urges?" Eddie swallowed hard, his voice raspy now, his own desire growing.

"The urge to take you and make you mine, whether you want it or not."

A hot flame shot through Eddie's core. Whether it was the nearness to Thomas's naked body, the smell of his blood, or the situation he was in, Eddie wasn't sure why he was suddenly so turned on. He only knew that he had to do something about it. He slid his hand onto Thomas's ass, drawing him closer. "What if I dominated you and made you submit to me? Would that help?"

Thomas's eyes blinked red, his vampire side emerging. His fangs lengthened, and a ragged breath rolled over his lips. "Yes, that would help."

Eddie pulled back, noticing Thomas's disappointed look at having severed the connection. "Good." He pointed to the leather chaise longue near one wall of the room. "Lie down on your stomach."

"What are you planning?"

"No questions!" Eddie ordered. "Lie down!"

Barely able to contain his excitement, Eddie watched as Thomas walked to the chaise longue and lowered himself onto it, taking a prone position. He followed him slowly, looking down at him as he reached him. Thomas was spread out like a feast, his thighs slightly parted, giving him a view of not only his tight backside, but also a glimpse of his balls. Then his eyes zeroed in on the cuts on his skin.

Slowly he bent over Thomas, bringing his mouth to his wounds, but Thomas moved underneath him, sliding away.

"What are you doing?" Thomas asked in an agitated voice.

"Isn't that pretty obvious? I'm going to heal your cuts. You're bleeding."

"Don't!"

Thomas's sharp voice got his hackles up. "So it's ok for you to drink my blood, but not for me to drink yours?" No way would he play by those lopsided rules. He grabbed Thomas's shoulders and pressed him back down on the chaise, using his body weight to subdue him as he struggled.

"You call that submitting?" Eddie ground out and jumped on him as if he were getting on a horse.

"Let go of me!" Thomas ordered.

"Not a chance." Eddie held his shoulders down and bent down, scooting back to sit on the top of Thomas's thighs.

"My blood, it's not good," Thomas claimed, making another attempt at stopping him.

But Eddie's tongue already darted out and licked over the first cut, collecting the blood. As the cut sealed, he closed his eyes and let the dark liquid run down his throat. His taste buds exploded and he pulled in a sharp breath.

"Not good? It's delicious!" And it made him feel strong. He'd never had vampire blood—not consciously anyway, since during his turning Luther had to have fed him—and he'd never known what kind of power rush it created. Without pausing, he licked over the next cut, lapping up the tantalizing drops and swallowing them.

His fingers dug into Thomas's shoulders, holding him down as he continued to struggle.

"I thought you wanted to be dominated," he teased and licked again. "Doesn't that mean you have to do what I want?"

"Stop it, Eddie, you're going too far!"

"On the contrary, I'm not going far enough." He scooted farther down, dipping his face lower until his mouth hovered over the cut on Thomas's ass cheek. He gave a tentative lick, then another long stroke over the cut. It mended almost instantly, but he didn't stop. Instead, he continued to caress Thomas by pressing kisses on his skin.

A moan broke the silence in the room, and it had come from Thomas, who, underneath Eddie, had stopped fighting, his muscles relaxing. Eddie released Thomas's shoulders, sliding his hands along his muscular torso until he reached his hips.

Eddie lifted his weight off Thomas, allowing him to lift himself onto his hands and knees. Automatically, as if he'd done it a hundred times, Eddie ran one hand along his crack and past the entrance to his dark portal.

He dove between Thomas's legs, touching his balls, cupping the precious stones in his palm.

A sharp hiss came from Thomas's lips. "Fuck, Eddie! You know what I need."

Strangely enough, he knew exactly what Thomas wanted. And what Eddie craved right now.

"Do you have any lube?"

Thomas pointed to a cabinet on the wall.

Releasing Thomas's balls, Eddie stood and walked to the cabinet, opening it. An array of sex toys lay neatly arranged on several shelves: dildos in all shapes and sizes, clamps, rings, handcuffs, and straps. His pulse kicked up. It appeared that Thomas was into some kinky shit. While he thought this would disgust him, no such feeling rose in him. On the contrary, it only seemed to make his cock harder.

Finding the tube of lubricant, he grabbed it and turned back to Thomas, colliding with his intense gaze. No other person had ever looked at him with such hunger in his eyes.

Setting the tube on top of the cabinet for a moment, he pulled his T-shirt over his head and tossed it on the floor. Not breaking eye contact, he opened the button of his pants and slid the zipper down, slowly peeling away the layer of leather that hid his hard-on. As he pushed the pants down and kicked off his shoes, he noticed Thomas licking his lips.

Without hesitation, he rid himself of his boxer briefs, allowing his erection to pop free.

Then he took the tube of lubricant and walked back to the chaise, basking in the admiring glow of Thomas's eyes. When he stopped before him, he opened the tube and pressed a dollop of it into his palm.

"I never thought you'd be the one to let . . . " Eddie didn't know how to put it without hurting Thomas's feelings.

" . . . let another man fuck me?" Thomas looked up at him. "Very few have. But with you, I want to feel everything."

Eddie took his erection into his hand and lubricated it. The thought of feeling Thomas's tight muscles around his cock in a few seconds almost drove him insane with lust. Impatiently, he moved between Thomas's spread thighs, his legs to either side of the chaise longue, remaining standing behind him. Then he squeezed more lube into his hand and brought it to Thomas's crack.

As he let his fingers slide down, a visible shiver went through Thomas. A moan followed. When he reached the tight ring of muscle that guarded the dark portal, Eddie rubbed over it with his lube-covered fingers, circling it like a tiger its prey. Power surged inside him, making his chest swell. He would be the one to take charge now. No longer was he the person who succumbed to Thomas seducing him with his alluring touch, leaving him defenseless and weak. Tonight, he would be the one to fuck Thomas until he was quivering and asking for mercy.

Virtually shuddering from anticipation, Eddie pressed his finger against Thomas's anus and felt the tight muscle give way, allowing him to slip knuckle-deep inside him.

A deep groan echoed through the room. Encouraged by it, Eddie thrust his finger deeper until it could go no farther. The tightness with which Thomas's interior muscles gripped his finger was intoxicating. His cock would never survive this.

"Fuck!" Thomas hissed.

"Yeah," Eddie murmured, his breath deserting him. He pulled his finger out slowly, then spread more lube over the entrance and repeated the action. The second time he entered, the motion was smoother, the lubricant making him slide more easily without taking away from the exhilarating sensation of feeling Thomas gripping him.

"You love being fucked, don't you?" he asked and moved his finger in and out in a steady rhythm.

Thomas panted, his hips rocking back and forth in synch with Eddie's thrusts. "Get on with it!" he ground out through clenched teeth.

He didn't have to be told twice. Pulling his finger from Thomas's ass, he brought his rock-hard cock in position. Holding on to Thomas's hip with one hand, he used the other to guide his cock as he pressed against the tight ring of muscle.

His knees virtually shaking from the excitement, he pressed inward, submerging the head of his cock in Thomas.

"Fuck!" he hissed, panting heavily as Thomas's muscles squeezed his sensitive tip. Not only would he not survive this, he'd come off as a green kid in front of Thomas by spilling himself when he wasn't even all the way inside him yet.

Taking a few breaths, he dared not move for fear of coming instantly. He'd never felt anything this tight.

"You okay?" Thomas asked, turning his head.

Eddie pulled his lower lip between his teeth, biting it to stave off his imminent orgasm. "I'm fine," he ground out.

"Good, then you won't mind this," Thomas answered with a strange gleam in his eyes and suddenly pushed back his hips, taking Eddie's cock into him to the hilt.

All air rushed from Eddie's lungs. His pulse raced, and instinctively, he gripped Thomas's hips with both hands, steadying himself. Without conscious thought, his body moved on its own, pulling back, then thrusting forward again. It was different from any sex he'd ever had. More intense, more urgent, more passionate.

Feeling the heat around his cock, and the intense pressure that surrounded him, accompanied by the smoothness of flesh gliding into flesh, drove him insane. He panted uncontrollably, moans and groans coming over his lips and mingling with Thomas's sounds of pleasure.

"You like that?" Eddie asked, moaning.

"You kidding me?" his lover pressed out, breathing hard. "I've never had better."

Pride spread in Eddie's chest. This vampire who was well over a hundred years old had never had a better lover than he? That admission spurred him on even more, and he drove his cock harder into him, thrusting deep. With each stroke, he drove himself closer to the inevitable. Yet, he couldn't slow himself down, couldn't stop plunging faster and harder into Thomas. As if driven by some unknown power, he continued.

His fingers had long ago turned into claws and were digging into Thomas's flesh, holding on to him for dear life. His vision was tinted red now, evidence that his eyes were glaring red. His fangs had descended and were fully extended, pushing past his lips. His vampire side had taken over, all hesitation and doubt about his actions gone. He was fucking a man, and he loved it, every single second of it. There was no shame, no embarrassment. Only a deep feeling of satisfaction. All he could feel now was Thomas, his channel squeezing him.

"You're so fucking tight!" he cried out and continued to thrust.

"Are you complaining?"

Eddie groaned. "Fuck no! But I'm not gonna last much longer."

Already now he could feel a tingling sensation in his balls, which had pulled up tight. His spine tensed and his tempo had increased to such a speed that a human would get dizzy watching them.

With a growl Thomas pushed back, doubling the impact of Eddie's next thrust.

"Oh fuck, I'm coming!" Eddie closed his eyes, threw his head back, and surrendered to the sensations washing over him. His orgasm hit him like a mega ocean wave, slamming him into his lover with such force that his knees buckled and he landed on top of him while his seed shot through his cock, filling Thomas's ass.

Underneath him Thomas's body jerked. "Fuck, yes!" he groaned as a visible shudder went through him, indicating his climax.

Breathlessly, Eddie continued to thrust, the movement now smoother than before. Thomas's convulsing muscles gripped him tightly, until both his and Thomas's orgasm ebbed.

Underneath him, Thomas breathed hard. "Fuck!" His hand reached back, sliding onto Eddie's ass, squeezing him lightly. "You can fuck me again anytime you want to."

Eddie felt a smile form on his lips. "Be careful what you offer, I might just take you up on it."

"Good," Thomas murmured.

30

Samson entered Zane's house, walking past the bald vampire who now shut the door behind him. "Thanks for letting us hold the meeting at your house. I didn't want to bring everybody to my place with Isabelle there. She picks up way too many adult conversations already."

"You won't be able to shield her forever," Zane answered. "Do you want me to have a chat with her, letting her know it's bad manners to listen in on conversations and then telepathically tell her mother?"

Samson chuckled. "She might just listen to you more than to me." After all, Zane was her godfather, her mentor for life, and if he wasn't mistaken, his nine-month-old daughter had a bit of a crush on him. "Everybody here yet?"

Zane motioned to the living room. "They're waiting."

"And Portia is gone?"

"Just as you requested. She went shopping with Maya to get a few final things for the baby shower."

Samson smiled. "Everybody is going nuts over this baby."

"Can't blame them. It's rare for a hybrid to be born."

"How about you and Portia? Any plans yet?"

Zane quickly shook his head. "Too early. I'm not ready to share her." Then he winked. "But it doesn't stop us from trying."

Samson slapped him on the shoulder. "Just watch out. It happens faster than you think." He walked into the living room and looked at the assembled, Zane following him and shutting the door behind them.

Cain and Haven stood at the fireplace, deep in conversation. Amaury sat in an armchair, his feet up on the coffee table, his eyes closed as if he were sleeping. Quinn and Gabriel sat on the couch, checking their iPhones for messages.

"Evening," Samson greeted them, drawing their attention to him.

Amaury opened his eyes, Cain and Haven stopped talking, and Quinn and Gabriel put away their iPhones.

"Thanks for coming here. I know this is not our usual place to conduct meetings, but it couldn't be helped."

"Yeah, why is that?" Amaury asked.

"I'll go into that in a minute. But first, what I'll tell you now has to remain in this room. You can't let anybody else know."

Serious faces looked back at him and heads nodded.

"Good, then let's get started."

"Shouldn't we wait for Thomas?" Gabriel asked.

Samson looked at his second-in-command. Thomas was of the same rank as the rest of the assembled vampires, and excluding him clearly looked like an oversight. "No. Thomas will have to stay out of this for reasons that will become clear shortly."

Samson rocked back on his heels. "The new vampires who've moved into our city are a danger to us and our way of life. More so than we could have ever imagined." He pointed to Zane who leaned against the armrest of the couch. "Zane and Thomas were following some leads last night and were able to track them to a building in Chinatown from which they seem to operate. We don't know yet how many followers they've brought in, but their leader, a vampire named Xander, claims more are coming every day."

Zane lifted his hand, a frown on his face. "How do you know his name? We didn't go in."

"Thomas did."

"What the—" Zane growled.

Samson raised his hand to stop him. "I know. It's against protocol. But he had his reasons. It was to protect you."

Zane shot up. "I need no fucking protection!"

"You do." He looked at his colleagues. "I'm afraid we all do. Xander and his people are no ordinary vampires."

"What the fuck is that supposed to mean?" Zane grumbled.

Samson glared at him. "If you'll shut up for once, I'll tell you."

Zane crossed his arms over his chest, but remained silent.

"You all remember when, a few months ago, a vampire named Keegan came after Rose to get back a list she'd taken from him?"

He noticed how Quinn instantly straightened and leaned forward, alert and curious.

"As some of you witnessed, Thomas and his maker fought each other with mind control. Unfortunately, it turns out that Keegan and Thomas aren't the only ones who have that kind of skill. Apparently Keegan sired many other vampires, who all have the same trait. They can all harness mind control in a way that makes them stronger than other vampires."

"Fuck!" Amaury cursed.

Samson could only echo his friend's sentiment. "Yes, because while all of us know how to use mind control, none of us would ever dare to use it against another vampire, unless somebody attacks us with mind control directly. We're aware of our limitations, and know that a mind control fight will lead to certain death. Whose depends on which vampire is stronger. However, that uncertainty is removed when it comes to Xander's followers: their mind control skills are superior to ours."

"Are you saying that whoever was sired by Keegan has that skill?" Gabriel asked.

"That's the information I have."

Gabriel sat forward on the sofa. "That means Thomas is as strong as they are. He can fight them. So why isn't he included in this discussion?"

"Thomas almost died during the confrontation with Keegan. I've therefore decided that he won't join in this fight."

It wasn't exactly the truth, nor was it an outright lie. But he couldn't violate Thomas's confidence and disclose that Thomas feared that any more contact with Keegan's protégés would push him over the edge and unleash the dark power within him. Thomas trusted him to keep his secret.

Haven stepped forward. "On the contrary, he's the ONLY one who can fight him, if what you say is true."

"I agree," Amaury added.

"No! My decision stands. We have to fight them with other means."

"And be annihilated in the process?" Gabriel questioned him, jumping up. "I respectfully disagree."

"What do they even want?" Quinn interrupted.

"To dominate the vampire world. They've started by driving decent vampires from the city, buying up their businesses for peanuts, threatening them. They killed Sergio and his mate when they refused to give in to their demands. What else do you want?" Samson tossed his friends a defiant glare.

"Is it confirmed that Xander's people did all this?" Gabriel asked.

"He admitted it to Thomas."

"Tell me another thing," Gabriel continued. "How is it that Thomas is still alive if he confronted Xander?"

Samson threw back his shoulders. "It doesn't matter how. It just matters that he was able to get away unscathed."

"I think it does, because it proves my point: Thomas is as strong as they are, if not stronger," Gabriel insisted. "Otherwise why wouldn't Xander have taken the opportunity to kill him? Why leave an enemy alive who can give us information about their group that may help us prepare against them?"

More than one pair of eyes shot to him, all of them waiting for an explanation. An explanation he couldn't give.

"Are you questioning my authority?" Samson thundered. He hated having to put Gabriel in his place by reminding him that he was the boss. He'd always looked at his friends as equals, not as subordinates, but today he had no choice but to issue his commands without taking his friends' concerns into account.

Gabriel glared back at him, his lips tightening into a thin line. "Very well. What do you suggest?" he asked after a pause.

"Good. Let's get prepared. We need a headcount of the newcomers. Their headquarters needs to be kept under 24-hour surveillance. Zane will give you the address in Chinatown. Follow anybody who leaves and find out where they're going, who they're meeting. Find out if they have any other safe houses apart from the one in Chinatown. Assign somebody to tail the guy who now runs Al's motorcycle shop. I want to know whom he meets with and where he goes. I also want you to assess the defensive features of their headquarters. How can we attack them there without causing civilian casualties? The place is located at the edge of Chinatown where it borders on North Beach. It's a densely populated area with lots of nightly activities. The area is packed with restaurants and bars that are open late into the night. Attacking their stronghold will draw attention to us. We have to find a way to draw them into a less populated area before we can strike."

"How?"

"I don't know yet. Put your heads together and come up with possible scenarios."

"Fine," Gabriel agreed.

Samson acknowledged his second-in-command's words, but knew it was a long shot to draw them away from their stronghold. If they had to fight Xander and his people in Chinatown, there would be human casualties, and he didn't relish that prospect. Besides, they would also be at risk of exposure as vampires, which was a whole other problem.

If only he could convince Thomas to change his mind and use the power he had to fight their enemies. Was there no way to convince him that he wouldn't succumb to the dark power and turn evil in the process? He'd known Thomas for over a century, and never even suspected the demons he fought against every day. Didn't that prove that Thomas was much stronger than he believed himself to be?

"Let's rock 'n roll," Samson announced and swept one last, long look over his friends, hoping that he wouldn't lose any of them in the coming fight.

31

At the chiming of the doorbell to her medical offices in the basement of her house, Maya took a deep breath and walked to the entrance door. She already knew who stood on the other side before she even opened the door.

"Hi Yvette, thanks for coming!"

Yvette smiled, crossing the threshold with her baby in her arms, a thick blanket wrapped around it. "Hi Maya. She just fell asleep. I hope the examination won't wake her again."

"Don't worry," Maya said and shut the door behind her. There would be no medical examination. Maya had already taken care of that before Cain had brought the baby to Yvette. She'd used it as a ruse to get Yvette to come to her house.

"Come!" She motioned Yvette to the stairs that led up to the main floor of the house, passing the door that led to her examination room.

Yvette hesitated. "But don't you want to examine her down here?"

"The heating died earlier today. It's freezing in there," she lied. "I've moved my instruments upstairs into the living room instead. We don't want the little one to feel uncomfortable."

Without another protest, Yvette walked upstairs and turned toward the door to the living room when she reached the landing.

"Go right in," Maya encouraged her, smiling to herself.

Yvette turned the knob, pushed the door inwards and stepped inside the room.

"Surprise!" several voices called out.

Yvette froze with a gasp rolling off her lips. "Oh, you guys!"

Maya entered the living room behind her. She'd decorated it with pink and white ribbons and stacked the presents in front of the fireplace. Everybody had helped out, and was now assembled and greeting Yvette enthusiastically, surrounding her to get their first glimpse at the baby: Rose, Delilah with her baby daughter, Ursula, Portia, and Nina.

"Oh, she's so cute," Rose professed.

"Look, she's opening her eyes," Nina said.

Delilah held Isabelle so she could get a look at the bundle in Yvette's arms too. "See the little baby? You were that small once too."

Isabelle reached her tiny hand out to stroke over the baby's face, but Delilah pulled her back quickly. "Careful, sweetheart, she's still tiny and fragile."

Maya watched how Yvette looked at the decorations and the presents. "I can't believe you did all this for me!" Then she turned her head to glance at Maya. "I'm so grateful."

Maya smiled back at her. She knew that Yvette wasn't thanking her for the baby shower, but rather for the fact that she'd given the orphan to her, rather than raising her as her own daughter. She could have easily made the request, and considering that Gabriel had seniority over Yvette, Samson would have had no qualms agreeing to it.

Despite the fact that she and Gabriel had unsuccessfully tried for a baby for many months now, she hadn't given up hope. She was half satyr, and this meant that she was fertile, while pure vampire females weren't. The next time she went into heat, she was positive that she would get pregnant. She just had no way of knowing when it would happen. Since she and Gabriel had bonded, she hadn't yet gone into heat, and she assumed that this was an event that didn't happen as frequently as she had assumed at first. Not that it stopped her and Gabriel from trying almost daily.

"Why don't I hold the baby while you start unpacking the presents?" Rose asked and stretched her arms out.

Rather reluctantly, Yvette handed the baby to her.

Rose chuckled. "Don't worry, I'll give her back!"

Yvette laughed nervously. "I know that, of course."

Nina dragged her to the couch and made her sit down. "I'll hand you the presents one by one."

As everybody huddled around Yvette and watched her as she unpacked one present after the other with "oohs" and "ahs" filling the room, and laughter and chuckles echoing off the walls, Maya couldn't stop her heart warming. This was her family, the people she cared about, and who cared about her.

"Have you decided what to call her?" Ursula suddenly asked.

Yvette stopped unpacking and looked at the baby that now looked up at Rose. "Haven and I are thinking either Lydia or Emily. Lydia was the name of his grandmother, and Emily was my grandmother's name. We can't decide."

"They're both great names," Delilah assured her. "You'll just have to see what fits better." Then she suddenly turned to Isabelle in her arms. "What's that sweetheart?" Mother and daughter locked eyes before Delilah looked back at Yvette. "Isabelle says the baby prefers Lydia."

Yvette raised an eyebrow. "But—"

"Well, let's try it out and see what name she responds to."

Maya watched with interest. Was Isabelle right?

Yvette shrugged. "I doubt that'll work." Then she looked at the baby, who still looked up at Rose.

"Emily," Yvette called out to her, but the baby didn't react. "Emily," she repeated. Then she sighed. "Lydia." Instantly, the baby turned its head and looked at her, smiling.

"I think you've got your answer," Delilah said.

Yvette chuckled. "If she starts making her own decisions this early, we're going to have our hands full."

The others laughed. Suddenly the baby started crying and Yvette reached for it, pulling her into her arms.

"What's wrong, Lydia?" she asked and rocked her in her arms.

"Maybe she's hungry," Delilah suggested. "Did you bring a bottle?"

Yvette nodded and pointed to the bag she'd set down on the floor earlier. She made a motion to get up, but Rose stopped her. "I'll get it." She rose and rummaged around in the bag until she pulled out the baby bottle.

Yvette tossed Delilah a questioning look. "Do I have to mix some blood into the formula?"

Delilah shook her head. "Too early. You'll need to wait until she bites somebody first. After that, she'll need blood regularly to supplement her human diet."

Yvette sighed. "How am I going to learn all this?"

Delilah smiled. "Don't worry! You'll get the hang of it. But without a doubt, this will change your life dramatically."

"No more bodyguard assignments for a while," Maya added. "Have you asked Gabriel for a leave of absence yet?"

Yvette's gaze collided with hers. A sliver of panic crept into Yvette's eyes. "I hadn't even thought that far yet. Oh my god, what if I'm completely useless as a mother? I don't know the first thing about babies."

The women chuckled.

"You're going to do just fine," Maya assured her and smiled. "You'll be a wonderful mother."

Yvette's eyes moistened, then a pink tear ran down her cheek.

32

Dressed only in his robe, Thomas watched Eddie walk to the door that led down into the garage. Two days and a night had passed since Eddie had surprised him in his dungeon. While they'd both had to go to work during the night, the two days they'd spent making love.

"Are you sure you have to leave already? Your shift doesn't start till nine."

Eddie tossed a look over his shoulder as he opened the door. "Nina wants me to stop by her place. I haven't seen her in a while." He descended the stairs, disappearing from Thomas's view.

Still not sated, Thomas followed him into the garage.

"Ah, fuck it," he cursed under his breath, unable to keep his lust in check. It seemed the more time he spent with his new lover, the less he was able to pull away from him. At the same time, he'd noticed something else. The dark power within him had remained entirely dormant while he and Eddie had lain in each other's arms. Yet now that Eddie was about to leave the house, he could feel it rising from its slumber. He wasn't ready to deal with it. He wanted a few more minutes of peace.

Thomas reached the last step when Eddie took his leather jacket from the hook and was about to put it on. Thomas grabbed it, pulling it from his grip, and tossed it onto the motorcycle. Without a word, he pulled Eddie into his arms and sank his mouth onto his.

A startled groan dislodged from Eddie's throat, but he gave no resistance. Instead, his arms snaked around Thomas's waist and slid onto his ass, grabbing his cheeks firmly and pulling him against his groin.

Coming up for air, Thomas moaned out his pleasure at feeling Eddie react to him. He couldn't imagine anything better in his life than the body of his lover pressed against him, his hands exploring him, his tongue dueling with his.

"Just ten minutes," Eddie rasped and tugged on the belt of Thomas's robe, releasing the knot.

Thomas felt like releasing a triumphant growl, but he restrained himself, and instead busied himself with opening Eddie's pants and shoving them down to his thighs.

"I love the way you get hard within seconds," Thomas whispered against the tempting column of Eddie's neck, planting hot kisses on his skin, while he wrapped his palm around Eddie's cock.

"You don't exactly give me a chance to ever get soft."

"Is that a complaint?" Thomas moved his hand up and down Eddie's erection.

"No complaint." Eddie's hand slid over Thomas's cock, squeezing him hard.

Thomas felt his heartbeat accelerate and his breath rush from his lungs. He loved the way Eddie touched him—not tentatively, but with determination, with a directness that told him that there was no doubt in his mind about what was going to happen next.

When Thomas dropped onto his knees and moved his head to Eddie's cock, Eddie's hands on his shoulders pulled him back. "I only have ten minutes."

"Trust me I'll only need two to make you come."

Eddie shook his head, his gaze locking with his. Lust and desire shone from his eyes, and something else flickered in them that Thomas couldn't interpret, when he unexpectedly said, "I wanna suck you too."

During the entire time they'd spent in bed together, Eddie had never sucked Thomas's cock, even though he'd used his hands to make him climax. And now, as they stood in the garage with only ten minutes to spare, Eddie wanted to go down on him?

"Fuck, Eddie!" Thomas let out a ragged breath. "You couldn't have chosen a better time for this?" Because feeling Eddie's mouth on him wasn't something he wanted to rush. He wanted to lay back in his soft sheets and luxuriate in the feel of Eddie's lips around him, his tongue sliding down his shaft, his teeth scraping along his skin.

"I want it now." Eddie stared at him, his eyes blazing. Then he lowered himself. Eddie pressed back with his hands against Thomas's shoulders, and within a second, Thomas found himself on his back, his robe falling open in the front.

His lover pushed his pants down to his ankles, his boots preventing him from ridding himself of the garment altogether. Then he turned around and moved, bringing his cock in line with Thomas's mouth. As Eddie bent over him, he reached for Thomas's thighs, spreading them. Then his head dipped lower, and he licked over the head of Thomas's erection.

Thomas almost exploded right there and then. Eddie's hips moved and suddenly his cock nudged at Thomas's lips. He parted them, taking him inside his mouth, sucking on him greedily, just as Eddie began to suck him in earnest.

There was no occasion to tell Eddie what this meant to him. Suddenly Thomas felt accepted by him, because Eddie was fully acknowledging his maleness by performing the most intimate sexual act on him without any sign of embarrassment or shame. On the contrary, the soft moans and sighs that came from Eddie's chest and blew against his cock were confirmation that Eddie was finally ready for him.

With tenderness and adoration, Thomas licked Eddie's cock, sucking him firmly and in a rhythm Eddie's body dictated while he cupped his balls in one hand, fondling the precious sac. But he found it hard to concentrate on pleasuring Eddie while his lover did the same to him. Eddie's hands forced him to angle his knees, giving him full access to his balls and ass.

When Eddie's fingers, moist from his saliva, slid over Thomas's balls, then dipped into the crease of his ass, Thomas groaned, his back arching off the concrete of the garage. But Eddie was giving him no reprieve to this sensual torture, because his dew-covered finger now circled his anus and pressed against it. The sucking motion on his cock intensified just as Eddie's finger breached his portal and drove into him.

Eddie's cock in Thomas's mouth jerked, reminding him of his lover's need. Bringing one hand to aid, he sucked him harder, letting him slide in and out of his mouth, while he squeezed Eddie's balls in concert with his motions.

He'd never thought that Eddie would be so enthusiastic about finger-fucking him, but this wasn't the first time he was doing it, nor, Thomas hoped, would it be the last. With every thrust, Eddie's head dipped lower, taking him deeper into his mouth, and with each movement, Eddie's ass lifted up in the air, his thighs spreading wider.

The temptation was getting too much, and Thomas extended the middle finger of his hand that was caressing Eddie's balls and bathed it in the saliva that was escaping from his mouth. Then he let his finger slide into the crack of Eddie's ass. Eddie jolted slightly, but then he eased back into the touch, and Thomas let his finger slide over the spot again, feeling the ring of muscle that was hidden there. He rimmed it, slowly at first, then faster, noticing how Eddie suddenly finger-fucked him harder and more rapidly, his mouth mimicking the movement. His hips pumped up and down and his ass pressed against Thomas's finger as if he wanted him to thrust inside.

Unable to resist the erotic pull of Eddie's movements, Thomas pushed past the tight muscle and plunged inside.

Above him, Eddie's body convulsed, and a second later, hot seed shot into Thomas's mouth. Eddie's orgasm triggered his own, making him explode in Eddie's mouth without having had time to warn him. He realized with joy that Eddie didn't pull back, and instead kept him in his mouth as wave after wave shot through his cock. His entire body felt weightless, and for a few moments his vision went black.

When Thomas finally released Eddie's cock, having licked him clean, with Eddie having done the same to him, he couldn't talk. It was hard enough to pump oxygen through his body. His lover was breathing as heavily as he, his cheek now resting on one of Thomas's thighs, his groin still braced over him.

"I've gotta go," Eddie murmured, pulling himself up.

When he turned, their eyes locked for a long moment, and Thomas recognized the promise in Eddie's gaze. Everything would work out all right between them.

33

"We have to split up or we're going to lose one of them," Cain said to Oliver, his patrolling partner for the night.

"We can't do that!" his colleague whispered back under his breath. "Gabriel's instructions were to stay together in teams."

"Things change," Cain said, shrugging. "There are times when you have to improvise. So go! You're taking the fat guy. I'll follow that other goon. And don't get too close. Those guys are dangerous."

Without waiting for a confirmation from Oliver, he turned into the next street, careful not to lose sight of the vampire he'd been trailing through half of San Francisco. He and his associate had left the house where Xander was holed up, and had made various stops throughout town. At every point, Cain and Oliver had watched carefully to make sure they weren't committing any atrocities, but it seemed that the two were simply on a reconnaissance mission. However, once they'd reached the Civic Center area, they'd parted ways.

Not knowing which of the two might possibly lead them to another hideout or more of their kind, Cain had made a quick decision. If Gabriel wanted to come down hard on him for it later, so be it. But he wasn't going to let this opportunity slip through his fingers.

Foot traffic thinned somewhat as he continued to follow the other vampire west on Market Street. There were fewer bars and restaurants. Cain had to stay farther back in order not to attract any attention.

For several blocks nothing unusual happened. At the turnaround of the tram that ran along Market Street, the vampire turned into the Castro, and Cain followed at a safe distance. The vapor trail the guy left behind reminded him of a cheap brothel. It practically overpowered the vampire's own scent.

There was more activity in the area he'd turned into, and Cain shortened the distance between him and the other vampire.

The man was of average height, dressed in casual clothes, without any distinguishing features. He looked average, yet at the same time something in his aura—which identified him as a vampire—seemed different from other vampires Cain had met. It was nothing he could actually see, but the closer he walked behind him, the more he could sense something radiating from him that he couldn't put a name to. He only knew that he didn't like it. Was this the superior mind control skill Samson had talked about? Strangely enough, he'd never noticed anything similar around Thomas, even though he had that same skill.

Following the vampire farther up the hill, Cain suddenly heard a voice he recognized. His head whirled to the side, and his eyes searched for the person. He saw her a second later: Roxanne was surrounded by three men who were clearly intoxicated.

"Step aside, or I'll have your balls!" Roxanne claimed, but the human idiots didn't take her seriously.

And why should they? They had no idea that the curvy woman who wore her black dress like a second skin could rip their balls out in less than fifteen seconds, should she wish to do so. For a moment, he contemplated helping her, but he wasn't entirely sure whether she would even appreciate his help. She was more than capable of dealing with those three drunkards herself and would probably even get annoyed at him for having interfered.

But just in case, he figured he needed to at least offer his help. "Roxanne, you need me to take care of them for you?" he called out to her from across the street.

Her gaze shifted to him and she shook her head. "Don't spoil my fun," she answered.

Turning back in the direction in which his suspect had been heading, he froze. There was no trace of him, even though the encounter and exchange with Roxanne had lasted less than fifteen seconds.

Cain inhaled deeply, and luckily he could still smell the cheap aftershave the vampire wore. He followed the trail, speeding up even as the street became steeper. It wound around a corner, and Cain stopped for a moment, sniffing again. The scent was becoming fainter.

Shit! He had to get closer.

Cain ran farther up the hill, his eyes searching for any sign of the vampire, his nose constantly examining the air around him until he finally had to admit that he'd lost him.

Cain looked around the neighborhood and realized that he'd reached Twin Peaks, the area where Thomas lived. What had the vampire wanted here? Or had he merely come up here to lead him on a wild goose chase? In any case, considering how close to Thomas's house he'd lost him, it was better to alert Thomas.

He oriented himself and turned right at the next street, then headed farther uphill. At the bend before Thomas's house, he heard a noise and stopped, remaining behind the bushes along the bordering property. He peeked out from his hiding place and saw the garage door of Thomas's house lifting. He was about to step forward and wave to Thomas, when his eyes zeroed in on the scene playing out in the garage. Surprise made him hold his breath.

Eddie sat on his motorcycle, the engine running. Thomas stood next to the bike, his arms around Eddie, his lips fused with the younger vampire's. Eddie leaned into him, one hand on Thomas's nape, his head angled for a passionate kiss, one that seemed to go on forever.

Thomas wore only a robe. Eddie was fully dressed in his motorcycle leathers. They looked like two lovers saying goodbye after making love. It was written as clearly on their faces as if they'd shouted it off the rooftops.

Cain stepped back behind the bushes, not wanting to watch their intimate embrace any longer. They deserved privacy, and would certainly not appreciate it if they knew they were being watched. After all, nobody at Scanguards knew they were lovers, which could only mean that they went to great lengths to hide their relationship. And he wasn't one to nose around in other people's business. If Thomas and Eddie didn't want anybody to know what was going on between them, he wouldn't be the one to divulge that secret.

He was only surprised at himself that he'd never noticed the chemistry between them. It was so clearly visible now. How had it escaped him all these months he'd been with Scanguards? He'd always considered himself a good judge of people, and figured he'd see beyond the things others were trying to hide. Obviously those two had fooled even him.

Cain turned back and quietly took a path leading between two houses to walk down the hill, not wanting to be seen by Eddie when he drove by with the motorcycle. He would call Thomas on the phone and tell him about the other vampire, so he would not suspect that his and Eddie's kiss had been witnessed.

34

Eddie parked his motorcycle in front of Quinn's Pacific Heights mansion and rushed up the stairs. The message he'd received had said to hurry. He rang the doorbell and waited. From the inside he could already hear several voices. Something was up. Before he could wonder what was going on, the door was opened by Quinn.

"I got here as fast as I could," Eddie said without proper greeting.

Quinn waved him inside. "Come in. You're one of the last. Thomas with you?"

Stiffening, Eddie shook his head. Did anybody know about him and Thomas? Had somebody noticed anything in the way they interacted at the office? "No, should he be?"

"Just thought he might be with you. He didn't reply to the text I sent him."

Eddie shrugged, trying to appear unaffected and walked past Quinn toward the source of the voices. The door to the living room was ajar. Eddie pushed it open farther and perused the room. He was surprised to see half of Scanguards assembled, and they'd brought their wives.

He turned his head to Quinn. "What's this about?"

"You'll find out when everybody else does. So, go and mingle."

He swept his gaze over the crowd and caught Samson's eyes. Noticing him motioning to approach, Eddie walked to him, stopping in front of him.

"Hey, Samson, you know what this is all about?"

"You'll find out. So, how did the meeting with Luther go?" Samson's eyes seemed to want to look through him.

Eddie evaded his gaze and feigned interest in a spot of dirt on his leather jacket. "Fine."

"Did you get what you wanted?" Samson continued.

No, he didn't get the answer that he'd wanted to hear, but he couldn't very well tell his boss about that without revealing what was going on. He still wasn't sure that he was okay with the direction his life was taking. As he looked past Samson, he noticed his sister talking to Portia. How disappointed would Nina be when she found out that her little brother was having sex with Thomas? Or did she already suspect it? And the rest of Scanguards, would they look at him in an odd way? Would they treat him differently? Would they too make fun of him like the boys in his high school?

"I don't mean to pry," Samson's voice drifted back to him.

"No. No, that's okay. Everything was all right. Luther seems well."

"Well, good then."

There was an awkward pause, but Eddie was saved from saying any more when Nina spotted him and waved to him. She said something to Portia, then walked toward him.

"Excuse me, there's Nina," he said to Samson, glad for the excuse, and strode toward his sister, meeting her halfway.

"Hey, Eddie," she greeted him with a smile and a hug. "I don't think I've ever seen as much of you since when we were living together."

She was right. Ever since she'd started looking for an apartment for him, they'd seen each other practically every day, or had at least talked on the phone. Nina was putting a lot of work into this apartment search, and he felt like an ass for leading her on. But this wasn't the time or the place to tell her to cool the search. There were too many people in the room who could eavesdrop.

"Getting sick of me?" he asked, grinning back at her to hide his guilty conscience.

She boxed him in the side. "No chance. So where's Thomas? Haven't seen him yet." Her eyes wandered around the room.

Defensiveness crept up in him. "How should I know?" Why did everybody have to ask him about Thomas as if they were an item?

Nina tilted her head, giving him a curious look. "Are you in a bad mood?"

"No, I'm not!" But if she kept going on about this, he would be very shortly.

"Hey, buddy," Blake's voice came from behind him, a hand landing on Eddie's shoulder, giving him an overly friendly pat. "Nina."

Eddie turned to look at the human. He wasn't mad at him or at Oliver anymore for having leaked that Thomas had feelings for him. Blake just couldn't help himself: he was a bit of a klutz. He meant well, but being the newest member of the extended Scanguards family, he still had lots to learn. As Rose and Quinn's 4th great-grandson, he had become part of their group overnight and, given the circumstances, he had adjusted surprisingly well.

"Blake. So what's this all about? Samson seemed to know but didn't say anything," Eddie asked.

"Your guess is as good as mine. Can't be long now. Almost everybody is here. Even Wesley." He pointed to the window where Wesley stood talking to his brother Haven, making wild gestures with his hands. Blake leaned in, lowering his booming voice. "He's been working on his witchcraft, and I don't think Haven is too pleased with the outcome of his experiments."

Nina drew her head closer. "What happened? I thought Haven was okay with Wesley trying to regain his witch powers."

Eddie had thought the same, and in fact he was grateful for it: Wesley's witchcraft had helped save Thomas's life when he'd fought his maker, Keegan. Had Wesley not cast a spell to break Keegan's concentration during the mind control fight he and Thomas had been locked into, Thomas could have perished in the fight. Even now, Eddie still shuddered at the thought.

"He already has some of his powers back. I've seen it," Eddie added.

Blake grinned. "Yeah, but apparently he has trouble controlling his powers. Last night when he was visiting to have a look at the baby, he was trying out some spells on Haven's two puppies and turned them into piglets. Haven was pissed to say the least."

"Oh no!" Nina laughed out loud.

Eddie couldn't suppress his own laugh. "That's too comical."

"Well, Yvette didn't think so. She's afraid of Wesley being around the baby now, because who knows what he might turn her into."

Nina stopped laughing. "She's got a point."

"Has he turned them back into puppies yet?" Eddie asked.

Blake gestured toward Haven, the witch-turned-vampire, and his witch brother. "Doesn't look like it. From what I could overhear, the place where Wesley buys his ingredients ran out of something he needs for the reversal spell."

"You mean those two puppies are still running around like pigs?" Eddie could virtually see them before his eyes.

Blake chuckled. "Yes, Bacon and Sausage are roaming Haven's house, driving everybody crazy."

"Bacon and Sausage?" Nina echoed.

"Yeah. Like the names? I'm going to suggest they rename the puppies. And maybe the names will stick even after Wesley has managed to turn them back into dogs." Mischief twinkled in Blake's eyes.

Eddie nudged him in the ribs. "You do that and Haven is going to have your hide."

Suddenly a tingling spread over his back and Eddie tried to ward off the bolt of desire that shot through his body. He didn't have to turn around to know who was approaching.

"What is that about Bacon and Sausage?" Thomas's voice sounded from only a few feet behind Eddie.

Only turning his head by a fraction to acknowledge Thomas's arrival, Eddie answered, "Blake's getting himself into trouble again by insulting Haven's puppies."

"Well, they're not puppies right now. More like ham and pork rinds," Blake shot back.

Thomas gave him a questioning look. "Do I want to know what this is about?"

Nina shook her head. "No, you don't. It's just Blake being silly. Again."

"You're calling me silly?" Blake asked. "That's outrageous!"

As Nina and Blake continued arguing about what constituted silly, Thomas stepped closer to Eddie. Eddie felt as if little charges of electricity were jumping from Thomas's body to his.

"Hey." The husky tone with which Thomas had spoken the single word made Eddie's throat go dry in an instant. He dared not respond, knowing that he wouldn't be able to utter a coherent sentence. Ever since he'd sucked Thomas in the garage, he knew something was going to change between them. When he'd felt Thomas's finger inside him for a brief moment and had come uncontrollably, he realized that he'd crossed a bridge from which there was no way back. And it scared the shit out of him. Because if he continued on this path, it would mean that his entire life had been a lie.

Eddie was about to return Thomas's greeting, when somebody started clapping loudly to gain everybody's attention. He turned to the source of the sound like everybody else, and noticed that Oliver and Ursula stood at the door to the living room, looking at the assembled.

"Thanks all for coming," Oliver started. "I know this was short notice, but I figured if I tried to coordinate ahead of time, our schedules would have been even more chaotic. Anyway, I didn't want to wait any longer." He smiled at Ursula, whose hand he was holding. "I've asked Ursula to marry me, and she said yes."

The crowd broke out in cheers. A few wolf whistles bounced around the room, some of the assembled started clapping, and the ones standing closest to the happy couple hugged them, congratulating them.

"Guess Cain owes me a hundred bucks," Thomas remarked, smiling.

Eddie nodded. "You were right."

"Thomas, you knew?" Nina asked.

He turned to her. "The signs were all there."

Eddie rolled his eyes. "Thomas saw him buy the ring."

Thomas chuckled. "Thanks for undermining my superiority." He ruffled Eddie's hair.

Immediately Eddie pulled back. Shit! How could Thomas just touch him like that in public? His gaze shot to Nina to see if she'd noticed it, but she seemed to be staring in Ursula's direction, trying to get a glimpse of her hand, which sported a massive diamond solitaire ring.

"Well, another bachelor off the market," Nina commented and looked at Eddie. "She's such a nice girl. So, little brother, how about you? Are you seeing anybody special?"

Panic surged through him. Nina had just handed him the perfect opportunity to come clean, to confess everything and tell the world that yes, indeed, he was seeing somebody special. And that this somebody was standing right next to him.

"And she'd better be at least as nice as Ursula, or I'm going to be very disappointed," Nina added. "I wouldn't mind becoming an aunt one day. Did I tell you about the baby shower? Yvette's baby is the cutest I've ever seen."

Eddie couldn't swallow past the lump that had formed in his throat. Nina had no idea about his leanings. How could he tell her that he liked a man? That there was no chance of him ever becoming a father, because he couldn't imagine ever being with a woman again.

"There's nobody right now," he choked out, feeling like an ass for not having the courage to confess what he really felt.

From the corner of his eye he saw Thomas's shoulders tense and his face turn expressionless.

"Mind if I steal your brother for a moment, Nina? We've got some training stuff to discuss."

"No prob," Nina said quickly.

Thomas put his hand on Eddie's elbow and pulled him through the crowd and into the kitchen in the back of the house without saying a word.

The kitchen was empty. Thomas shut the door behind them, releasing his grip. "What the fuck was that?"

Becoming defensive, Eddie lifted his chin. "What was what?"

"Don't pretend you don't know what just happened out there. First you shrink back from me when I touch your hair, and then you lie to your sister. So there's nobody special in your life, is there? Because I'm nobody to you."

Eddie felt his heartbeat kick up. "I didn't say that!"

"That's exactly what you said! So what is this between us? You just want to live out some gay fantasies you're having? But you don't want to commit to it, because you're ashamed of it. Just like you're ashamed of me."

"I'm not! But I can't do this. I can't tell Nina. Not now. Not yet."

"Then when? When will there ever be the right time to tell your sister and your friends that we're lovers?"

Eddie shrank back, his back hitting the kitchen counter behind him.

"Yes, lovers. We've been lovers from the moment you kissed me on that construction site, since the moment you let me touch you. But you can't admit that, can you?"

Eddie tried to evade Thomas's intense gaze, but he couldn't make himself turn his head. "You're asking too much from me."

"Too much? Eddie, the only thing I'm asking is for you to be honest about who you are."

"I can't disappoint Nina."

"Disappoint? Is that what you feel? That admitting that you're with me will be a disappointment for your sister?" Thomas's nostrils flared and his eyes suddenly started glaring red. "So you won't stand up and be a man, but you'll continue to use me, is that it? Because that's what you're doing. You come to my bed and let me suck you, kiss you and touch you. And I let you fuck me, because I wanna give you everything you desire. How does it make you feel to fuck a gay man?" Thomas tossed him a hurt glare. "You're using me for sex, because you know I can't turn you down. You know that I'm irrevocably in love with you, and that's why you think you can string me along until maybe one day you're ready to man up? Until one day you're ready to admit that you're gay too. It doesn't work that way!"

Irrevocably in love? Eddie's heart raced. Thomas had never before talked about love. Lust and desire, yes, but love. No, he'd never said those words before.

"Didn't you just hear what Nina said? She wants me to find a nice girl and have children. She has no idea." How could he burst her bubble like that? He'd promised himself never to disappoint her again. Never to hurt her again. But it seemed he had to hurt somebody: either Nina or Thomas.

"God forbid your sister found out that you sucked my cock and liked it!" Thomas hissed. "I'd never figured you for a coward, Eddie."

"I'm no coward!" he ground out, fury rising from his gut, his fangs itching now.

"Then make a fucking decision. Now! If what happened between us was more to you than just fucking and experimenting, then you have to come out of the closet and admit what you are."

Eddie hesitated. Admit that he was gay? He shuddered at the thought, remembering the words of his foster mother when she'd caught him with the other boy, the taunts in high school, and his sister's face. Would she understand? Would she love him the same way? She was all he had. His family.

"I guess I have my answer," Thomas said, his voice flat and emotionless. "It meant nothing to you." He turned to the side door leading out of the house and turned the knob.

"Please give me time. Please, Thomas. I need to think on it."

Without a word, Thomas exited and pulled the door shut behind him.

Eddie let out a heavy sigh. "Shit!" He hadn't been prepared for this. He'd hurt Thomas with his inability to commit to their relationship. Because that was what they were having: a relationship. Thomas was his boyfriend. And by the looks of it, they'd just broken up.

35

Thomas stormed out of the house, Eddie's words chasing him. What was there to think on? Eddie wanted to have his cake and eat it too. He clearly enjoyed the sex they'd been having, but he wanted to continue leading a straight life on the surface, so he wouldn't rock the boat with his sister and his friends. Because deep down, Eddie was still ashamed of his desires, even though when they were alone, he'd surrendered in all ways but one. Thomas had hoped that tonight they would breach that last barrier too, because he'd been almost certain that Eddie would have surrendered to him tonight and allowed him to take his virgin ass. But their fight had changed all that.

Thomas could have kept his mouth shut, not saying anything to Eddie about how this made him feel, but when he'd answered his sister and said that there was nobody special in his life, Thomas had seen red. It had hurt to hear his lover say those words while he'd had to stand there silently. By the time they'd reached the kitchen, he'd already felt his dark power rise in his chest, making it impossible to pull back and cage the beast. He'd wanted this confrontation, because he wanted Eddie to confess that they had something special, that what was growing between them was not just sex, but affection, love. But by doing so, he'd pushed him away.

"Fuck!" Thomas cursed and swung himself onto his motorcycle, inserting and turning the key, hitting the start button, and letting the engine roar to life. He pulled into the quiet street and raced down the hill until he had to stop at a stop sign. There was no traffic. He was about to pull into the intersection, when he saw a dark figure emerge from the shadows and step into the light of the street lamp.

Shock made him almost lose his balance on the motorcycle. What he saw was impossible. He squeezed his eyes shut and blinked them open again.

"Christ!" he hissed.

The man walked toward him, his gait casual and relaxed. "Not my name, that's for sure, but I never cared much about what you called me, lover, as long as you talked to me."

Kasper, his maker, the man who'd died in front of Thomas's eyes months earlier, stopped in front of the motorcycle. The dark power radiating from him left absolutely no uncertainty that this was indeed his maker.

Thomas found his voice again. "You're dead."

A wistful smile crossed Kasper's face. "Ah, yes, that incident was unfortunate. But let's not talk about that right now. We have other things to discuss."

Kasper killed the engine, and removed the key. Suddenly there was only silence around them. Reluctantly, Thomas dismounted and rolled his bike to the sidewalk, parking it. His entire body was tense and alert. His dark power simmered just below the surface, and he knew he could strike Kasper the instant he felt any danger.

"The only thing we have to discuss is why you're alive," Thomas answered. There had to be an explanation for it. No vampire had ever come back after being turned into dust. "You turned into dust in front of me. I *saw* you die."

"Are you sure it was I?" Kasper smiled.

Thomas narrowed his eyes. There had been no doubt.

"Later, I'll feed your curiosity, but first, there's something we'll have to settle." Kasper looked up and down the street, but it was deserted. "Your lover, Eddie. I'm afraid he's not honest with you."

"How—?"

Kasper raised his hand. "I've had my people watch you and him." He shook his head. "He's cute, I give you that, but really, can you not see that he's just playing with you?"

Defiantly, Thomas squared his stance. "He's not playing with me. Stay out of this. You'd better tell me what you want."

"Isn't that evident? I want you back, my sweet Thomas. You've had your fun. You've sown your wild oats. Now it's time to return and claim what's yours. To sit by my side as we rule the world of the vampires."

"You're out of your fucking mind if you think I'll ever return to you!"

"You've got nothing else. I overheard your fight with your lover. But that's not all. I know what he really thinks. I know what he does behind your back." He pulled an iPhone from his pocket and tapped on it. "Did you know that he's been planning to leave you all along?"

At Kasper's treacherous words, the dark power inside Thomas roared, wanting to burst to the surface. He sensed it growing stronger, drawn to the power that Kasper was exuding. "You're lying!"

"Am I?" He tapped something on his iPhone, then held it up.

Thomas instantly recognized Nina's voice coming from the device. *"What didn't you like about the flat I showed you earlier?"*

"It's not in the right neighborhood. I told you I didn't want to live in Noe Valley," Eddie's voice replied.

Surprise and dread filled him. Eddie was discussing apartments with Nina. Why?

"That's not considered Noe Valley. It's practically the Mission. And I thought you said you'd like living in the Mission," Nina continued.

"Fine. But it was also too expensive. I don't want to pay that much in rent. I just want something small, just something for myself."

Thomas felt his heart stutter to a halt. There was no doubt about what Eddie was saying. He wanted to move out. He searched for an explanation. Maybe this was an old recording, something that Eddie had discussed with his sister way before he and Eddie had become lovers.

"This proves nothing!" he said to Kasper. "You can't prove that this recording is even recent."

"Can't I?" Kasper grinned wickedly. "Continue to listen."

Thomas sucked in a breath, about to protest, when Nina's voice sounded from the speakers of the iPhone again. *"I guess then you're not going to like the one in the Marina that I saw."*

"The Marina is on landfill, Sis. After that earthquake three days ago, I'm not interested in living on anything but bedrock. Even Thomas's house shook pretty heavily. I don't even want to know—"

Kasper switched off the recording. But Thomas didn't need to hear any more. There had been an earthquake three days earlier, the only major one since Eddie had moved in with him. There was no doubt now that the conversation between Nina and Eddie had taken place earlier that day. And Eddie had even admitted to needing to see Nina when he'd left the house.

Thomas felt a sharp spear of pain lodge in his chest. Right after they'd made love there on the floor of his garage, Eddie had gone out to look at an apartment so he could move out. Eddie had planned all along to leave him. He'd never had any intention of continuing their relationship. All he'd wanted was some sexual experimentation.

The feeling of betrayal that now rushed through him wasn't anything he'd ever experienced. He sensed his hands trembling and his knees going soft as all hope left his body. Eddie didn't love him, despite the intimacies they'd shared. It had all been an illusion. A lie.

Fury charged through him, igniting his cells and rattling on the door to the cage in which he kept his dark power locked away.

"He used you," Kasper said, his voice penetrating the fog in Thomas's mind.

Used. Yes, he felt used. Like an old toy a kid played with once, and then discarded because his friends didn't find it acceptable.

"You'll show him that you don't need him!" Kasper continued, the words sinking deeper into Thomas's mind, making inroads there.

"I don't need him," Thomas repeated. No, he needed no lying, deceitful lover in his life.

The dark power in him agreed and pushed against the door of its cage, shoving it open. A roar went through his body.

"Yes, you feel it now, don't you?" Kasper coaxed. "It's been chained up for too long, hasn't it?"

Thomas sensed the power as it was drawn to Kasper and the power swirling around him freely now. Bright sparks illuminated the shadows around them. Thomas closed his eyes and let the energy flow, for the first time in his life not putting any reins on the beast inside him.

"Welcome back!" Kasper put his hand on his shoulder, but Thomas instantly shook it off.

Glaring at him, he snarled, "You owe me an explanation! Talk now! And talk fast. I might not know how to control my powers the way you do, but I have nothing to lose anymore. Do you hear me? Nothing! And that makes me dangerous."

Kasper's face remained impassive despite Thomas's threat. "What I tell you now will forever be our secret. None of my followers know. And they can never find out."

Thomas didn't answer. He would make no promises to Kasper or anybody else. Never again. He lifted his clenched fist, his fangs descending. A sheen of red color tinted his vision. Electrical sparks released from his hands. "Talk!"

Kasper nodded briefly. "The man your people killed was my identical twin, Keegan."

Thomas's heartbeat shot up. Twins? There had been two of them? How had he never found out about Kasper's twin?

"Yes, there were always two of us, but we lived as one. To everybody else, we were known as Kasper. We traded places to emphasize our strengths and to control our followers. We could be at two places at the same time, giving the impression that we were more powerful than any other vampire." He paused.

Thomas could barely trust his ears. Was that the reason why he'd often thought that Kasper had a split personality, being kind and loving one minute and violent and uncaring the next? Because they were two different people parading as one?

"Don't get me wrong. We *were* more powerful than others, because our blood made us stronger. And the dark power ran equally strong in both of us. Nobody could tell us apart. Not even you, my sweet Thomas. Not even you."

Anger flared up inside Thomas. "You lied to me all this time."

Kasper shook his head, smiling. "On the contrary. I never did. Keegan was the one who caused you all this pain. He was the one who went out to fuck anything in a skirt. He wasn't into men, you know. He loved women only. So I can assure you, you only had sex with me, and I was true to you."

Thomas scoffed. "Yeah, right! You fucked around on me just the same." He hadn't forgotten the woman who'd sucked Kasper the night of Thomas's turning. "You liked women too. You said so yourself."

"I admit, I swing both ways; however, after I met you, I only slept with you. There were no other men, and no more women. Keegan was the one who flaunted his sexual exploits for all to see, and there was nothing I could do to make you understand that there was no need for your jealousy. He and I had an agreement never to divulge the fact that we were two people. Everything hinged on it. As one, we were strong; as two individuals, we would have faltered."

Kasper sighed.

Thomas stared at him, stunned by his revelations. But did it really change anything after so long a time? It didn't change the fact that the reason he'd left Kasper was because he was cruel and violent, not because he was unfaithful.

"You used your powers to hurt people in the most violent way I've ever seen."

"No. I didn't. Keegan was the one who couldn't control his powers. His outbursts were violent. He had no compassion. That's what made us so different. I had empathy for others; he didn't have that capacity. It was what ultimately led to his death. I warned him. But he wouldn't listen, and pursued a path that I couldn't pull him back from. I tried. I followed him, and then I found you. I couldn't interfere in the fight between you. It would have exposed me, and I might have met the same end as my brother. But believe me when I tell you, I wasn't rooting for him during that fight, I was wishing for you to win."

Thomas felt a shiver run down his spine. Could he trust his ears? Had it really been Keegan who'd committed all those atrocities? Was Kasper blameless? He shook his head.

"Please don't tell me you were a choirboy. You weren't a saint back then, and you're not a saint now! The way Sergio and his mate were killed has your handwriting all over it. Don't deny it!"

"Ah, yes, a very unfortunate incident. And the one who is responsible for it has been punished. I'm afraid some of my followers still cling to methods that my brother instilled in them. I've been trying to retrain them since his demise, but some of these ways are so ingrained that they're hard to eradicate. I prefer cleaner methods to achieve my goal."

"Yes, and what is your goal, Kasper?" Thomas asked, still suspicious of his maker and former lover's motives.

"You know what it is. I told you the night I met you. It is for our kind to be accepted. To be free to live the way we choose, without persecution, without restraints. I thought you wanted that too. That's why you joined me back then. Has that changed?"

Thomas didn't answer immediately. His deepest wish was still the same: to be loved for what he was and not be judged just because he was different. "I have the respect of my colleagues."

"Are you so sure about that?"

Thomas narrowed his eyes. "What are you insinuating?"

"Did you know that Samson held a secret meeting at Zane's house the other night?"

He didn't know, but it didn't have to mean anything. "That's irrelevant."

"You say that because you don't know what was discussed at the meeting. Did you know that Samson told your colleagues about your secret?"

"He would never break his promise," Thomas protested without hesitating.

"Don't be so naive. See, that's your problem. You always assume the best in people when you should assume the worst. Samson betrayed you just like Eddie did."

"No! You can't prove that!" Thomas desperately tried to cling to his belief that his oldest friend and colleague was keeping his word.

"Just like I couldn't prove that Eddie betrayed you?" Kasper let out a bitter laugh and raised his iPhone again. "Care to listen to what Samson told them?"

Don't do it! a voice inside him pleaded. *Don't listen to it. It'll only make it worse. Eddie betrayed you. They all betrayed you. You're nothing to them. Nothing. It was all a lie.*

He sucked in a breath.

Feel the power! It's yours!

Thomas sensed a bolt of electricity shoot through him and felt the dark power physically now. It was all around him, cocooning him, keeping him safe, protecting him. It was all he could trust in now, because his trust in Scanguards and his old friends had vanished.

He put his hand over Kasper's iPhone. "No. There's no need."

Kasper released a sigh of relief and let the tension flow from his body. It always took a lot of energy to influence another vampire without triggering his self-defense instincts and his fighting back with mind control. Luckily, he'd provoked Thomas long enough for his dark power to emerge, and thus given him a way in. Kasper had allowed his own power to connect with Thomas's so his former lover would accept the thoughts Kasper had sent to his mind as his own. It had only taken a little shove to push him over the edge.

When Thomas had continued to question him and his motives, he'd had to think fast to turn the situation around. Because despite the fact that Eddie had betrayed him, Thomas had still clung to his association with Scanguards.

No longer.

By the time Thomas found out that Samson hadn't betrayed his confidence, he'd be so deep within the pull of the dark power that he wouldn't find a way out of it anymore, even if he tried. Kasper would make sure of it. Thomas would be surrounded by him and his followers day and night, and the collective dark powers that swirled around them would drug Thomas and make his own power stronger so that he wouldn't have the strength to fight against it anymore.

Nothing would be strong enough to pull him back. He'd seen it before with his other protégés, the ones who'd fought against it at first, only to lose the fight. They had become loyal and docile, just as Thomas would. Maybe not docile, though, since for Thomas, he had other plans. Because Thomas was stronger than all of them together. Thomas just didn't know it yet.

Luring Thomas back into his bed would take longer, but Kasper was nothing if not patient. He'd waited over a hundred years for this; he could wait a few weeks longer. And once they had blood-bonded, Thomas's power would be his, and together they would be invincible.

"Come home now, Thomas, where you belong."

36

He hadn't slept a wink all day. Thomas hadn't come home after storming out of Quinn's house. Eddie had waited up for him all day, pacing in the living room and listening for the familiar sound of Thomas's bike approaching the property. But Thomas had not returned. With every hour, Eddie's mood had turned grimmer. Had Thomas gone out to the Castro to pick up some willing human to have sex with?

Jealousy made his gut burn from the inside, when he knew he had no right to feel such emotion. After all, he'd been the one driving Thomas away, and most likely into the arms of another man. He hadn't been prepared for Thomas's demand to commit to him right there and then. It wasn't the right time or the right place. He hadn't expected Thomas to react like this and simply leave and stay away all day. Clearly he'd hurt Thomas more than he'd realized.

And one other thing was clear now too: he didn't want his relationship with his lover to end. And for sure he didn't want Thomas to find another lover. At that thought, his fangs itched for a vicious bite. If he found Thomas with another lover, he'd rip that stranger's throat out. He hoped for both his and Thomas's sake that Thomas had spent the day in his office at Scanguards to cool off, rather than fucking another man.

As soon as the sun set, Eddie jumped onto his motorcycle and raced down the hill, ignoring all rules of traffic on his way to Scanguards' headquarters. After parking his bike, he charged past the security guy at the door, flashing his ID, and took the stairs to the top floor, too impatient to wait for the elevator.

On the executive floor, he walked down the long corridor and headed for Thomas's office. The door was closed. Without knocking, he opened it and entered.

The office was empty. He sniffed, but there was no fresh scent that would indicate that Thomas had been here in the last twenty-four hours.

"Fuck!" he cursed.

He took a few steadying breaths and reached for his cell, then paused. Would Thomas even pick it up if he knew it was he? And besides, what would he even say to him on the phone? This was a conversation where he needed to look him in the eye. Frustrated, he shoved the phone back into his pocket and left the office, shutting the door behind him.

In the hallway, he rushed past Cain.

"Hey, Eddie, what's up?"

Eddie didn't even look back at him and continued walking. "Nothing. Gotta run an errand." Then he pushed the door to the stairs open and ran downstairs and out a side exit, not wanting to run into anybody else and be delayed. He had to find Thomas before the situation escalated even more.

It took him only minutes to reach the Castro, where Thomas's favorite hangouts were located. This would be where he would pick up guys. The area was teeming with gay men of all ages. With Thomas's handsome looks, he wouldn't have any problem finding a willing bedmate within seconds. Guys were always coming on to him. Eddie had seen it often enough when they'd been out on patrol together. It had always annoyed Eddie, and he wondered now if even back then he'd been jealous. He could admit it to himself now: the thought that right now, Thomas was in the arms of another man was eating him up from the inside.

One by one, Eddie searched the bars in the Castro and kept his eyes open for a sign of Thomas's motorcycle. At the bars where Thomas was known, he even asked the bartenders if they'd seen him, but the answer was always the same.

"Not in a while."

Deflated, Eddie left the last bar in the Castro and walked back to his bike. When he reached it, he closed his eyes for a moment. Where had Thomas disappeared to? If he hadn't been in the Castro to pick up some guy, then where was he?

A terrible thought invaded his mind. What if Thomas had harmed himself? What if the rejection had been too much for him? His hands shaking now, he jerked his cell phone from his jacket and dialed Thomas's number.

"Please pick up," he whispered to himself.

But the phone only rang and rang until Thomas's voicemail kicked in.

***

Gabriel typed his password a second time, but the notice flashed on his computer once more: *password expired.*

"Crap!" he cursed. Security procedures around IT were so tight at Scanguards that all employees had to change their password every month, and if they missed the two-day grace period, they had to get IT to reset the password.

Gabriel dialed the number for the IT desk and drummed his fingers on the desk.

"IT support," a bored male voice answered.

"Yeah, this is Gabriel Giles. I need you to reset my password."

"One moment," he said.

"Don't put me on hold!" Gabriel answered, but it was too late. There was already a click in the line, and insipid elevator music sounded in his ears.

Gabriel growled. Did this idiot in IT not know who he was dealing with?

Seconds ticked by, then suddenly there was another click in the line.

"I'm sorry, Mr. Giles, but I don't have access to the executives' security profiles. Those are handled exclusively by Thomas. I can put you through to him."

"Don't bother!"

Gabriel slammed the phone down and shot up from his desk. As a director, he shouldn't have to jump through hoops just to access the system. Grumbling to himself, he left his office and turned to the one next to him. *Thomas Brown, Director, IT*, it said on the plaque next to it.

Gabriel knocked impatiently and opened the door without waiting for a reply.

"Thomas, you've gotta—" He stopped in his tracks. The office was empty.

Annoyed he turned back and pulled his cell phone from his pocket, speed dialing Thomas's number. It rang several times.

"You've reached Thomas. Leave me a message," the voice recording echoed in his ear.

"Where are you?" Gabriel bellowed into the phone. "I need that fucking password reset."

He disconnected the phone and looked down the corridor, seeing Cain come around the corner.

"You seen Thomas?" he called out to Cain.

"No, I haven't. Have you asked Eddie? He came out of Thomas's office earlier."

Gabriel nodded his thanks and dialed Eddie's cell phone.

It took several rings before Eddie finally picked up.

"Gabriel? What can I do?"

"Where's Thomas? My fucking password expired and he's the only one who can reset it."

There was a pause, and Gabriel almost thought that the cell connection had been interrupted.

"Eddie?"

"Uhm, Gabriel. Thomas didn't come home yesterday. I haven't seen him since the party at Quinn's house."

"What?" Disbelief coursed through him.

"I don't know where Thomas is, and he's not picking up his phone."

From the corner of his eyes he noticed Cain approach, curiosity flashing over his face.

"And you didn't report that?"

"Hey, he's got a right to privacy."

Anger shot through Gabriel. "There's no fucking privacy! If somebody from Scanguards disappears, there's a protocol to adhere to. You should know better!"

Pissed off, he disconnected the call and met Cain's inquisitive stare.

"What's going on?"

Gabriel motioned to the phone. "Thomas didn't come home. He disappeared after the party."

"You mean not even Eddie knows where he is?" Cain's voice was colored with surprise. "But . . . "

"We have to find him."

"You think something happened to him?" Cain asked.

Gabriel ignored the question, not wanting to think of the many possibilities of what could have happened. He hoped that Thomas was simply out on a binge, enjoying a day of sex and blood, and was still in some guy's bed, even though Thomas was too conscientious to not have called the office and told somebody where he could be found in an emergency.

"Find out if he left any messages with the front desk," Gabriel instructed Cain.

"I'm on it."

37

Samson sat in his office at Scanguards, having been alerted to Thomas's disappearance hours earlier, when the door flung open.

"Now tell me what's really going on!" Gabriel thundered, charging inside and pounding his fist onto Samson's desk. "And no more bullshit!"

Samson jumped up, glaring at him. "What the fuck is this?"

"I'll tell you what it is: Cain just called from his patrol. He saw Thomas at Xander's headquarters in Chinatown. And he looked like he was there of his own free will."

"Ah shit!" Samson cursed. "I was afraid this would happen." He ran his hand through his thick, dark hair.

"What the fuck is that supposed to mean?"

Samson pointed to a chair. "Sit down, Gabriel."

Gabriel folded his arms over his chest. "I'd rather stand."

"Suit yourself." Samson paused. "Thomas came to me the other night. After he'd confronted Xander. Everything I told you and the others when we met at Zane's house is true. But I left something out. I'm afraid Thomas carries a dark power in him, the same dark power his maker had. The same that's ruling Xander and his people. Thomas has struggled to suppress this power for all his life. But now that these vampires have come here, his power senses them, and is drawn to them. He told me that it's getting harder and harder for him not to act on it, not to succumb to its pull."

"Fuck!" Gabriel hissed. "Why didn't you warn us? We could have had somebody watch Thomas day and night. We could have prevented this!"

"I couldn't tell you. I gave him my word!"

"Fuck that! Look where that got us! Thomas has joined them!"

"We can't know that for certain," Samson protested, but he knew he spoke more out of hope than conviction.

"We have to do something," Gabriel urged him.

Samson nodded, his shoulders feeling the weight of responsibility on them. "We have to convince him to come back to us."

***

Samson stepped out of the shadows when he finally saw the door open. He'd sent Thomas several messages to his cell, and later emailed him after realizing that Thomas had switched his phone off. It appeared that Thomas was finally responding by leaving the house in Chinatown.

Behind Samson, his friends Amaury, Gabriel, and Zane remained in the background, even though he realized that Thomas would be able to sense them, just as Samson realized that Thomas wasn't alone. Remaining in the shadow of the covered entry, too far back to see his face, stood another vampire.

Samson crossed the street halfway and perused his surroundings once more. There was barely any traffic this time of night, and since the shops on this small side street were closed, nobody else seemed to be around.

"What do you want?" Thomas asked, his words clipped, the friendliness that normally colored his voice wiped from it as if they were strangers. No, worse: as if they were enemies.

"We need to talk, alone." Samson motioned his head to the stranger in the shadows.

"If that were the case, you would have come alone too," Thomas retorted, his gaze drifting past Samson's shoulders.

"We're all friends—"

"Friends don't break promises," Thomas interrupted. A snarl ripped from his throat. "Friends don't betray friends."

"I didn't betray you! It's the dark power in you talking. You have to fight it, Thomas!"

"No, on the contrary. I don't have to fight it anymore. Because I've got nothing left to lose." His jaw set into a hard line as if he were choking back an emotion so powerful it was about to overwhelm him.

"That's not true, Thomas. You have a great life with us. Everybody at Scanguards loves you and respects you. We need you!"

Thomas expelled a bitter laugh. "A great life? That's easy for you to say, Samson. And for all of you too," he added and looked toward the shadows where his three colleagues stood in silence. "You all have somebody who loves you. A mate. I have nothing! You understand? Nothing! The one person I loved betrayed me. Do you know what that feels like?"

For a second, Samson didn't understand who Thomas was talking about. Then he ventured a guess. "Eddie?"

The pain in Thomas's eyes confirmed that he was right.

"But you always knew that Eddie could never be yours. He's straight." And Thomas had always accepted that. Samson knew that for a fact. So why was this suddenly an issue?

"Leave me alone, Samson. I can't do this any longer. I can't live the way you want me to live."

"Don't do this, Thomas! That's not you!" He pointed to the person behind Thomas. "You're not like them. You're not cruel. You're not evil."

"How would you know? I've never shown you what I've hidden all my life. You've only seen what I allowed you to see. All of you! You don't know me at all!" Thomas turned.

Samson gave his friends a signal, and they rushed forward. If Thomas wasn't coming voluntarily, they'd force him. "Come back to us!"

Thomas spun on his heels, his eyes glaring red as he focused them on Samson.

"Shit!" Samson cursed, realizing what was going to happen. He steeled himself for the assault, but there was no defense against it.

The first bolt of pain drilled into his mind, almost blinding him, the second knocked him several yards back. He landed on his ass, a rib cracking as he slammed against the curb.

Amaury, Zane, and Gabriel charged forward, but a bolt of lightning coming from Thomas's outstretched hands stopped them. "No farther, or you'll all die!"

Disbelief rolled over Samson as he pulled himself up. This wasn't Thomas. This wasn't the gentle biker he'd known all his life. Somebody was pulling the strings behind the scenes, and as long as they couldn't separate Thomas from his puppet master, they couldn't pull him back from the path he'd chosen.

"We're leaving. For now," Samson conceded.

But they'd come back, and next time they'd bring an army. Whatever it took, they'd get Thomas back.

***

"I'm proud of you," Kasper said, patting him on the shoulder.

Thomas shook off his hand and walked to the fireplace in the living room where a low fire was burning. Despite it, he felt a chill creep into his bones. He'd felt it ever since he'd joined Kasper. As if all warmth had left him and ice was now running in his veins.

"There was no need to be out there with me. Or did you not trust me to handle them?"

"I don't trust them," Kasper deflected. "And I was right. They were trying to bring you back to their side. With force, as it turns out. Are those the actions of friends?"

Inside him, the dark power churned, pushing fury up his chest. "No."

"I protect those I love." Kasper's voice dropped to a husky murmur and Thomas felt him draw closer. He'd so far evaded all of Kasper's attempts at physical intimacy, and he wasn't in the mood for it now either.

"I want to be alone."

Kasper sighed, stopping in his approach. "Very well. Rest for a while. There's much to be done. And I need you well rested."

Thomas nodded and waited for Kasper to leave the room before he pressed his forehead against the mantle and braced his hands to either side. His head ached from the fight with Samson. And his heart beat frantically. He didn't like how he felt, how the dark power made him indifferent to the feelings and concerns of others. He felt nothing, only emptiness. Was this how his life would be now? He couldn't live like this. The tiny traces of scruples that emerged from his heart grew and made themselves increasingly felt.

He was jolted backwards instantly and felt the dark power inside him beat against the scruples that kept invading his mind. He'd been able to defeat the evil inside him for so many years, but it appeared that the ability had deserted him. He felt under its thrall, captive and bound. Was there no way back for him? No way to regain his humanity?

He glanced at the wood that was stacked up next to the fireplace, and bent down to toss another piece on the fire, when he felt something in his pocket. He reached inside and felt the stake that he carried with him at all times. He pulled it from his pocket and stared at it.

Maybe there was one way to defeat the power and destroy the hold it had over him.

Gripping the stake tightly in his right palm, he brought its tip to his chest. Swallowing hard, he clasped his other hand over it and took a breath. His thoughts went to Eddie and the way he'd looked at him that night before he'd driven off: with such promise in his eyes. Yet it had all been a lie.

He felt a sob rip from his chest, and closed his eyes. With all his strength, he thrust the stake against his heart, but he met resistance. His hands worked against an invisible foe, fighting to keep hold of the stake, struggling not to be pulled back. The tension in his shoulders increased and with a violent jolt his hands were ripped to the side, losing their grip on the stake. It tumbled into the fire as Thomas was thrown back. Disbelief coursed through him. His power was getting so strong that it was controlling his body now, and it wouldn't allow him to take his own life, because doing so would extinguish the power itself. And the power wanted to survive.

"Thomas," Xander's voice intruded from behind.

Thomas swiveled, furious at being interrupted, and lashed a glare at the vampire. Murderous thoughts boiled up inside him and he stretched his arms toward him, snarling.

"I said I wanted to be alone!"

Before his eyes, Xander's hands went around his own neck and he started squeezing it. Xander stared at him, stunned at his own actions. But Thomas continued to exert mind control on him and made him squeeze harder. Xander's attempts at fighting him off with mind control were futile. In fact, Thomas felt barely any power coming from him, whereas on the night he'd first entered this house, Xander had easily fought him off. None of that power was evident now.

Was it possible that Xander had had help that night? Had Kasper been able to channel his own power into Xander to help his follower defeat Thomas? To fool him into thinking all his followers were stronger and more powerful than they were?

Thomas released his mental hold on Xander, who then dropped his arms and coughed.

"Get out of my sight! Or I'll crush you!" he warned him.

With a panicked look on his face, Xander stumbled from the room.

Inside Thomas, the dark power started to settle. It had gotten its due for now. It had proven its superiority and been appeased. But for how long?

38

Eddie heard the ringing of his cell phone via his Bluetooth-equipped helmet as he navigated through light traffic. He'd been aimlessly combing the city for Thomas. Without success. With every hour that had passed, he felt worse because he knew this was his fault. Thomas had disappeared because of him, so it was his responsibility to find him.

He answered the call. "Yes?"

"Thought you should know. We know where Thomas is," Cain said.

Eddie's heart leapt, a weight lifting off his shoulders. Now everything would turn out all right. He'd go and see him and talk to him. Confess what he really felt in his heart, and apologize. "Where?"

"Uhm, he's with Xander and his people."

Shock made his heart stop. "They captured him? Fuck!" His hands curled into claws and his fangs descended. He'd get those bastards and skin them alive if they hurt Thomas.

"No, Eddie. They didn't."

"But you just said—"

"He joined them," Cain interrupted.

"Joined? He would never!" Eddie tried to wrap his brain around the information as he slowed his motorcycle.

"Afraid so. I figured you'd want to know, given you and he . . . " There was a pregnant pause on the other end of the line. "Listen, it's none of my business, but if you love him, now might be the time to help him. If anybody can get through to him, it's you."

Stunned, Eddie sucked in a breath of air. How could Cain know that he loved Thomas when he'd only just realized it himself? "How did you find out?"

"I saw you and him kissing in his garage. I didn't mean to spy on you; I just happened to come by."

"Fuck!" Eddie hissed.

"Hey," Cain said quickly. "I'm not judging. Whatever floats your boat. I'm just saying if there's anything you and he have to air out to make up—"

"Make up?"

"It's pretty obvious. When you guys were at Oliver's party, there was some tension. And then Thomas left early. Listen, I don't care what this is about. None of my business. But if there's anything you can do . . . Samson tried, but didn't get through to him. Amaury told me that Thomas claims he's got nothing left to lose."

"Ah shit," Eddie cursed. Thomas had snapped because of him. "No need to say any more. Who's on guard in Chinatown?"

"Jay, why?"

"Call him and tell him I'll relieve him in fifteen minutes."

"What are you planning?"

What he'd been planning all along. "I'm going to talk to Thomas." And if talking wasn't enough, he might just have to drop to one knee. Hadn't Thomas once said that he didn't find it old fashioned to drop to one's knee? Well, suddenly, Eddie didn't find it old fashioned anymore either.

Eddie turned his motorcycle around and headed for Chinatown, reaching it in record time. He parked the bike and walked to the dark entryway where Jay stood waiting.

"Any movement?" Eddie asked by way of greeting.

Jay shook his head. "Nobody entered or exited in the entire two hours I've been here. It's all yours."

Eddie lifted his hand, bidding him goodbye and looked at the house across the street. The lights were on in several rooms, but he couldn't detect any movements inside the house. He shoved a hand through his hair, brushing it away from his face, and realized that it was a gesture he'd picked up from Thomas.

During the many months they'd lived together, he'd grown so used to Thomas. What had started out as a mentorship had morphed into a friendship, and now that he'd driven Thomas away, he finally realized how much his friendship meant to him. But friendship alone wasn't enough anymore. In the last week, his feelings for Thomas had deepened and turned from friendship into love in the blink of an eye. It was time to man up, as Thomas had demanded. He was ready now.

With determined steps, Eddie crossed the street and walked up the few steps to the entrance door of the house. He rang the doorbell, once, twice, then a third time. He strained to listen, but no sounds came from the inside.

"Thomas!" he called out. "It's me, Eddie!"

Thomas would hear him, he was convinced of it. Still, nobody came to the door. Frustrated, he exhaled. But he wouldn't give up now. He'd come this far and wouldn't let a flimsy door stop him.

He looked to his right. Or a window. Bracing himself at the railing with one hand, he kicked his leg up, shoving his booted foot through the glass, which shattered on impact. He reached inside it with his hand and unlocked the sash, then pushed it open. Hoisting himself up, he crawled through the narrow opening.

When he was inside, he jumped up instantly, ready to defend himself should one of Xander's people already be waiting for him, but to his surprise, he was alone in the foyer. Even a human should have heard his forced entry. In a house full of vampires, they should have been on him like dogs on a mailman. Something was wrong.

His gut constricting with unease, he walked farther into the house. There was a large living room on this floor, the door of which stood wide open. It was warm inside, but equally empty. Eddie glanced at the fireplace: a low fire was still crackling there, evidence that whoever had been here couldn't have left too long ago.

Eddie turned and continued his search, his senses alert to be prepared for a possible ambush as he walked up the stairs. Most rooms on the second floor were bedrooms interspersed with several bathrooms. The windows were hung with heavy drapes, and the disorder in the rooms indicated that the inhabitants had left in a hurry. But how?

The house had been watched ever since they'd found out that it was Xander's headquarters. And Jay had confirmed that nobody had come or left.

His surveillance of the top floor didn't yield any other results. It was just as empty as the other floors. Frustrated, he walked down to the first floor and looked around once more. He turned to the living room, letting his eyes wander over the furniture and the wood-paneled walls. Then he marched back into the hallway. The door to the half bath stood open. Besides a toilet and a sink, a large, floor-to-ceiling mirror graced one wall. Eddie saw no reflection of himself in it and turned away from the useless item.

An errant thought penetrated his mind. If he still had to shave, he would probably have had a hard time doing it without the help of a mirror. Vampires didn't reflect in mirrors, so it was rare that a vampire had any in his home.

Eddie whirled back to the half bath. He walked inside and looked at the sink. The mirror above it was missing, just as in many homes belonging to vampires. His gaze swept back to the full-size mirror. It didn't belong here. If somebody had gone through the pains of removing the mirror above the sink, why had he left the tall mirror standing? It made no sense. Unless the mirror served another purpose.

His heart beating faster than usual, he ran his hands around the frame of the mirror, feeling for any indentation or hook, when his fingers encountered a groove on one side. He pressed against it and heard a click. Gripping the frame, he pulled the mirror toward him, away from the wall and peered behind it. A dark tunnel opened up before him. He sniffed and smelled the scent of vampires who'd used it only recently.

His vampire vision was sufficient for him to see into the tunnel and realize that it was empty. Without hesitation, he walked into it and followed it around a bend. By his estimation, it was at least a hundred feet long, most likely longer, and when it suddenly stopped after another turn, he found himself in front of a door. He listened for any sounds, and heard cars going by.

Stunned, he turned the knob and pulled the door toward him, opening it only a sliver to peek outside. He was at street level. He opened the door wider and stepped out onto the pavement, searching for a street sign. He found it instantly and realized that the hidden tunnel had led him to a street parallel to the one Xander's headquarters stood on. The vampires had snuck out this way while Scanguards had watched the front, unaware of the secret escape route.

"Shit!" he cursed and pulled his cell phone from his pocket.

As he speed-dialed Gabriel's number, he rushed back to where he'd parked his motorcycle.

"Yes?" Gabriel's tense voice came through the line.

"The house in Chinatown is empty. Thomas is gone. They're all gone." The words suddenly sank in, and his heart constricted as if somebody were squeezing it with an iron fist. He needed to find Thomas.

"How the fuck—?"

"I found a secret walkway leading to the street behind it," Eddie interrupted him.

"Shit!"

Having reached his motorcycle, Eddie swung himself onto it, jammed the key into the ignition, turned it, and hit the starter button. The engine howled and he kicked away the stand.

"I'll be at HQ in fifteen minutes."

Without waiting for Gabriel's answer, he disconnected the call.

Now he could only hope that Thomas hadn't disabled the GPS chip in his own cell phone yet. He had to hurry to get to the IT lab at Scanguards to run a trace and see if he could locate him via his phone. Quickly, Eddie dialed the IT lab's number so they could start setting up the trace. He didn't even want to think what to do if that didn't work, because the prospect of losing Thomas hurt more than he'd ever imagined anything could hurt. Thomas was his best friend and the only lover he'd ever wanted. He needed Thomas like he needed his next breath, and living without him for the rest of eternity was unimaginable.

39

The elevator doors opened, and Eddie rushed onto the executive floor of Scanguards' headquarters. He'd already been in the IT lab and run a trace on Thomas's phone, with disappointing results: Thomas had disabled his phone, making it impossible to be located.

The floor was buzzing with activity. He almost collided with Nina as she came around a corner.

"Eddie!"

"Fuck, Nina, what are you doing here? You're not even allowed on this floor."

Nina rolled her eyes. "For your information, the no-humans rule on the executive floor doesn't apply to blood-bonded mates. And besides, have you forgotten that you were supposed to meet me?"

Eddie ran a shaky hand through his hair and down his nape, feeling the perspiration that had built there. "What for?" His mind drew a blank.

"To look at that apartment near the waterfront. I told you about it. Don't tell me you've already forgotten. Gee, can't you put those things in your calendar?"

Eddie sighed. Maybe this was as good a time as any to come clean. "Nina, I'm not moving out."

She stared at him, her eyes widening in surprise. "What?"

Eddie put his hand around her arm and pulled her into the copier room. "We need to talk."

Nina looked up at him, a frown building on her face. "I hate it when somebody starts a conversation like that. It never ends well."

"You might have a point there," he admitted, hesitating for a moment. He rocked back on his heels, shoving his hands into his pockets. "There's something you need to know." He took a deep breath. "Nina, I'm gay. And Thomas is my lover."

He expelled a breath and looked away, not wanting to see the disappointment in her eyes. Not a word came from his sister, only stunned silence greeted him. He swallowed past the lump in his throat.

"I'm sorry," he murmured. "I didn't choose this. It just happened. And I can't make it undone. I am what I am. I didn't mean to disappoint you again."

When a soft palm touched his forearm, he jerked his head up.

Nina looked at him, her brown eyes focused on him. "Disappoint me? Oh, Eddie, you're not disappointing me. You're my brother, my family. I love you no matter what." She sighed. "Looks like my *gaydar* is completely off these days. I really didn't see this coming."

He tentatively returned her smile. Was she accepting him the way he was?

"How long have you been hiding this from me?"

He shrugged. "I'm not sure, Sis. I guess I've always known, but I suppressed it so much that I never realized what was going on inside me. But when I was turned, everything changed. My . . . uh . . . desires became stronger, you know. And then when I overheard somebody say that Thomas has the hots for me, I guess it triggered something in me."

"You overheard somebody?"

"Long story. Doesn't matter anymore. It happened, and I'm glad for it now. But I screwed up, Nina. I screwed up royally." He sighed heavily, bringing his hands to his face, holding back the sob that wanted to escape from his chest.

Nina reached for him and stroked his cheek. "Screwed up how?"

He met her eyes and saw concern there. And something else: acceptance. How could he have ever doubted that she would still love him?

"Thomas wanted me to come out and admit that I'm gay. I couldn't do it. I rejected him, Nina. I hurt him. That's why he's gone over to the other side. He's joined those vampires who are committing those crimes all over the city. Because I was too much of a coward to stand up and tell everybody that I love him. Hell, I couldn't even tell Thomas that I love him."

"But you do love him?"

Eddie nodded. "With all my heart. I can't lose him, Nina. I can't."

Nina wrapped her arms around him. "Then you'll have to do everything in your power to get him back."

He hugged her closely to him.

"Whatever you need, I'll be there for you," she whispered.

"Thank you." Reluctantly he released her. Then he opened the door to the hallway. "You should go home now. We have a lot of things to take care of tonight."

She nodded and followed him out into the corridor. "Call me as soon as you hear something."

"I will. And I'm sorry I made you look for apartments."

She smiled in response, and he watched her walk toward the elevator.

Behind him a door opened. "Eddie! You're here."

Eddie turned to see Gabriel motion him to his office, his face grim. "Just got back."

"Good. Before you do anything else, you'll need to reactivate my password. The idiots in IT said they don't have access, and I can't do anything without going into our systems."

Eddie marched past Gabriel and fell into the chair behind his desk, opening up a new window on the monitor. "I should be able to get in. Thomas gave me access to the management profiles."

"That's the best news I've heard all night," Gabriel replied, looking over Eddie's shoulder.

Eddie logged into the control system and navigated to the correct screen, scrolling down the list of names to find Gabriel's.

"Here you are," he murmured to himself and selected Gabriel's profile. A new screen popped up and Eddie started typing. He hit enter, but the line he'd been filling in didn't populate with the new password. Instead, a beep sounded.

"What the fuck?" he cursed and typed the password again. Another beep sounded.

"What's wrong?" Gabriel asked.

"I don't know." Eddie felt perspiration running down his nape and disappearing under the collar of his T-shirt. Suspicion crept up his spine like fast-growing ivy and curled around his neck like a boa constrictor. He minimized the window and opened up a different one, then logged into it. He clicked on the first icon that popped up and tried to open it, but a pop-up told him 'access denied'. The sight made his blood freeze in his veins.

"Shit! Shit! Shit!"

He clicked on the next icon and tried to open it, but the same thing happened.

"Eddie, what's going on?" Gabriel asked, his voice now more agitated than before.

"My access to the data nodes was revoked."

"English please!" Gabriel barked.

"I can't do anything in our IT system anymore."

"But you just logged in!" Gabriel protested.

Eddie clenched his teeth. "And now somebody's thrown me out."

"Who?"

Eddie turned to look over his shoulder, staring straight at Gabriel. "Thomas." More beeps made him look back at the screen. More windows popped up, all saying 'access denied.'

"He's revoking everybody's access. Gabriel, he's shutting us down."

"Oh, fuck!" Gabriel cursed. "What is he planning?"

Before Eddie could answer, a deafening alarm bell started to ring. It was accompanied by strobe lights in the hallway. He knew instantly what it meant.

"He's locking us in."

"Stop him!" Gabriel yelled.

Eddie jumped up. "I've gotta get to the servers in the basement." As he ran into the corridor, others came running from their offices.

Samson charged out of his office. "Who's doing this?"

"Thomas. He's shutting us down!" Eddie replied as he ran past him and pushed the door to the stairs open.

He knew the elevator would already be disabled. His heart stopped for a moment. Had Nina made it down in time and exited the building? Concern for his sister made him run faster. The server room was the only place where he could get into the system via a backdoor and immobilize Thomas.

Eddie reached the basement and grabbed the handle of the door that led to the hallway, but was flung back against the wall instantly. An electric shock had catapulted him back. The door was electrified.

"Fuck!"

He labored to regain his breath and lifted himself up on shaky legs, bracing himself with his hands on his thighs for a moment. Things were worse than he'd expected. Thomas was using all weapons at his disposal.

Eddie rushed up the stairs again, reaching the executive floor a few moments later. Gabriel, Samson, Zane, and several others congregated in the hallway. They turned their heads to him as he charged in, their eyes full of questions.

"Thomas is in the building!"

"Did you see him?" Samson asked.

Eddie shook his head. "He sealed off the basement. The access door is electrified. He must be in the server room."

Curses bounced against the walls of the hallway.

"He's got us by the throat," Samson said, his mouth set in a grim line.

Suddenly loud banging could be heard from the direction of the elevator, coupled with a faint voice. "Help! Help me!"

A bolt of panic shot through Eddie as he ran toward the elevator, just as Amaury came running from the other side.

"Nina!" Eddie called out, but his voice was drowned out by Amaury's.

"Nina! Chérie! We'll get you out!"

40

Thomas looked over his shoulder, watching as Kasper instructed his men to sweep all rooms in the basement and guard the electrified door leading to the stairs. Xander stood close, waiting.

With all of Kasper's disciples assembled in such close proximity, Thomas sensed their powers more intensely now. In fact, he could almost isolate which strand of power belonged to which vampire as if they were colored ribbons hanging around a maypole. The power flowing from Kasper was by far the strongest, and his own power was drawn to it as to a magnet.

Thomas had used his keycard to gain access to the building via the parking garage, making sure, by remotely logging into Scanguards' intranet, that his access had not been restricted. Not that he would have had to worry about that: there was nobody in the entire company who would have been able to shut him out. Nobody had a higher IT clearance than he. Besides, he'd surprised them by attacking where they thought they were safest. They hadn't seen this coming.

Kasper had planted the idea in him that a clean takeover would be best for all involved.

"It's time to issue our demands," Kasper said now, turning to him. "Everything is in place, isn't it?"

Thomas nodded slowly, looking back at the surveillance monitors in front of him. He checked all entrance points and verified that they were locked. Nobody would be able to enter or exit the building without his permission.

"Everything is set. Nobody moves without me knowing about it."

"Then let's get this show on the road."

Thomas typed a command into the keyboard in front of him, then pulled the microphone close to his mouth.

"Will Samson hear you no matter where he is?" Kasper asked.

"The intercom broadcasts into every room in this building. Everybody will hear what I've got to say."

"Do it!"

Thomas pressed the button at the base of the microphone. He inhaled slowly. "By now, you probably all know that I've taken over this building." He exchanged a look with Kasper, before continuing, "Samson, I've finally found my way back to my roots. I am what I am. And Kasper has shown me the way. I can't deny the power in me any longer. And now, with Kasper by my side, I've claimed that power. I will no longer hide from it."

Thomas closed his eyes for a moment, feeling a strange feeling in his gut that was trying to work itself up into his chest. Using his dark power, he forced it down.

"I've helped you build this company, and I realize now that none of you are worthy to run it. I've proven that today. You're my prisoners now. Had you bothered to curb my authority and put checks and balances in place to stop me from overstepping my domain, this would have never happened. As it is, you let me implement fail-safes that I am now using against you. You shouldn't have trusted me."

Because trust was a dangerous thing. He'd trusted Eddie to keep his heart safe, and Eddie had tossed it to the dogs. Eddie had betrayed him in the worst possible way. The pain, still fresh and ever-present, sent another painful spear through his heart. He'd hoped that by claiming his dark power and exercising it, the pain would vanish, just as all other feelings of concern for his fellow vampires had vanished. Where he'd been a caring man before, there was simply a void. He felt nothing. Nothing but the pain of Eddie's betrayal. Nothing could ever stamp it out.

"I won't bore you any longer. Here's what you'll do, Samson. You'll sign Scanguards over to me. Amaury and Gabriel will do the same with their interests in the company. You have ten minutes. I'm opening up the intercom in your office for you to respond."

He was about to press the intercom button to switch off the microphone when Kasper stopped him and bent to it. "I'm afraid my dear Thomas is far too nice. This is Kasper, his maker. And I am a little less patient than he is. Sign the company over to us or the human currently stuck in the elevator dies." A grin spread on his lips, then he pressed the button, muting the intercom.

Thomas's glance shot to the monitors in front of him, searching for the video feed that showed the interior of the elevator. Nina's blond locks were easy to distinguish against the dark lining of the interior.

Stunned, he looked up at his maker. Kasper had assured him earlier that nobody would die tonight.

***

Eddie exchanged a frantic look with Amaury.

"Shit!" Eddie cursed. "We've gotta get her out now!"

His brother-in-law's fingernails had already turned into claws, and he now tried to jam the sharp edges in between the two doors to try to pry them apart. His neck muscles tensed and he breathed heavily.

"Where's the fucking manual release?" Eddie cried out, rushing to Amaury's side, falling to his knees and trying to do the same as Amaury, lower down. But the doors didn't move.

"There's a panel somewhere," Cain answered from behind.

"Find it!" Amaury ordered.

Eddie heard Nina's panicked voice from inside the elevator. "Get me out of here, Amaury, please! Before he does it!"

Eddie had nearly forgotten that the intercom could be heard in the elevator too. Nina had heard every single word of Kasper's threat.

Amaury's expression was gloomy. "It'll be all right, chérie. We're nearly there," he lied. Then lower, he whispered to Eddie, anguish in his face. "I can't lose her."

His last word was drowned out by Samson's voice coming over the intercom. "Thomas, stop this madness. We know this is not your doing. You're being manipulated. Whoever this man is who claims to be Kasper, you know it can't be he. Kasper is dead. He has no power over you anymore. We can work all this out. We're friends. You'd never hurt your friends."

Then Thomas's voice cut in again. Eddie felt his heart bleed as he heard it, cold and emotionless. "You're wrong, Samson. Kasper is very much alive. He and I belong together. He can give me the love I need. The love that I deserve."

Eddie knew instantly that the last words were meant for him, not for Samson. Thomas was craving his love, and it was Eddie's fault that he now turned to an evil man like Kasper. How Kasper could still be alive when he'd seen him die in front of his own eyes, Eddie didn't know. But what he did know was that Kasper was evil. Thomas had said so himself after his mind control fight with him a few months earlier. Thomas hated his maker.

"Check the printer in your office, Samson," Thomas's voice continued over the intercom. "The contract is there. Sign it, you, Gabriel, and Amaury. When you're done, let me know."

There was a click, and silence descended on the floor. All Eddie heard was Amaury's heavy breathing as he continued to try to pry the doors apart.

"The elevator doors won't open," Kasper's voice suddenly sounded over the loudspeakers. "There's no use in trying. And the manual release you're looking for has been disabled."

Then a loud sound from the elevator, coupled with a shriek from Nina, tore through the hallway. Within a second, the sound stopped, but Nina's crying could be heard through the doors.

"Sign the fucking papers, or next time I won't just drop her half a floor. I'll drop her all the way to the basement," Kasper announced.

"I'm going to kill that fucking bastard!" Amaury screamed.

"I'll sign the papers," Samson's voice came over the loudspeaker.

Eddie charged to the open door of Samson's office, watching as his boss took several sheets of paper from the printer. "Don't!"

Samson spun around. "You heard him. He's going to kill your sister if I don't give in to his demand."

"And he'll also kill her once you sign. If this man is really Kasper—and I have no idea how that's possible—but if that man in the basement is Thomas's maker, then he's evil to the core. He will kill any and all of us just because he can. He's toying with us, don't you see that? He's enjoying the power Thomas gave him over us. We're the mice, and he's the cat. The only person who can stop him is Thomas."

Samson slammed his fist on the desk. "Thomas is under his thrall. I could feel it when I confronted him at the house earlier. He's not himself. He said he's got nothing left to lose. Thomas won't help us. We've lost him. All we can do is try to save Nina ourselves."

Eddie gave a slow shake of his head. "There's one other way." He walked around Samson's desk and reached for the microphone. "I'll bring him back to us. Because I'm the reason he left us."

Samson stepped aside, a look of curiosity on his face. When Eddie looked past him, he noticed his colleagues at the door.

"What's going on?" Zane asked.

Eddie sat down in Samson's chair and leaned over the microphone, then pushed the button. "Thomas, it's Eddie. I know you probably don't want to listen to me right now, but there's something I've got to say to you and to everybody here at Scanguards." He paused, collecting his courage. "I'm gay, and I'm not ashamed of it anymore. Because of you, I've finally found who I really am."

He noticed the surprised looks on his colleagues' faces, but continued concentrating on his speech. "Thomas, I'm sorry for what happened at Oliver's party. I was wrong to reject you. I was afraid. But I'm no longer afraid. Thomas, I love you. Not just as a friend. I love you as my partner, my lover, my forever. I didn't mean to hurt you. I beg you to forgive me. You once said that for the right person, you would fall on your knees. Thomas, if you'll come back to me, I'll fall on my knees. Because you're the only person I ever wanted and needed. I love you."

Eddie clicked the button to mute the intercom and looked up. He sensed moisture in his eyes, but felt no embarrassment when he looked at his colleagues. With understanding in their eyes they looked back at him.

41

". . . I love you."

Eddie's words echoed in Thomas's mind, ricocheting inside him like a stray bullet. Was he hallucinating, or had he really just heard Eddie confess his love for him in front of all of Scanguards? Eddie had to have known that the intercom would broadcast his words into every room in the building. Still, he'd said them. He'd come out publicly.

"You can't possibly believe what he's saying!" Kasper sniped next to him. "It's clearly a ploy to get you to surrender control over Scanguards." He pointed his finger up to the loudspeaker from which the words had echoed. "He's lying to you. As soon as you give up, he'll recant. His colleagues probably put him up to it since they know how you feel about him. It's all a lie. He doesn't love you. Not like I do!"

Thomas recognized desperation when he smelled it. And Kasper was desperate to save the day. It meant Kasper too had heard the sincerity in Eddie's words. They were true. Thomas felt it in his heart. As it warmed and pushed against the dark power that surrounded it, he suddenly felt an invading force. It was subtle, yet he recognized it: Kasper had slipped into his mind and was hiding within the layers of Thomas's dark powers. He recognized it so clearly now, almost as if feeling Eddie's love had opened his eyes and lifted the veil that had hung over him for the last few days. Just as Eddie's love now gave him the strength to push the dark power away.

There was only one thing he could do now.

"You're right, Kasper. It's a ploy. And I'm going to tell him just what I think of that."

Kasper grinned with a self-congratulatory smirk. "That's my man."

Thomas pressed the button for the intercom and chose his words carefully. "That was a nice speech, Eddie. Congratulations. If only it were true. Even if it were, it's too late. Because, you see, you computer genius, the key was always *I love Eddie*. You can have that now, I won't need it anymore. So I'm gonna let you mull that one over, you IT wannabe. Because this is the last thing you'll hear from me until this is done." He switched off the microphone.

"What the fuck was that garbage?" Kasper growled and glared at him.

"As I said, I told him what I think of the crap he fed me. I fed him the same nonsense. He'll get it!"

Thomas hoped so with all his heart, because what was hidden in his garbled speech was his password to the company's systems. Since Thomas had disabled everybody else's login, only his own login now had control over Scanguards. If Eddie could figure out that he'd just been handed the password to Thomas's login, he would be able to take over control. In the meantime, Thomas had to buy some time.

Keeping one eye on the computer screen, Thomas stood up and put his hand on Kasper's arm. Then he motioned to Xander, who was standing a few yards away from them.

"Why don't you ask Xander to help the others guard the doors?" He stroked suggestively over Kasper's arm.

A spark ignited in Kasper's eyes. Without looking away from Thomas, he issued his order. "Xander go join the others."

Thomas waited until Xander had left the room. The door was still open, but it didn't matter. There was an illusion of privacy and it was all Thomas needed now.

"I don't want there to be any more lies between us," Thomas started and pulled his hand off Kasper's arm.

A disappointed glance was Kasper's answer. "There are no lies between us."

"There are things you haven't explained to me. And if this is going to work between us, then I have to know everything."

"But you know everything," Kasper protested.

Thomas turned away, clandestinely glancing at the computer screen to see if anything was happening. But the curser blinked evenly.

"You told me that Keegan was the one who committed all those atrocities. And you claimed that your followers were still doing the same, but that you didn't order the torture of Sergio and his mate."

He heard a quick intake of breath behind him.

"Don't get me wrong, I have nothing against a little torture when it's warranted," Thomas lied. "But I'd expect you to be honest with me about it. How can we be partners when you hide things from me?" He paused for a moment. "And if you want a blood-bond, then you have to be honest with me."

He turned back to face Kasper, looking at his stunned expression. Yes, he'd guessed right: Kasper not only wanted him back, he wanted a bond, one that was stronger than anything else, one that would make them both stronger by combining their dark powers.

"You do want a blood-bond, don't you?" He placed his hand back on Kasper's arm.

"Yes!" Kasper stepped closer as if he wanted to kiss him, but Thomas turned his head to the side.

"Then tell me the truth. Tell me everything. As your future mate, I deserve it." Thomas almost choked on the words. He couldn't imagine anything viler than bonding with Kasper. He never again wanted to be in contact with such evil.

As he waited for Kasper's answer, Thomas perceived a movement on the computer screen. Lines of code scrolled over it. He suppressed the sigh of relief that wanted to burst from his chest. Soon this would be over.

"Well, if you put it that way," Kasper hedged, "you're right, of course. Keegan and I were much more similar than I would like to admit. Apart from our sexual appetites of course. Those were very different. But the dark power in us craves the same tributes. You feel it in yourself too, don't you?"

Thomas nodded automatically, still avoiding Kasper's gaze. "I feel the urge to hurt somebody." And that wasn't even a lie.

"Yes, it feels good, doesn't it? Just as it felt good when I forced Sergio to hurt his mate."

"You were there yourself?" Thomas suppressed the impulse to slice Kasper's throat open at the knowledge that he'd done the deed himself.

"I never miss an opportunity like that. When I realized that Sergio wasn't going to play ball, I called a few of my followers so they could watch and learn." Kasper leaned closer, dropping his voice. "From time to time, you'll have to do similar things to show them who's the master. If they don't fear you, they'll start to think they're more powerful than you. You never want that to happen."

Bile rose in Thomas's stomach. He forced a few words over his lips to continue buying Eddie and his colleagues more time. "Just like you killed Wu, your attorney."

"He deserved it. Greedy bastard. And what a sniveling little weasel. He found out that I had a twin brother, and he was going to tell Xander and the others. It would have undermined my authority."

"I understand. And Keegan, when he came to San Francisco, you followed him."

The smile was evident in Kasper's voice when he answered, "As I told you before, that's how I found you. At first, I wanted to help my brother, but when I realized who he was fighting against, I had to make a choice. I chose not to intervene. I couldn't very well let you die. Besides, I was growing sick of sharing the throne with him. His antics were getting on my nerves. Brother or not, he had to go. Between you and me, Scanguards did me a favor by getting rid of him. And as an added bonus, they also killed the men who were with him. There were no other witnesses, and when I returned to my followers, they weren't the wiser. Nobody knew of Keegan's death, because to them there'd never been a Keegan."

"So it worked out perfectly for you," Thomas concluded.

"I couldn't have planned it any better. Now you and I are reunited." Kasper's hand came up to cup Thomas's chin, and he pulled his face back to him. He lowered his lips and Thomas felt an ice-cold shiver run down his spine.

A rumbling sound came from the outside, and Kasper suddenly pulled back. "What the fuck is that?" he called out to the hallway.

"The elevator!" Xander shouted. "It's moving!"

"Shit!" Kasper cursed, then looked back at Thomas. "Make it stop!" he commanded.

Thomas used both his hands to catapult Kasper away from him, slamming him against a desk. "No!"

Kasper's eyes widened, recognition illuminating them. "You betrayed me!"

"And now I'm going to destroy you!" Thomas promised and focused all his mental power on his maker, just as he heard the ping of the elevator announcing that it had reached the basement. "Go to hell, Kasper, where you belong!"

42

Eddie nodded to Samson, giving him the signal to open the door. As it swung open, Eddie and Amaury rushed into the basement corridor, their semi-automatic guns pointed straight ahead while unleashing a barrage of silver bullets toward the unsuspecting vampires who were shooting into the empty elevator as its doors opened.

Several of their opponents fell instantly, disintegrating slowly as the silver bullets burned them from the inside, until their forms were mere ash. The others sought shelter in the offices lining the hallway.

"Did you leave me any?" Zane shouted as he charged into the hallway.

Eddie motioned to one of the open doors one of the vampires had disappeared into. "Be my guest."

As Zane approached the room, covered by Samson, Eddie locked eyes with Amaury and pointed to another room. Amaury nodded.

Eddie pressed himself along the wall next to the door, then took a deep breath, steeling himself for the assault. In vampire speed, he whirled around, stepping into the doorframe, his eyes spotting his enemy instantly. His gun was pointed at its target, but before he could pull the trigger, a flash of energy pierced through his head as if somebody had stuck a knife into it. Instinct told him that the vampire was attacking him with mind control, even though he'd never experienced firsthand what it felt like.

The pain that shot through him was something he'd never felt before. His knees buckled and his hand holding the gun lowered. At the same time, his own mind tried to ward off the attack. But he wasn't prepared.

Shit!

The vampire gave him a nasty grin, then he lifted his gun and aimed at Eddie. Frozen by the mind control the vampire exerted on him, Eddie couldn't move. Fuck, he would die here without having had a chance to feel Thomas's arms around him once more.

The sound of a bullet tore past him, and suddenly, the invisible chains that had held him in place loosened, and the pain in his head ceased. Stunned, he stared at his attacker and saw blood running from a wound in his forehead. The vampire's eyes looked at him with a blank stare and then his face started crumbling from the inside, ash flaking off his skin, before he collapsed in a heap of dust.

"You're welcome," Amaury said from behind him.

Eddie turned and nodded gratefully to his brother-in-law. "Let's get the rest of them."

Peering out into the corridor, he saw more Scanguards personnel rush in from the door to the stairs, guns at the ready.

Eddie rushed in the other direction, heading for the server room. Amaury remained on his heels. At the next open door, he stopped and peered in, seeing Zane battling with one of the assailants as Samson had fallen to his knees, pressing his hands to his temples, his face distorted in agony.

"Fuck!" Eddie cursed and aimed at the vampire who was fighting with Zane, but Zane was in the way. Eddie didn't have a clear shot. He hesitated for a moment, but then made a decision. "Zane, drop!"

Instantly, Zane dove to the floor, giving him a clear line of sight. Eddie pulled the trigger and the silver bullet hit the target. His hours at the shooting range had paid off.

He didn't wait to see the vampire disintegrate into dust, but instead rushed to the end of the corridor, where the server room was located. Before he even reached the open door, he already knew what was going on inside it. The sparks flying around in the room illuminated the corridor in short bursts.

When he peered into the room, a sense of déjà vu overcame him. He'd seen the exact same scene a few months earlier. Thomas was engaged in a mental fight with his maker, Kasper, or Keegan as he'd called himself then. And the man looked exactly like Keegan. How it was possible, Eddie didn't know and didn't care. All he cared about was ending this fight and saving Thomas.

Without hesitation, he aimed. But just like Zane, Thomas whirled around his opponent, not giving him a clear shot.

"Thomas!" he shouted. "Get down!"

But Thomas didn't react, too engaged in the mental fight. It was questionable whether he heard him at all.

"Fuck!" Eddie cursed and leveled his gun in Kasper's direction.

His hand shook, and sweat dripped from his forehead. Then a calming hand touched his shoulder.

"Wait for it," Zane said, his voice soothing. "Aim at where he's going to be, not where he is now. Then squeeze the trigger. Just like I taught you. What Portia said is true. I did compliment you on being an excellent marksman."

Zane's confidence in him lent him strength, and he forced his heartbeat to slow down, taking steadying breaths.

"Just squeeze," Zane repeated.

Calming his mind, Eddie gave control over to his body and fired the gun. His heart stopped. The sparks that had rendered the air electrical ceased. The mind control fight was over.

Eddie stared at Thomas and Kasper, searching for the place where his bullet had entered. Kasper's head suddenly turned to him, and shock coursed through Eddie's body. Had he missed?

Then a trickle of blood ran from Kasper's ear down his neck. As if watching TV in slow motion, Eddie watched Kasper's body disintegrate into ash from the inside out.

Eddie felt his body shake uncontrollably and reached for the doorframe to support himself. Then his eyes locked with Thomas's and strength returned to his limbs. He pushed himself away from the door and dropped his gun onto the nearest desk.

With a determined gait, he walked to Thomas, stopping right in front of him. "I don't care who sees us; I have to do this."

Putting his hand to Thomas's nape, he pulled him close and sank his lips onto him, searing Thomas's mouth with a passionate kiss. Eddie drove his tongue between his lover's parted lips, savoring the masculine taste and the powerful strokes with which Thomas responded to his kiss. Strong arms drew him closer, holding him tightly. Eddie groaned as he felt Thomas's hard body rub against his. He slipped one hand over Thomas's ass and squeezed, pressing him closer and making him aware of his need.

When Thomas finally pushed against him, severing the kiss and bringing some distance between them, he let it happen only reluctantly. "We've gotta stop," Thomas whispered against his lips. "We're not alone."

Only now did Eddie hear the clearing of throats from behind him. "I'm not ashamed of you. Of us."

Thomas smiled at him, his eyes twinkling with affection, acknowledging his admission without a word. Then he stroked his knuckles over Eddie's cheek.

Eddie turned around to face his colleagues, who all stood just inside the server room, looking in different directions, some of them staring at their shoes, slightly embarrassed. Nina stood among them, smiling brightly at him, the fear she'd experienced in the elevator wiped from her face. He returned her smile.

"You can look again," Eddie said.

Several pairs of eyes landed on him and Thomas. Then, deliberately, he took Thomas's hand into his, earning a smile from his lover.

Thomas sighed. "I'm sorry about what happened. I had no control over what I was doing. Kasper . . ." Thomas pointed to where his maker's ash covered the floor.

Samson nodded. "You did the right thing in the end by giving Eddie your password."

"It took me a few minutes to figure it out. First I thought you'd gone completely crazy. You've never called me a computer genius or an IT wannabe before. It made no sense," Eddie explained.

"That was the point," Thomas confirmed. "I knew you'd try to figure it out because what I said to you was gibberish. I know how your mind works."

Eddie nodded, then motioned to the heap of ash on the floor. "What about him? Who was he?"

Thomas sighed. "Kasper, my maker."

"But Kasper was already dead! Rose shot him months ago!" Eddie protested.

Thomas shook his head. "That's what we all thought. But the vampire who died that night wasn't Kasper, he was his twin, Keegan. Nobody knew he had a twin, not even I. He fooled us all."

Surprised grunts echoed in the room.

"Is it over now?" Samson asked.

Thomas gave his boss a long look. "I don't know Samson. I honestly don't know. The dark power is still inside me. It'll always be there."

"You were able to defeat it tonight. You defied Kasper by giving Eddie your password. And then you attacked Kasper. There must have been a reason why you were able to fight against it," Samson suggested.

Eddie looked intently at Thomas, who turned to him and locked eyes with him. "There was a reason. When you confessed your love for me I felt stronger, and I was able to fight against the influence that Kasper had over me. I was able to fight the dark power inside me because your love filled my heart."

Eddie pressed his hand over Thomas's heart. "Then you'll never again have to worry about the dark power inside you controlling you. Because my love will always be there." He leaned in.

"Uh, guys, before you kiss again," Gabriel interrupted, "can you please restore our logins so we can get this place back in shape and cleaned up?"

Thomas smirked. "I think that can be arranged."

43

Thomas wrapped the towel around his lower half out of habit and stepped out of his ensuite bathroom. His bedroom was bathed in the soft light given off by a single bedside lamp. His eyes roamed over the bed and drank in the sight before him.

"I know now that I've always dreamed of this: to wait in your bed for you," Eddie said and lifted the thin duvet off his body, pushing it aside. "Naked." He put his palm around his erection and stroked it suggestively. "And hard."

Thomas let his eyes wander over Eddie's nude form, his defined, hairless chest, the hard planes of his abdominal muscles, the thatch of dark blond hair that surrounded his cock, and down to the strong thighs that would soon wrap around his hips when Thomas plunged into him.

Thomas felt the urge to pinch himself to make sure this wasn't a dream. But he knew it was a dream—a dream that had finally come true. Eddie lay in his bed, naked, and hungry for sex. No, not just sex, he corrected himself, hungry to make love. But before he touched Eddie, he had to do one thing.

His heart beating into his throat, Thomas approached the bed, but instead of joining Eddie on it, he dropped down to one knee and brought his hand in front of his body, revealing the small, velvet-covered box he held in it.

Eddie instantly reared up and moved to the edge of the bed, dropping his feet onto the floor, his eyes wide with the realization of what Thomas intended to do.

"Thomas—"

"Please, let me do this my way," Thomas urged, locking eyes with him.

Silently, Eddie nodded.

"I loved you from the moment I first saw you. My heart broke in that same instant, because I was convinced that you could never return my feelings. But I'm a sucker for torture, so I took you in nevertheless. I mentored other vampires before, but they never lived with me. But you—I wanted you close. Even though every day was filled with pain, the bittersweet joy I experienced when you were with me made up for that."

Eddie stroked his fingers over Thomas's lips. "I'm so sorry. I was so blind. Everybody saw it, everybody but me."

Thomas took Eddie's hand and kissed his fingertips. "Nobody was ever meant to see what I felt for you. I was determined to keep those feelings locked away. But you can't lock up love. It always finds a way. Eddie, I know all this has happened in a whirlwind for you, but for me, this has been a long time coming. Just having you in my bed was never going to be enough for me."

Eddie's lips parted and he leaned closer, his breath washing over Thomas's face. "I meant every word I said over the intercom. Every single word."

Thomas smiled, his heart warming at Eddie's reassuring words. He looked down at the box in his hand and opened it, revealing the platinum band sitting on a red velvet cushion.

An intake of breath made him look at Eddie, who stared at the ring.

"I bought this for you the night you sucked me in the garage. I knew then that our relationship was changing. And I wanted you to know then that you weren't just any lover for me. I wanted you to know that if you committed to me, I'd lay the world at your feet."

Eddie's hand on his chin pulled his face closer. "I don't want the world. I only need you. I know that now." Then he smiled. "So, are you going to get on with this proposal or do I need to fall to my knees now and ask you instead?"

"You're impatient, you know that?"

"Yes, because I wasted over a year not making love to you. I've got some catching up to do." Eddie brushed his lips over Thomas's, then pulled back again. Their gazes locked. "Ask me so I can finally do what I need to do."

A spear of excitement shot through Thomas, and he pushed back the tears of joy that threatened to unman him. "Will you marry me?"

Eddie put his hand on Thomas's nape, bringing his mouth to hover over his lips. "I thought you'd never ask." He sighed. "Yes! Of course I will." He pressed a kiss onto Thomas's lips, then released him just as quickly, before Thomas could even enjoy the sensation.

When Eddie lowered his gaze, Thomas realized that he was still holding the jewelry box in his hand.

"Oh!" he said, suddenly realizing what Eddie was waiting for. Thomas took his hand. "Sorry. This is the first time I've done this." He slipped the ring onto Eddie's finger.

"And it will be the only time," Eddie promised. "I'll never let you go."

Thomas pulled Eddie into an embrace, lowering him onto the bed behind him, while he freed himself of the towel. He covered Eddie with his body, the skin-on-skin contact fueling his desire. "I have no intention of ever leaving you."

"Good." Then Eddie all of a sudden pushed against him, rolling Thomas onto his back. Straddling him, he now sat above him. "I was going to do this on my knees, but I guess this position works too."

Thomas raised an inquiring eyebrow, then looked pointedly at Eddie's cock. "With you, any position works for me."

Eddie shook his head, chuckling. "Do you ever think of anything but sex?"

Thomas pressed his hard-on against Eddie. "Don't play coy with me now. I know you want this."

Eddie lowered his body over him, his lips within inches of Thomas's. "Yes, I want this. I want you taking me, making me yours. I want to feel you ride me long and hard, and then I want to feel you come inside me."

Eddie's seductive words made him moan out loud. "Fuck, Eddie, if you don't let me get on with it right now, I'm not going to last more than ten seconds."

"Patience, my sweet lover. There's something else I want from you first."

"What?" Thomas growled impatiently, his hands gripping Eddie's hips to grind against him with more pressure. His cock slid against Eddie's, making the fire in his belly flare up.

"I want more than just marriage. I want a blood-bond."

Eddie's words made him rear up in shock, bringing them both to sit up, Eddie still straddling him.

"Eddie, it's impossible! We can't!"

"Are you trying to tell me that two male vampires can't bond?"

Thomas shook his head. "No! Theoretically, it's possible. But you and I, we can't."

Eddie pulled back, a hurt look spreading over his face. "Are you saying you don't want to?"

Reaching for him before he had a chance to lift himself off his lap, Thomas stopped him. "I want to, I do, but I can't." When Eddie simply stared at him, he continued, "I thought you understood that I can never blood-bond with anybody. Kasper's blood, it's evil. How can I share that with you? How can I subject you to that? I love you, Eddie, I love you more than my life. That's why I can't do this to you. Marriage will have to be enough."

Slowly, Eddie eased back onto him, his hands gripping Thomas's shoulders. Understanding dawned on his face. Then he slowly moved his head from side to side. "So that's why you didn't want me to lick your wounds." He sighed. "Oh, Thomas, have you already forgotten what happened tonight?"

Not understanding what Eddie was referring to, Thomas answered with a questioning look.

"You were able to fight the dark power with my love. Together we're stronger than the evil in Kasper's blood. Much stronger. Because we love each other."

Eddie's gentle press against his shoulders urged him to lower himself back onto the sheets.

"You can't be sure of that."

"I am sure. Our love will protect us both." Eddie rocked his hips against Thomas's groin, eliciting a soft moan from him. "Now let me ask you again." He looked down to his knees, which were braced to either side of Thomas's hips. "Guess I am on my knees after all, just like I'd planned it." Raising his gaze back to Thomas, he continued, "Will you blood-bond with me?"

The love and affection shining from Eddie's eyes invaded Thomas's entire body, capturing every cell and spreading warmth and peace. Instinctively, he knew that Eddie was right. They would defeat the dark power together, because their love was stronger.

"Yes, I want to blood-bond with you." And now that he'd made the decision, he couldn't wait a moment longer. "Now."

"Yes, now," Eddie agreed. "With your beautiful big cock inside me."

Thomas couldn't have imagined it any more perfect. He flipped them, bringing Eddie underneath him. Gazing into the eyes of his lover, he spread Eddie's legs, making space for himself. "I've waited for this for so long."

His hand trailed down to Eddie's cock, squeezing him briefly before sliding over his balls, caressing them softly. Then he slipped a finger farther back, and noticed how Eddie brought his knees up, placing his feet flat on the bed.

Eddie hissed out a moan. "I missed your touch."

"You'll never go another day without my touch," Thomas replied.

"Promise?"

Thomas smiled up at him. "You're going to beg me to give you a breather, that's how often I'll touch you."

"I don't need a breather," Eddie whispered. "I need your cock. Now!"

Thomas bent over him, bringing his mouth to Eddie's lips, capturing them with a kiss. Eddie's lips parted, and his tongue immediately stroked against Thomas's, inviting him in to explore him. Thomas groaned out his pleasure, reveling in Eddie's masculine taste, a mixture of leather and wood, of musk and innocence. As he delved deeper, he felt Eddie's arms pressing him closer, one sliding onto his ass, squeezing him, while Eddie ground his cock against him in the same rhythm as his tongue responded to Thomas.

Even the night Eddie had sucked him, his kiss hadn't been as passionate as it was now. It was as if all barriers between them had finally been removed, and they were free to show their love for each other.

Breathing hard, Thomas ripped his mouth from Eddie's and stared into his lust-drugged eyes. "I can't wait any longer." His cock was aching for release. And his heart was impatient to claim his mate.

"Then take me. Make me yours forever."

Thomas lifted himself off Eddie and reached for the bedside table. He opened the drawer and pulled out a tube of lubricant. When he turned back to Eddie, he noticed how he was turning onto his stomach.

"No," Thomas stopped him, meeting his questioning look. "I want to look into your eyes when I'm inside you. Turn onto your back."

Eddie complied without a word, stretching out on the sheets, his knees raised again, his thighs spread wide. "Like this?" he asked and swept a seductive gaze over Thomas, before resting his eyes on Thomas's erection.

Thomas moved closer and squeezed a dollop of lubricant onto his fingers. "Perfect." As he settled between Eddie's thighs and brought his hand to his crack, he continued looking into Eddie's eyes.

"I'll be gentle. Just relax into it."

Thomas slipped one lube-covered finger into Eddie's crack and slid farther back. Automatically, Eddie brought his knees closer to his torso, giving him more access, opening himself up. Thomas felt the tight ring of muscle that guarded Eddie's dark channel and rubbed his finger over it, slowly and gently.

Eddie's eyelids fluttered. "Oh!" he let out on a sigh.

"Yes, just relax," Thomas cooed. "Let me take care of you." He continued rubbing against the spot until Eddie pressed against his finger. Adding more lubricant, Thomas pushed against the muscle and breached it, his finger slipping inside it to the first knuckle.

Eddie moaned out loud.

"Am I hurting you?"

"God no! Give me more."

Spurred on by Eddie's words, Thomas slid deeper inside him, still slowly and gently, but without stopping, until his entire finger was enveloped. Feeling Eddie's interior muscles clench around him sent a bolt of desire through him. His cock wouldn't survive Eddie's virgin ass for long; he knew it instinctively.

"God, you're tight," Thomas said.

"Just like you were when I was inside you," Eddie responded, lust blazing from his eyes. "Now fuck me."

"You're not quite ready," Thomas cautioned and withdrew his finger, only to add more lubricant and slide back in a moment later.

Eddie bucked against him, taking his finger deeper. "I'm ready."

Eddie's eagerness warmed his heart, but he wasn't fooled. His lover wasn't ready to take his cock yet. He would be soon though.

"I'll get you ready," Thomas promised and thrust his finger deeper and harder, increasing his tempo. With satisfaction, he watched how Eddie's eyes rolled back and uncontrolled moans tumbled from his parted lips, while his body moved in synch with Thomas's thrusts.

"Soon," Thomas whispered as he added a second finger to the first and plunged deep.

Eddie's back lifted off the mattress, then crashed back down, a groan dislodging from his chest. "Fuck, yes!"

As he finger-fucked him with two digits now, Thomas felt his own body heat rise with desire. His cock had already oozed pre-cum, and if he wasn't careful he would come just by watching himself pleasure Eddie. Seeing the vampire he loved respond to him so freely, and with such passion, drove him wild with lust.

"Oh, fuck it!" Thomas cursed and pulled his fingers from Eddie's ass, lathered his own cock with lubricant, and positioned himself at Eddie's entrance.

As the tip of his cock brushed against Eddie's hole, Thomas looked deep into his lover's eyes. "I love you."

Eddie's lips echoed the words silently just as Thomas pushed forward and drove inside, seating himself to the hilt.

Eddie gasped, a visible shudder racing through his body.

"Are you okay?" Concern spread in Thomas, and he stilled in his movements.

"Fuck, you're big!"

Thomas pulled back, but Eddie's hands on his hips stopped him from withdrawing his cock completely.

"Don't you dare stop now!" A wicked grin spread on Eddie's face. "I think I like big." Thomas felt Eddie's hands draw him back toward him, making him plunge back into him.

Eddie's eyes flashed red at him and from his parted lips, Thomas now noticed his fangs extending. "Yes, I do like big, and hard, and deep."

Thomas couldn't stop a smile from curving his lips. "How hard?"

"I'm a vampire, Thomas. I can take it as hard as you can deliver it."

"A man after my own heart." Before the last word had left his lips, Thomas plunged deep into Eddie, his movements still slow, but with every thrust and every withdrawal, he sped the rhythm, and with every moan coming from Eddie, he gave more of his control over to his body, allowing himself to bathe in the sensations his connection with Eddie conjured up in him.

Eddie's tight muscles squeezed him hard, but the plentiful lubrication made every thrust a smooth slide into heaven. Heat engulfed his erection and Eddie's channel kept him prisoner in a prison he never wanted to escape from.

Not even in his dreams had it been this good. Reality was more exciting than any dream could have ever been. They were two male bodies, moving in synch with each other, their hands caressing, their mouths fused in a passionate kiss. Against his stomach, Thomas felt Eddie's hard cock pulse, the heat of it driving a spear of desire into him, adding to the thrill of finally taking the man he loved and making him his. Of possessing him, just as Eddie possessed him. His heart, his soul.

Thomas lifted his lips from Eddie's, unable to hold back any longer. "Now," he whispered and felt his lover nod.

Thomas's fangs descended. Eddie tilted his neck to the side in invitation. Without haste, he lowered his mouth and scraped his fangs against the tender skin.

"I love you, Thomas."

Closing his eyes, Thomas drove his fangs into Eddie's skin and pulled on the plump vein. Simultaneously, he felt the sharp tips of Eddie's fangs pierce his shoulder.

While his cock continued to thrust into Eddie, Eddie's rich blood spread in Thomas's mouth, its taste exploding on his tongue. He swallowed it down, letting it coat his throat, and felt all tension flow from his body. Everything around him seemed to disappear. The dark power in him retreated farther and farther until he could sense it no longer.

At the same time, he felt another force invading him. This invasion he welcomed. Love and peace spread in his mind as he opened up the wall around his heart. He felt the pull of Eddie's fangs on his vein more intensely now, just as he could feel Eddie's imminent orgasm.

I'm coming, he heard Eddie's thought in his mind as clearly as if he'd spoken the words.

I'm right there with you, Thomas replied without speaking.

When Eddie's muscles convulsed around his cock a moment later, and cum shot from Eddie's cock against Thomas's stomach, Thomas felt his own cock jerk, and sensed his semen as it charged through his erection and exploded from the tip, filling his lover in hot spurts. His body shook with the waves of his orgasm, wringing every last bit of energy from him until he collapsed on top of Eddie, unable to move a single limb. He couldn't prevent his body from trembling, and noticed that Eddie was shaking too.

Too exhausted to speak, Thomas reached out with his mind. *You're mine now.*

And you're mine, he heard Eddie's voice in his head.

Then Eddie moved his head, bringing his lips to Thomas's, brushing them against him.

"You can do this anytime you want to."

Thomas lifted his head. "You shouldn't give me carte blanche like that, because your sweet ass is going to be so sore for the next century that you're going to curse me."

"Just for the next century?" Eddie teased.

Thomas felt a laugh build in his chest. As he released it and Eddie joined in the laughter, happiness cocooned him like a thick blanket. He knew then that the dark power in his blood would never be able to rise again as it would forever be locked away by love.

~ ~ ~

ABOUT THE AUTHOR

Tina Folsom was born in Germany and has been living in English speaking countries for over 25 years, the last 14 of them in San Francisco, where she's married to an American.

Tina has always been a bit of a globe trotter: after living in Lausanne, Switzerland, she briefly worked on a cruise ship in the Mediterranean, then lived a year in Munich, before moving to London. There, she became an accountant. But after 8 years she decided to move overseas.

In New York she studied drama at the American Academy of Dramatic Arts, then moved to Los Angeles a year later to pursue studies in screenwriting. This is also where she met her husband, who she followed to San Francisco three months after first meeting him.

In San Francisco, Tina worked as a tax accountant and even opened her own firm, then went into real estate, however, she missed writing. In 2008 she wrote her first romance and never looked back.

She's always loved vampires and decided that vampire and paranormal romance was her calling. She now has 32 novels in English and several dozens in other languages (Spanish, German, and French) and continues to write, as well as have her existing novels translated.

For more about Tina Folsom:

www.tinawritesromance.com
http://www.facebook.com/TinaFolsomFans
Twitter: @Tina_Folsom
Email: tina@tinawritesromance.com